Changeling Press, LLC

ChangelingPress.com

Black Star
A Sci-Fi Futuristic Alien Adventure
Marteeka Karland

Black Star
A Sci-Fi Futuristic Alien Adventure
Marteeka Karland

All rights reserved.
Copyright ©2025 Marteeka Karland

ISBN: 978-1-60521-939-4

Publisher:
Changeling Press LLC
315 N. Centre St.
Martinsburg, WV 25404
ChangelingPress.com

Printed in the U.S.A.

Editor: Katriena Knights
Cover Artist: Marteeka Karland

The individual stories in this anthology have been previously released in E-Book format.

Table of Contents

Black Star Princess
A Sci-Fi Futuristic Alien Adventure
Marteeka Karland

One of only a very few cyborg vessels, the *Black Star* is a prize everyone wants, but no one can attain -- much like its pilot, Nadira. The youngest to ever hold that rank, and the only woman aboard, she has created her persona out of self-preservation. What she doesn't count on is finding a man she simply can't resist.

But can even Mikiel, a powerful captain of the enemy fleet, tame the woman known simply as Black Star Princess?

Chapter One

"I need more power to the maneuvering drive!" Sweat streamed down Nadira's face and neck as she gripped the forward and lateral control sticks with a firm but gentle hand. If she gripped too hard, she might miss one of the many fine vibrations running through this great ship, and that might mean the end of freedom as they knew it. This was definitely not the way she had envisioned a battle to be. Just one more thing to prove how green she was at her job.

"There *is* no more power! You're going to have to do the best you can with what you've got."

"Take it from life support if you have to, Captain. They're smaller and more maneuverable than we are, and I promise you they *will* kick our asses if I can't turn her."

An explosion rocked the *Black Star*, and Nadira had to hang on to her control panel to keep from losing her seat.

"Three more ships bearing 10830 by 424, closing fast, sir," Damon, the grizzled second in command, announced in his gruff, harsh voice. "That's a total of seven Asalian War Slavers."

"I have faith our --" His sarcastic pause grated on Nadira's nerves. "-- legendary pilot will get us out of this." Captain Barnus sat back in the captain's seat and crossed his arms. The pompous windbag had made it his personal mission to see her fail and removed as pilot of the Empire's newest -- and most advanced -- cyborg space ship, *Black Star*. If he refused to give her what she needed to get them out of this, he might do more than that. He might get them all captured and enslaved.

Nadira glanced at Damon before turning her

eyes back to her console. The various viewscreens showed the space surrounding the *Black Star* and where their enemies were positioned. "I can't do it with what you're giving me to work with," she bit out.

Before anyone could say anything else, the *Black Star* shuddered and pitched as one of the Slavers fired on them.

"Direct hit! Aft starboard quarter!"

Nadira blocked out everything possible at this point. They were sitting ducks. Asalian War Slavers were the most maneuverable, heavily armed ships in the known galaxy. The *Black Star* might be the most feared ship in the Vok'nair Empire, but there was a limit to what she could do, especially since she hadn't bonded with her pilot.

That was the whole point of being a cyborg war ship. The *Black Star* was supposed to use the enhanced telepathic stimulators given her by the makers to bond with the pilot, captain, or second in command -- most usually the pilot. Unfortunately, *Black Star* hadn't bonded with any of them.

Nadira guided the ship as it swerved and danced around the Slavers, putting herself in the middle. Yes, the *Black Star* was a very large ship, but the Asalians were notoriously careful with their people. She was betting they wouldn't risk their own ships being caught in the line of fire.

"Target lasers and missiles. Shoot to kill."

"Asalians aren't a mortal threat, Captain," Damon said, his voice matter-of-fact. "There's no reason to do more than disable --"

"I said," Captain Barnus snarled angrily over the top of Damon, "shoot to kill."

Nadira knew she could do anything it took to prevent her ship from being destroyed, but she refused to kill others to ensure the safety of her ship unless it was a last resort. Asalians took slaves. They did not kill. Given what she needed, she was confident she could outfly them.

She readjusted her hold on the stick and braced herself to react the moment weapons control fired. The *Black Star* would let her know when to move -- whether or not they had bonded -- if she just paid attention to the vibrations flowing through the ship. If Captain Dumbass wouldn't do this the easy way, she'd have to do it the hard way.

The Slavers surrounded them now. She could almost feel them bracing themselves for an attack. Nadira was certain she had puzzled them by putting herself in such a vulnerable situation.

There! A minute loss of vibration in the controls. Power being diverted from all systems save life support to fire the massive guns of the *Black Star*. Her plan was to bank hard to port, but before the signal got from her brain to her hands, the ship lurched in the exact maneuver she'd planned. Fortunately, the laser shot went wide, striking its target, but not destroying it as intended.

Captain Barnus bellowed angrily at her, but she blocked him out. Nadira didn't have time to contemplate what had just happened because firing at the Asalians would definitely bring retaliation. She had to keep at least one Slaver in their line of fire or they were as good as captured.

A volley of laser fire from three of the Slavers narrowly missed them as she swerved and swooped from one Slaver ship to the next, finally settling on the one she figured to be the command ship. It was slightly larger than the others, though no other markings indicated it to be any different. Having studied every scrap of information the Empire had on the Asalians, she knew Slavers didn't travel in groups without having one ship in command of the others.

She put herself behind the larger ship, effectively shadowing it. Nadira matched the Slaver move for move -- no matter how extreme. She wasn't sure how the *Black Star* managed several of the sharp turns and climbs and dives. The creaking metal was a testament to the stress, but the ship obeyed her commands perfectly. Pride swelled within her. If it was possible for a cyborg ship to have a consciousness -- something she had begun to doubt when she hadn't been able to link to the *Black Star* -- this one recognized her as a friend. *Finally!* The ship might not have formed a bond with her yet, but she was very close. Trust was building between them, and that was the key.

Renewed hope that she might get them out of this brought an adrenaline surge through her veins. The Slaver she was using to shield the *Black Star* couldn't shake her. If she could force him into leading her toward open space, she might be able to use the jump engines to get them into hyperspace. It would seriously strain their resources, and they would be helpless once they exited to normal space until they'd had a chance to generate more power, but it would secure their escape from the Slavers. She just had to calculate their jump to be as close to a Vok'nair base as possible.

The Slaver tried a banking maneuver to rejoin its comrades, but Nadira anticipated and effectively cut the ship off. The move left the *Black Star* exposed to the other Slavers for a short time, and several volleys of laser and missile fire streamed toward them. One missile struck the port aft quarter shield, and there was an enormous *whoosh* as the shields on the *Black Star* buckled without even a moment's resistance. Nadira lost her breath as the equivalent of an anguished, terror filled scream engulfed her mind. *Black Star*!

Unfortunately for the Slaver, a shield-crippling missile -- shot by its comrade -- glanced off the smaller ship, effectively neutralizing its shields, as well. In that moment, Nadira knew she'd lost this game of cat and mouse.

She had two choices. She could duck back behind the Slaver, or she could make a run for empty space. The problem was the missiles. Asalian missiles were programmed to seek out specific generic parts of any ship they came into contact with. Engines, primary hull, even shield resonance, all had a specific energy signature. The Asalians had refined the detection of these signatures to a fine art. Unfortunately, Nadira had no idea what the Slavers would do next. If they were only looking to disable *Black Star*'s engines, moving behind the command Slaver wouldn't hurt anyone. On the other hand, if they were good and pissed off, looking to breach the *Black Star*'s hull, putting the Slaver between herself and the missiles might be a death sentence for everyone aboard the Slaver if someone decided taking out the *Black Star* was worth the sacrifice. It wasn't like the Asalians to risk their own ships -- quite the opposite -- but it wasn't like them to shoot a shield missile so close to one of their own, either. One more indecision in the heat of battle. Perhaps she wasn't as good as everyone thought.

While she had no qualms about disabling a ship to secure the escape of her own, she didn't know if she was ready to sacrifice a ship whose government the Empire wasn't officially at war with. Asalians captured. They didn't destroy. Usually.

But was she willing to take that chance?

* * *

That incompetent bastard! Squad Commander Mikiel Anjoom wanted nothing more than to beat the living hell out of Captain Norus. The man was too ambitious for anyone's good. In his zeal to capture the infamous *Black Star*, he had effectively rendered Mikiel's own Command Slave, *Sword Breaker*, defenseless. *Black Star* could easily destroy them.

To make matters worse, Mikiel simply could not shake the larger ship. The pilot was effectively using him as a shield between the *Black Star* and his squadron. Whoever he was, he was doing a damned good job of it, too. The Slavers should have outflown the much larger ship with no effort at all. Instead, this damned pilot was flying circles around them all.

Seven Slavers to one ship should have been more than enough. Apparently, the Empire's claim the ship was a super weapon wasn't as much of an exaggeration as the Asalian Coalition believed.

Without warning, the *Black Star* disengaged and headed to deep space.

I have her, Commander! I have her! Norus's excited, disembodied voice broke the disciplined silence of Mikiel's crew. Mikiel scowled. The man simply had no self-control. He hated people with no self-control. During battles, every Asalian soldier relied on computer signals fed directly into their brains via a psycom unit. The absence of unnecessary chaos gave a commander a tremendous advantage, allowing him to notice the slightest changes in the sound of his ship.

"You will stand down, Captain!" No way. There was no way it could be this simple to capture the *Black Star* after the ride that ship had taken them on. It had to be a trap.

And let you claim responsibility for this great victory? Norus answered. Mikiel had to grit his teeth to keep from dressing down the subordinate over the open comm. *I will take this for my family and my ship.* The arrogant bastard was going to get himself killed and lose a valuable ship and crew in the process.

"You will stand down, or surrender your rank." He bit out the words and gripped the arms of his chair. The cold metal bit into his palms, but the pain was a welcome reminder to keep his focus or he could very well give the *Black Star* the same opening Norus was offering -- playing the enemy's game, not his own.

No response from the squad's second ship, but looking at the tactical viewer, Mikiel could see for himself Norus was doing exactly what he'd told the other man not to do.

Norus's ship, *Great Sword*, broke formation and tried to engage the *Black Star*. The larger, faster ship easily left Norus behind. A volley of weapons fire from the *Black Star* leapt from her rear guns and *Great Sword* took a direct hit that buckled her forward shields.

The smaller ship slowed as the *Black Star* accelerated but one last missile leapt from the *Black Star* and streaked toward the doomed *Great Sword*.

The death of the ship was not instantaneous. A gaping hole formed where the ship's command deck had been, and a series of explosions rocked through her hull. Comm chatter from all levels of the vessel let Mikiel know the crew was trying to abandon ship before it was too late. Mikiel knew from grim experience not many -- if any -- would escape.

He listened in silence while the crew of the *Great Sword* tried to get to undamaged sections of the ship. Mikiel deployed android manned shuttles in an effort to get as many of the crew out as possible.

Before the first transport left *Sword Breaker*, however, the *Great Sword*'s fuel ignited in a brief flash of plasma fire and the ship literally disintegrated before their eyes.

Mikiel slowly leaned back in his seat, fingers digging into the steel of the captain's chair again. Anger surged through him, anger and grief. He had lost a good crew, but if Norus wasn't already dead, he'd have killed the man himself.

"Do we pursue the *Black Star*, Sir?" *Sword Breaker*'s pilot didn't sound at all eager to continue this battle. Mikiel couldn't blame him. Any pilot who could fly a ship that size in such extreme maneuvers wasn't someone to take on lightly.

"Anxious to pit your skills against her pilot again?" He couldn't help tormenting Ranier. He was good, but he needed to be taken down a peg or two. Perhaps he'd be easier to be around.

"Are you kidding?" Ranier turned in his seat and looked directly at Mikiel. "If he can fly circles around me in a ship as big as the *Black Star*, no way I want to meet him in battle again. I was just trying to do my duty."

Quiet chuckles broke out around the command center. Mikiel only smiled. The young man hadn't done so bad. He *had* moved them aside at the last moment, otherwise they'd all be dead. "By the way, that was a lucky move you made, Ranier. You probably saved us all."

The other man cleared his throat. "Much as I'd sincerely love to take the credit for that, Sir, I can't. The ship did it on her own."

Mikiel raised an eyebrow. "Has she linked with you?"

"No, Sir. You may think this sounds crazy -- I

know I do -- but I think she linked with the *Black Star*."

"Explain." His barked order came out harsher than he'd intended, but he had to know.

"The nav computer, Sir. I almost didn't notice it -- it was only a blip -- but when I went back and checked the log there was an encoded signal that originated from the *Black Star*. It was so fast, there was no way it could have been meant for a human to execute it and no way a human had time to send the command in the heat of battle."

Mikiel had to restrain himself from cringing. That was the worst possible scenario. Ships weren't supposed to be able to link without the benefit of at least one human surrogate. If this was true, then they needed to get the link with that ship and find out what he knew. If the Vok'nair operated anything like the Asalians, the most likely link would be with either the captain, second in command, or the pilot. Security was probably compromised. It also made going after the *Black Star* all the more crucial. No matter what the crew wanted, no matter what he wanted, they had to engage the *Black Star* again. If that ship could link with their own, they had to either capture or destroy her. Besides, that ship was a huge morale boost for the Empire's troops. Without her, there was a chance something would give in the "non-war" between his Coalition and the Vok'nair Empire. His mission was to take that ship. Failing that, he was authorized to destroy her.

"Much as I'd love to tuck tail between our legs and take the remains of the squadron home, we can't. We have a job to do. Our lives, and the lives of every man and woman in this unit, do not matter. What matters is capturing the *Black Star* and making the ship part of the Asalian Coalition, or, failing that, destroying her." He sat up straighter before signaling the entire squad. "This is Squad Commander Mikiel. We are pursuing the *Black Star* with the intent of capturing her. If capture is unsuccessful, we have instructions to destroy her. Given the danger of the situation, and the destruction of the *Great Sword*, you will transfer all female slaves and nonessential male slaves to the *Broad Sword* and the *Gem of Maylar*. These two ships are to return to the Asalian home world to avoid unnecessary loss of life. You have fifteen standard minutes to comply before we leave this sector. That is all."

The tension in the command center was palpable. An order to destroy any vessel was far from common. Apparently, the Asalian Coalition didn't want anyone else to have the *Black Star*. He was beginning to understand why, since the ship appeared to be at least semi-sentient. Besides, with the possibility that the *Black Star* had breached their security systems, they couldn't let her get back to the safety of a Vok'nair base.

As his squadron made the necessary preparations, Mikiel mulled over his instructions to the main fleet. The Empire and the Coalition weren't at war. Exactly. It was more of a face-off -- who could gain the subtle upper hand without actually engaging. Both sides always vehemently denied the rare skirmishes between the two groups, so if a soldier -- or ship of soldiers -- was captured, he was left at the mercy of his captors.

For Imperials, it meant a life of slavery. For Asalians it usually meant death. Mikiel had barely managed to escape before such a fate befell him. He knew first-hand how Imperials treated their prisoners. At least the Asalians treated their slaves well -- there were strict laws outlining the rights of slaves. They were taken care of and allowed to develop their natural born talents. In many ways, it was a good life.

He was brought out of his deep thoughts as the last of his ships signaled their readiness. With a few final instructions to the *Broad Sword* and the *Gem of Maylor*, Mikiel gave the order to follow the *Black Star*. The only thing that had gone right in that battle was the beacon they'd placed on the *Black Star's* hull. They had a good lock and a strong signal. It was only a matter of time before they engaged the other ship, hopefully for the last time.

Chapter Two

Once the *Black Star* entered hyperspace, Captain Barnus exploded.

"You stupid bitch!" Nadira couldn't stop the yelp of pain and surprise that escaped her throat when Barnus hit her, then yanked her out of her seat by her hair. "You could have gotten us all killed! We could have taken out two or three of those bloody Asalians if you hadn't sabotaged my firing pattern!"

"Captain!" Damon's normally soft, raspy voice cut through the room like a Madorian laser blade.

Barnus whipped around, taking Nadira with him, and pointed at Damon with a shaky hand. "Keep quiet, or I'll relieve you of your station, as well!"

Before Nadira or Damon could protest, the ship lurched and bucked as the jump engines screamed in protest. The *Black Star* was thrown violently out of hyperspace, tumbling end over end, tossing everyone around like rag dolls.

"Evasive maneuvers! Evasive maneuvers!" Captain Barnus bellowed. It didn't do any good. She couldn't even crawl to the pilot's station the way the ship was pitching. The unplanned exit from hyperspace had thrown the *Black Star* out of control. Nadira prayed they were in open space.

She struggled to move toward her station, but with the artificial gravity, the tumbling created a centrifugal force far greater than normal gravity. Her limbs were so heavy, she got muscle cramps from simply trying to raise them from the deck. She was pinned by her own weight.

From the corner of her eye, she saw Damon flip a couple of switches on his console -- thank the Stars he'd been in his seat when this started -- and the artificial gravity disappeared. Unfortunately, that meant everyone tumbled in all directions.

Nadira felt like she was submerged in water with everything around her constantly moving. It took her a moment to work through the disorientation, but she managed to finally make a concerted effort toward her station. Once there, she strapped herself in and grabbed the control stick. Immediately, she made adjustments in pitch and yaw, bringing them out of the spin they'd been thrown into.

The tumbling lessened immediately, and within a few moments stopped altogether. As she automatically checked their position and scanned the area, the reason for their situation became clear. Four Slavers surrounded them, one of them directly in their line of flight. They weren't out of danger yet. She'd just bet their weapons were hot and trained on the *Black Star*. While they watched, another company of Slavers emerged behind them -- all part of the same group of ships they had just engaged.

"*Black Star. Black Star.* You will surrender and prepare to be boarded, or you will be destroyed. Will you comply?"

"Like hell." Captain Barnus started to say something else -- most likely something to further piss off the Asalians -- but Damon grabbed his hand in what looked like a very painful grip.

"No. You will not endanger this crew again." Over the years, Nadira had learned to read Damon's body language and facial expressions pretty well. She liked the man, mostly because he was the only man she'd ever known who hadn't tried to hit on her, but also because of his commitment to the ship and the crew as well as to her. He made sure they all functioned as a single unit, emphasizing the need to work together. He'd even made the men she'd rejected quit calling her the Black Star Princess. He'd said if Nadira had a holier than thou attitude, it was because she understood her job aboard the *Black Star*. She was the pilot, not a sperm receptacle. Nadira knew defending her honor wasn't the real reason he'd reprimanded them, though she appreciated Damon's harsh words to those foolish enough to let him hear their comments.

When Barnus started to protest, Damon spun the other man around and clipped him neatly across the jaw. Barnus's head snapped to the side and he stood there a moment before crumpling to the deck, unconscious.

Nadira was stunned. She looked at Damon, wide-eyed. "What have you done?"

"Either committed an act of treason, or saved this ship from the biggest mistake the Vok'nair Empire has ever made."

"*Black Star. Black Star.* You will surrender and prepare to be boarded. Comply or be destroyed." The Asalian Slavers weren't going to wait much longer.

"Communications." Damon didn't take his eyes from Nadira. "Signal our surrender, but with terms."

"By your command, Sir." The young officer's voice squeaked. Fine lot *this* crew had turned into. The best the great Vok'nair Empire had to offer, and all of them scared beyond imagination. All of them except Damon. He should have been captain of this vessel, not Barnus -- and he would have been, too, if not for her. Unfortunately for the *Black Star*, Damon had taken another assignment. As her bodyguard. As the pilot of the Empire's flagship, and the only female aboard, it was thought she might need extra protection.

"I'll get us out of this, Nadira."

"I know," she said matter-of-factly. "I never doubted it."

"That makes one of us," he muttered. "This may be harder than anyone thinks."

"*Black Star.* You will send your captain, second in command, and pilot for negotiations. You have thirty standard minutes to comply. A security team will meet your shuttle in the main docking lock. The area will be indicated with beacon lights. Do you understand?"

Nadira shivered. Why was she included in this party? She had a sinking feeling she didn't want to know.

"Signal our understanding and have security meet us in the shuttle hangar. Our esteemed captain might not agree with leaving his ship." Nadira knew she didn't want to. "And when we get back, I want gravity restored and this ship spaceworthy enough to get us back to a Vok'nair base."

Captain Barnus was indeed opposed to leaving the ship, but Damon and the security team didn't give him much choice. Bound and gagged, he left the *Black Star* a most unwilling ambassador.

The transport to the Slaver took exactly thirteen and one half standard minutes. Nadira felt every second of them. Her nerves were strung so tight, she could barely pilot the shuttle the short distance. Neither she nor Damon spoke, and Barnus could only offer muffled grunts.

Once they were locked with the Slaver, Damon turned to her. "Let me do the talking." His quiet, raspy voice projected calm that belied the almost palpable tension. Nadira could see Damon's unease in the way he held himself so erect. He didn't like this any more than she did, but under the circumstances, they didn't really have a choice. Though why they had asked her to join the party was still a mystery. There was nothing she could offer in any negotiation.

"You don't have to tell me twice."

"Agree with anything I suggest and don't let them see any hesitation on your part."

"Understood."

Before he opened the hatch, Damon gave her a reassuring smile as he readjusted his hold on Barnus. Nadira placed her hand on the scan pad and the air lock began to click and whir. In a few seconds, the door slid open with a hiss.

The corridor was so dimly lit Nadira couldn't see anything at first. As her eyes adjusted, however, she could see shadowy outlines of five or six very large people.

"Which one is captain of the *Black Star*?" Nadira couldn't tell who spoke, but the voice was masculine, very deep, and obviously in charge.

"This one." Damon pulled Barnus up beside him. Barnus's eyes went wide with fear as he looked from Damon to the Asalians.

There was a brief pause before the Asalian in charge responded. "I will need verification." There was no emotion in his voice, nothing to indicate his mood or state of mind.

"Understandable. I'm sure you have the Empire's registry of ships and their command crew. You can verify him by DNA."

"Agreed. You will come with us."

Nadira's eyes had adjusted to the darkness somewhat and she was able to better focus on their hosts. All five were very tall. Their body armor was dark and bulky, so it was hard to get an idea of their exact build, but Nadira knew there was no way she could take any of them on in hand-to-hand combat.

Any idea of armed combat went out the airlock when they were searched and their weapons confiscated. With Asalians all around them, there was no way to return to their shuttle unless they were given permission.

She didn't like this.

Nadira exchanged a look with Damon. He looked as impassive as the Asalian sounded. Nadira wondered if he was as calm inside as he seemed outside. Damon didn't resist when they were led to a large room with an oval table surrounded by chairs. Nothing else graced the chamber's interior. It looked as impassive as the Asalian himself. The guards took their stations on either side of the door, silent but large in their presence.

"Please be seated." The Asalian gestured to the table and turned to a control panel on the wall. When he touched it, the lights brightened slightly. He turned. Nadira's breath caught and that negative feeling she'd had about this whole situation got worse. This man was a predator.

His gaze passed over her briefly before acknowledging both Damon and Barnus, but his attention came back to her and they stared at each other for several very long minutes. She felt...

Uneasy.

It was like he'd decided he *owned* her, and wanted to see what he'd purchased. She had the strangest urge to cover herself, and it was all she could do not to fidget. She didn't think fidgeting would help their situation.

He wasn't handsome by any standard, but he was striking. Nothing about his face seemed ordinary. He had a square face, with a strong, straight jawline, chiseled cheekbones and those piercing, cobalt blue eyes. His head was shaved clean, but black eyebrows slashed at an angle over his eyes.

Nadira tried to match him stare for stare, but his penetrating gaze seemed to command submission. She shivered, and her skin prickled as if she'd stepped into the freezing cold. The man terrified her. Why was he so focused on her?

"We're here." Damon broke the building tension. The Asalian continued to regard her for several more moments. After a brief pause, he turned his attention back to Damon. Damon continued to speak as if the Asalian's concentration had been on him the entire time. "Since you've agreed to meet us, I sincerely hope we can work out terms we can both live with."

"I would have introductions first and verification of your identity." His accent was strange and harsh, but the quality of his voice reminded her strongly of Damon's -- raspy and quiet. This was a man who didn't have to yell at his troops to be obeyed.

"Of course. An oversight in protocol on my part. Forgive me," Damon conceded without hesitation. He rose smoothly, gently nudging Nadira to do the same, and bowed slightly at the waist. "I am Damon Singh, second in command of the *Black Star*."

"Mikiel Anjoom, commander of this vessel and the surrounding squadron. You said this one is captain?" He indicated Barnus with a raised eyebrow; otherwise there was no indication of any emotion.

"He is. Captain Hom Barnus."

"And why is he bound thus?"

"Captain Barnus has been relieved of duty. Regardless of the outcome of the previous battles, it is not the policy of the Vok'nair Empire to fire with the intent of destruction unless there is an imminent threat of death. I know the Asalians do not kill unless there is a good reason."

"Unfortunately, second in command, I cannot say the same for the Vok'nairs. I had the pleasure of spending many months as a prisoner of war at the behest of your government."

Both men looked at one another, neither backing down, sizing each other up. Nadira was far from the timid type, but she was next, and the last thing she wanted was Mikiel Anjoom's unsettling stare directed at her again. When her shoulder touched Damon's arm, she realized she was inching closer and closer to her commander and friend. Ideally, she could hide behind his larger frame, but somehow she knew Commander Anjoom hadn't forgotten her, nor would he. He wasn't the type of man to forget anything.

"If he is the captain, and you are the second, then the woman must be the pilot. Yes?"

Nadira's heart thudded in her chest. As nerve-wracking as the battle had been, this was worse. When he leveled his gaze on her once again, she broke out in a fine sheen of sweat, and she had to clench her hands into fists to keep them from shaking. Still, she met his eyes, trying not to flinch. She didn't intend to show any weakness to this enemy.

"Nadira Greyson." Damon stepped slightly in front of her even as he made the introduction, and she loved him for it. He was twenty years her senior, and though it had always irked her before, she was grateful he treated her like he might a daughter. She hated to think she needed his protection, but this was one time she wouldn't argue with him over it.

Mikiel raised one dark brow and, if possible, looked even scarier than before. "The Black Star Princess? She is your mate?"

Nadira started, and her gaze flew to Mikiel's

face. How the hell had her stupid nickname made it beyond the bounds of the *Black Star*?

"No."

"Your lover?"

"No, but she is under my command, and therefore under my protection, and I have no tolerance for that title."

"I see." Mikiel's eyes shifted from Damon to Nadira, a flash of annoyance crossing his features.

There was a brief period of silence while the two men stared at each other. Mikiel's guards held an identity pad to each of them for their palm prints. Damon not so subtly shouldered himself more securely in front of Nadira and gripped her hand in his own behind his back.

"I think we should discuss our current situation, Commander. We need to get back to our ship."

Mikiel sat back in his chair and steepled his hands. Nadira had a sinking feeling he was plotting something. She didn't trust him.

Damon urged Nadira to sit as he did so himself. She sat, but on the edge of her chair. She was too edgy to sit back and twiddle her thumbs. Commander Mikiel's attention kept coming back to her and there was something new in his eyes. Lust. It wasn't overt or overwhelming, but just knowing it was there made the hair stand up on her neck.

"What did you have in mind, second in command Damon Singh?"

"I'll give you Captain Barnus in exchange for the freedom of my ship and crew."

"A fine arrangement for you, but what's in it for me?"

"The captain of the *Black Star* would be quite a trophy."

"The *Black Star* would be a better one." He hadn't missed a beat, hadn't hesitated.

"I can't deny that, but we're out here in the middle of nowhere. Even with the four ships you have with you, I doubt there would be enough room for all the prisoners you'd have. Even if you left them aboard the *Black Star*, you'd be vastly outnumbered. Are you really willing to kill everyone on board for a trophy?"

"Well, actually --" Mikiel crossed his arms over his chest and looked Damon dead in the face. "-- that's exactly what I've been instructed to do."

Chapter Three

In all his years in service to the Coalition, and all the slaves he'd owned, he had never come across anyone who piqued his curiosity like the woman on the other side of the table, and he wasn't sure why. Yes, she was striking, but he'd known women more beautiful. Also, he certainly didn't know a woman -- or man, for that matter -- who could handle a ship like she could, but it wasn't that.

He'd had time to study her several times since they'd arrived on the *Sword Breaker* and the more he learned of her, the more he liked her. It wasn't just her appearance, but her spirit. She was scared -- probably beyond anything she'd ever known -- but she was holding her own. The only obvious sign she was uneasy was the finger that kept finding and twirling a strand of hair that had come loose from the thick knot of white-blonde hair at the nape of her neck.

At first, he'd just wondered what it would be like to see how far he could push her before she either fought back or her spirit broke. But his wayward thoughts kept wondering what all that hair would look like draped around her naked body. He could have any number of women -- had at his disposal at least five on this ship alone -- but none of them piqued his curiosity like she did, and he wasn't sure why. He did suspect she might have been the *Black Star*'s human connection, but that wasn't it, either.

The more he thought about it the more it grew into an obsession. He'd just bet there was more to this little wench than met the eye. When Damon Singh suggested taking the captain and letting the rest of them go, he got an idea. "Is this all a set up then? A trick?" Damon didn't seem convinced. The man was apparently a good strategist.

"No trick. I've been ordered to either capture the *Black Star*, or, failing that, destroy her."

"Then why haven't you done so?"

Mikiel didn't say anything for a moment or two, letting their situation sink in. "Because you have something I want."

"Aside from our ship, I assume."

"I'd be willing to spare the lives of your crew and let you retain possession of the *Black Star* for a price."

The other man sat back in his chair and crossed his arms over his chest. "It must be a high price if you're willing to give me that much. What do you want?"

Mikiel looked Nadira straight in her silver-blue eyes. He wanted to see her reaction when he answered. "I want your pilot." It was a good bargain. Mikiel knew with him holding Nadira, Singh wasn't likely to go far.

"Absolutely not!" Damon Singh's outraged explosion was expected, given how he had protected the woman until this point. "We've offered to give you the captain in exchange for our vessel. It would do both our governments good. Neither of us loses."

"That's exactly my point. I have the upper hand, and my superior will not be pleased to find I've let the *Black Star* go -- no matter what else I gain -- and I might as well get something out of it. I want her." Mikiel loved watching her eyes widen. His only regret was the fear he saw in them. Fear, however, could be used to his advantage. If he could keep it focused, he could keep control of her until she gave control to him willingly.

"I will *not* give you a member of my crew for you to use as a sex slave!" Damon's contempt was obvious, if misplaced.

"Who said anything about a sex slave?" Mikiel deliberately eyed Nadira up and down. "I already have men and women more --" He paused a beat, adding more than a touch of insult. "-- suited to that task. My interest in your crewmember is her skill as a pilot. She can best serve me as a free woman, but --" He leaned closer to Nadira, driving home his point. "-- if she doesn't perform as she should, slavery is still a viable option."

He didn't miss the flush of embarrassment and fear crossing Nadira's face, but he did notice something he had missed before. There was a large, bluish red bruise across her left cheek. By next day cycle, she'd have one painful black eye.

"What happened to your face?" Mikiel knew the question came out harsh, but he didn't care. Out of nowhere, the mark of violence across this woman's face almost made his blood boil. "Who did this?"

"The good captain has a bit of a temper." Damon grunted as he folded his arms over his chest. "Why do you think he's bound and gagged?"

Mikiel stood and crossed the space between himself and Captain Barnus and backhanded the man with as much force as he could. The other man's head snapped to the side and he slumped over the table unconscious.

"Women should not be treated that way in any culture. Slave or not."

Damon stood, pulling Nadira to her feet as well, and placed himself between her and Mikiel. "I will not let you take her, Asalian."

"You cannot stop me, Vok'nair."

"I have to try."

Mikiel knew Damon wouldn't agree to simply

turn Nadira over to him, and it would come down to who was stronger. Fortunately, in that Mikiel had the upper hand. "You have no hope of stopping me. You are obviously a good commander and take your responsibilities to your crew very seriously, but this is one battle you cannot win." If anything, Damon's features hardened even more, but he didn't say anything. There was nothing he *could* say.

"Damon," the girl whispered, "I'll be OK. The *Black Star* and her crew are more important than me. Get her away from here."

Few things surprised Mikiel, but this did. He'd have bet his ship she'd never been this scared in her entire life, yet she was willing to sacrifice herself for the good of her ship. He doubted there were many among his own crew willing to do the same.

Damon's fists clenched at his sides, but he nodded slowly. "It doesn't appear as if I have much choice, Nadira." Mikiel didn't miss her reaction. The blood drained from her face and she swayed slightly, but she locked her knees and bit her lip in an effort to stay upright. The little wench was made of sterner stuff than she looked.

"What about the captain?" Damon bit out.

"I'll keep him, too. This man is responsible for more deaths in your prison camps than I am in open battle. He will make an interesting addition to the auction block." Mikiel turned to the guards at the door. "Take Captain Barnus to the sick unit. Make sure there are no lasting injuries, then put him in a holding cell."

"Yes, Commander." The guard, Ishmiel, nodded to his partner and the two men dragged Barnus out. Before the door closed again, Ishmiel returned, having passed his prisoner to one of the guards outside the door. "The woman?"

"I'll take care of her. Escort our guest back to his shuttle. Make sure he is safely aboard his own ship before we leave the sector."

"As you command, Sir."

Once the new captain of the *Black Star* and Ishmiel were gone, Mikiel regarded his new crewmember. Her black uniform and light body armor covered her from the throat down. It was, however, form fitting instead of baggy as the men's had been. Her feet were booted and her hands gloved. She was shaped generously enough. Her waist was tiny, her hips and breasts flared almost dramatically. It would be interesting to see what was underneath all that armored black leather.

His cock twitched, and he did his best to squash the thought dead in its tracks. She was here because of her skill as a pilot and her ability to bond with ships -- no other reason.

"Life as you know it has changed as of this moment, Nadira. If you do as you're told and learn this ship as well as you knew the *Black Star*, I'll see to it you get to continue to fly."

Her eyes widened and she almost took a step forward before she stopped herself. "What do you mean?"

"I mean, if you prove you can fly this ship as well as you did the *Black Star*, I'd have no problem replacing my pilot with you."

"And earn myself another enemy in a place already full of enemies? I think I'll pass."

Mikiel allowed annoyance to lace his next words. "We don't operate that way. You'll learn that in time. Everyone has a place. The better you learn your chosen skill, the farther you progress." He could still see skepticism in her eyes, so he added, "Not everyone is cut out to be a sex slave, my dear. That takes unique talents indeed, and unless I miss my guess, you've concentrated too hard on being a pilot to perfect those particular skills."

When she blushed again, he knew he'd hit close to the mark. Still, she took a deep breath and stood straighter. "What do I have to do?"

Chapter Four

Nadira stood smartly at attention. Her heart threatened to beat through her chest, so hard was its pounding. She was a prisoner. There would be no rescue. There never was. Anyone captured by the Asalians was simply listed as "missing" and never seen or heard from again. There were whispers that even those who managed to escape were denied entry back into Vok'nair space. The Empire didn't deal well with those who failed it.

"I think you need some time to think about what you need to do to best serve this ship. This is your new life, Nadira. Adapt."

He turned and headed out the door and down the corridor. Nadira fell into step behind him. No way was she going to make him tell her twice. He was right. She had to adapt and do so quickly. She wasn't convinced by all his assurances about the way his society functioned, but if she could at least keep out of trouble and in his good graces, so much the better.

As she followed him, she couldn't help but admire the layout of the vessel. Had she not known this was a ship of war, she might have mistaken it for a luxury ship. Unlike the corridors in the section leading from the air locks, the halls in the main crew area were brightly lit. Lightly cushioned, beige carpet covered the floors, muffling their steps. The walls held various display panels every few meters, but were otherwise decorated with unobtrusive artwork.

Then there was the commander himself. Harsh didn't begin to describe him. His whole body was hard angles and raw power. The heavy body armor masked his true contours, but it couldn't alter the sheer size of him. He was big. Damned big. And she had no difficulty imagining powerful musculature underneath all that armor. He was not a man to let his body go soft and risk making himself vulnerable.

He frightened her, but she couldn't help but be curious as to the flesh and blood man beneath the commander's armor. It was enough to send a sexual thrill shooting through her.

She was so lost in thought she almost ran into Mikiel when he stopped and turned toward her. In fact, she would have had he not caught her upper arms. When her gaze snapped to his, his eyes commanded her to focus on what she was doing. He was too intense, his presence too overwhelming. Worse, she could see her own sexual hunger mirrored in his eyes.

His grip tightened on her arms and she thought he might pull her to him, but he didn't. Instead, he turned her toward the door. When Mikiel pressed a hand to the wall scanner the door slid open and he directed her inside.

"This is my chamber. You'll stay here until I get you someplace else to live. There should be everything you need, including suitable clothing." That rankled somewhat, but she didn't have time to say anything even if she'd had the nerve to. Mikiel was already turning to leave. With a sharp *hiss* the door slid shut, locking Nadira inside.

For several minutes, she just stood there. This couldn't be happening. This could *not* be happening! There was no way she had what it took to take on a man the likes of this one.

Worse, Mikiel was right to assume she didn't have many sexual skills. In fact, she didn't have any. Nadira was one of only a handful of females the Empire had deemed capable of completing military training, and she had started her career as a star pilot before she'd started her monthly cycles. As a result, it had been drilled into her not to have physical relationships. Such would undermine her position among the men on her ship as well as create unnecessary strife. As far as everyone there was concerned, she was untouchable. The fact was, Nadira was a virgin and had assumed she would stay that way for a very long time.

Not anymore. There was simply no way she could be sure he hadn't lied to her, or that she wouldn't do something to make him change his mind.

She sighed. Since she was going to be here a while, she decided to look around, explore her temporary home. There were three separate rooms. The main room and bedchamber were combined, the large inviting bed the only thing that didn't reflect the occupant. The rest of the room was stark, harsh, with only necessities decorating the space. A smaller room served as a work area, with computers and graphic map screens.

But the chamber that interested her most was the bathing chamber. When she walked into the spacious room, lights automatically came up and the bathing pool began to fill with water. Steam rose gently from the surface as it filled. *Real water!* It was a luxury she hadn't had on the *Black Star*. After months in space, she was finally going to get a real bath.

There were mirrors all around the bath, and it was impossible not to catch her reflection. She'd never given thought to her body before, but now it was foremost on her mind. Mikiel had said she wouldn't be a sex slave, but it was hard not to think about that type of life. This whole situation was terrifying enough as it was, but to think that she might have to spend her time on this ship being ridiculed because her form wasn't pleasing was something else altogether. She eyed herself now with a critical eye.

Her hair was probably her best feature. Long and lustrous, its thick tresses flowed down her back and tickled her ass -- her worst feature -- when she moved. While she had a small waist, her butt and thighs, though strong and firm, were round and fleshy. Not at all attractive. When she turned back around, she noticed her breasts rising and falling with each breath she took. They were too big, but still firm and high. As she pinned her hair back up, her arms grabbed her attention. She flexed and extended them, but there was no denying the extra flesh she carried on her upper arms.

No. She definitely wouldn't make a good sex slave. Her only hope was that the commander would hold to his promise that she could still be a pilot if she proved good enough.

Pushing those thoughts from her mind, she stepped into the bath and immediately the sting of the hot water gave way to a pleasant warmth that seeped its way into her tense muscles. The groan that slipped past her lips couldn't be helped. It felt lovely to be submerged in warm water again. When the jets started to gently but firmly pummel her back, legs and feet with water deep within the pool, she knew she'd found heaven.

She sat back in an indentation built into the wall of the pool and relaxed. This might be the only time she'd have the opportunity to do so, and she fully intended to take advantage of it.

Thinking back on her time in the commanding presence of her new "boss," there was something about the way he looked at her that made her feel different than she'd ever felt before. Not beautiful, or sexy, but sensual. He looked at her as if he'd like nothing more than to explore her body for his own pleasure. His hot gaze also promised he'd give as good as he got, but Nadira instinctively knew it wouldn't be as simple as that. He looked at her as if her sole purpose in the universe was to please him in every way he wanted. Any pleasure she received would happen only if it pleased him to do so.

The idea gave her a perverse surge of lust. To be used as a plaything for a man to take his pleasure from. To exist only to please him lest he move on to another. It should have made her feel degraded, like she was no more important as a person than the artificially intelligent androids that did most of the heavy labor throughout the Empire, but instead, it made her feel...

Powerful. She could have power over the pleasure of such a dominant man and make him *want* to return to her -- and only her -- because she did things to him that felt better than anything done by any other man or woman at his disposal.

If she was good enough. Pure fantasy, but what a heady thought! It made her cunt tingle.

The jets continued their delicious massage, and it wasn't long before she shifted her position so that one of them pointed between her legs. She gasped when the stream of water brushed her clit. Jumping with the unaccustomed contact, she moved out of the jet's path, only to readjust her position so that it shot straight at her once again. It didn't take long for the persistent stream to create very pleasant sensations within her core. Pleasure shot through her, so intense she had to bite the inside of her cheek to keep from crying out. In a sudden burst of energy, her world exploded. Her sight narrowed and spots of light pricked her vision as she reached her orgasm.

Breathing hard, Nadira let the sensations fade away and slumped in the water. She sat there for several moments before realizing she might not have long before Mikiel returned.

"Was that your first climax?" The familiar deep, rumbling voice from the doorway made her jump, and it took a moment for the question to penetrate the pleasurable haze fogging her brain.

When she found her voice, all she could manage was a shaky, "No."

"Have you cleansed yourself?"

"I --"

"Yes or no?"

She shifted in the water to cover her breasts beneath its surface. "No."

Without another word, Mikiel began ridding himself of his clothes. Off balance as she was, Nadira couldn't take her eyes off him. As each inch of flesh was bared, her body did things it had never done before. Her stomach fluttered when his abdominal muscles rippled, and her nipples tightened beneath the water. Mikiel seemed to be unaware of his effect on her -- which was good as far as Nadira was concerned.

He slid his pants down his hips and stepped out of his shoes. Powerful, muscular legs bunched and undulated with each movement. Heavily muscled arms and shoulders were the final testament of how correct her assumption had been that he took great care of his body.

When he finally stood and started toward Nadira, she saw the semi-erect flesh of his cock for the first time. Even in a flaccid state it was impressive, and she couldn't help but wonder what it would feel like. Mikiel might not be what she considered "handsome," but his body was a work of art. It was as if he had been fashioned out of her deepest, darkest, wildest fantasies. She didn't *want* to see him as anything other than her "master" at worst, her enemy at best, but seeing him like this made her see him as a man. Nothing more.

Nadira resisted the urge to move away from him as he stepped into the bath and settled himself in the water. When he opened a bottle of liquid cleanser, a crisp, clean fragrance of mint spilled into the room.

He took her arm and pulled her toward him. When his arms closed around her, she caught a brief glimpse of lust on his face before he turned her around and removed the clip from her hair. White-blonde tresses spilled down her back and into the water. She wanted to protest, but bit her lip to keep from it.

Mikiel guided her to a depression in the bath so that she sat in the water slightly lower than chest high. He was behind her, his legs at her back. "Rest your head on my knee." Nadira wasn't exactly sure what he wanted, but moved to do his bidding and found she didn't have to understand what he wanted. His hands guided her into position.

She lay face up with the back of her neck resting on his strong thigh and her hair floating gently in the water behind her. He scooped water over her head and when he started massaging the wonderfully scented soap into her hair, she couldn't suppress the groan. His fingers worked through her hair, then on her scalp. The cleansing gel tingled and cooled the sensitive skin underneath his fingertips. Mikiel urged her to lean her head back farther and he rinsed the soap from her hair in careful but methodical movements. The air felt cool as the peaks of her breasts emerged from the warm water as she was repositioned.

Once her hair was clean, Mikiel began to cleanse

her skin with the same lightly scented soap. He soaped her limbs and it seemed like he was going through movements he'd done hundreds of times. The methodical motions were designed to do nothing more than cleanse her, and she almost allowed herself to relax and let him pamper her.

As he caressed her from head to toe, her mind focused on the sexual abilities of the incredible man touching her so intimately. What kind of lover would he make? Would sex simply be a means of release for him, or would he expect her to draw out his pleasure until he tired of the game? Would he make sure she enjoyed herself or would he take what he wanted and leave her to find her release on her own? Would he train her to please in the manner Asalian men liked, then rid himself of her? All these questions flew through her mind before she finally landed on, *Does he find me physically appealing*? Moon and Stars! She hoped he kept his word that she wouldn't be a slave. She didn't think she could handle the emotional ride involved.

With that line of thought, it didn't take long for her to interpret his ministrations as sexual. It seemed like he might have lingered on her breasts longer than was necessary and, after a few passes over her fleshy globes, Nadira wanted to squirm. The moan that escaped her lips was slight, but any doubt Mikiel heard her moan and knew exactly what it meant evaporated when she saw the hot look of lust in his eyes.

With a growl, Mikiel hefted her out of the water and his lips closed over one nipple. Nadira didn't even try to stem the cry this time. The sensations flowing through her were overwhelming, and she knew that if this man chose to take her body as he had done to countless others, she wouldn't raise her voice in protest. In fact, she thought she might even beg him to continue should he stop now.

She arched into him and her fingers found his bare scalp -- seemingly on their own because she couldn't remember raising her arms -- and she held him to her as tightly as she could. When she felt one of his hands push between her thighs, she parted her legs eagerly. Nadira screamed the second his large, callused hand touched her clit. Mikiel stroked it several times before plunging his fingers inside her and Nadira rocked her hips in time to his movements. It didn't take long before she felt the tingling sensation start, centering around her clit and pussy.

When Mikiel pulled his mouth from her breast and looked at her, Nadira's breath caught. This man was as affected by their intimate moment as she was. An orgasm like none other she'd ever experienced washed over her, and spasms seized her body. A reflex action caused her to wrap her arms around Mikiel and cling to him, her lifeline in a sea of sensation.

When her climax passed, her eyelids grew heavy but she made an effort to hold them open. As she focused on his eyes once again, she found a trace of annoyance but as he continued to stroke her cunt and clit, his expression grew more and more filled with lust and possession. Now it seemed like everything he'd done had been designed to give the master a better sense of the property he'd newly attained. Even if she wasn't really a slave, she felt like one in that moment.

When Mikiel had stopped caressing her pussy, he urged her to sit, then stand. Once he'd exited the bath and dried himself, he helped her out and dried her with gentle but brisk movements, leaving her the towel to finish herself. Finally, Mikiel said the one thing Nadira had hoped to be able to keep to herself, at least for a little while. Now she had to deal with it. "You are untouched."

She felt her cheeks heat up. Never having had sex before wasn't something she'd ever been embarrassed about. Then again, it had never seemed important before now. As it was, there was a very real chance she wouldn't remain a virgin much longer if her bath was any indication. She didn't want to answer Mikiel, but something in his eyes told her it would be in her best interest to answer quickly and truthfully.

"Well, I've had orgasms, but --"

"Have you been with a man or not? It's not a difficult concept." His clipped, brisk question made her flinch when she would have preferred to stand her ground, but standing there in nothing but a towel gave her a feeling of utter helplessness. She was so far out of her element, so off balance, she couldn't shut out her emotional responses like she was able to in the pilot's seat. As it was, she was tense, stiff.

When she flew the *Black Star*, the one thing she relied on was her ability to pay attention to every little vibration within the ship, no matter what was going on around her. Now she felt like she was too focused on what was in front of her. It felt like she was flying blind. "No. I haven't."

His only response was a slight grunt before he took the towel from her and directed her to the bedchamber. Mikiel hardly spared her another glance. "I have arranged for you to have access to my computer if you wish it. You'll find everything you need to know about flying a ship of this class. My study is open to you."

Nadira knew an order when she heard one.

She was relieved, of course. Having to be in the same room with Mikiel after what had just happened was more than she was prepared to deal with emotionally.

Cold chills covered her body and she shivered. It reminded her she was still unclothed and her hair was still wet. She was definitely chilly, and promptly went in search of clothing. What she found was a sleek black flight suit that covered her from throat to ankle yet still managed to hide very little. It hugged every curve of her body, showing every imperfection she had. Sighing, she recognized there was little she could do. This was obviously the way he wanted her dressed and she'd simply have to deal with it. With a shrug, she decided to block it out by doing exactly what Mikiel suggested. She'd learn this ship as well as she knew the *Black Star*. She might not be able to do that solely by computer, but she could go a long way toward her goal.

Going to Mikiel's private workstation, she sat and tucked her legs underneath her in the large, high-backed, padded chair and pressed her palm to the screen imbedded in the surface of his desk. When the welcome popped up on the three-dimensional screen, Nadira started her studies.

Chapter Five

Mikiel dropped to his bed. All he wanted was to close his eyes and rest for a week. What the *fuck* had he just done? He had taken Nadira for her piloting skills. Nothing more. He *had* to remember that. Without her full attention on learning how to fly *Sword Breaker* as efficiently as she had the *Black Star*, she wouldn't be able to bond with the *Sword Breaker*. At present, *Sword Breaker* was the only Asalian vessel to be equipped with cyborg intelligence -- computers combined with human brain cells -- but who knew how many the Vok'nair had. So far, no one had been able to bond with *Sword Breaker*. Who knew how many Vok'nair vessels had been bonded.

When he'd seen the way the *Black Star* moved and fought, he knew he had to find out everything he could about her pilot. When the *Sword Breaker* had been commissioned, the ultimate goal had been for the three key people aboard a ship to bond with it -- the captain, the second in command, and the pilot. Given the degree of skill with which the *Black Star* had moved, of those three people, the pilot had been the most likely to have bonded with the ship. It was still possible one or both of the others had bonded as well, but given the fact that they hadn't pursued yet, he figured they either didn't have a good bond, or hadn't bonded at all. With the addition of Nadira to his crew, he began to think there might be a possibility of finding the key to this stupid three-quarter cyborg, one-quarter human tin can. The only reason the Asalian Coalition had built *Sword Breaker* in the first place was to keep up with the Vok'nairs' technology. It was a colossal waste of time, materials, and manpower as far as he was concerned.

Still, he had to make sure she stayed focused,

and fucking her until they were both sated and sleepy would not accomplish his goals. If anyone was going to bond with his ship, it was Nadira. He knew it in his gut.

Now he had to be strong, had to live up to the reputation of the cold and calculating commander he'd worked so hard to achieve. There was more at stake here than his engorged cock.

As he lay there, remembering how silky her skin had felt, how beautifully she'd responded to him, that aforementioned engorged cock twitched as if reminding him it still needed attention. Ignoring it wasn't an option, not when it was this hard.

Touching Nadira had been the worst kind of heaven. Once he'd slipped his fingers inside her and knew beyond a doubt she was a virgin, a quick fuck was out of the question. Sex with a virgin might be a heady thought, but there were invariably messy emotional complications. Always on the part of said virgin. Mikiel wasn't the kind of man to be with only one woman.

But what a fuck it would be! He took his dick in one hand and squeezed gently. It pulsed in his hand as if eager to begin. Pulling up, then down, he stroked himself steadily at first, wanting only to get off quickly. It was working, too, until the image of Nadira's lips enveloping his cock popped into his head. The air left his lungs and for a moment he couldn't breathe. In his mind, she looked at him, drawing her lips up the shaft and letting go of the head with a popping sound before wrapping her lips around him once again and starting over.

On second thought, he wanted this to last as long as it could. The possibility of actually getting Nadira into this position was virtually zero, and the image was too damned good to rush. He wondered what she would think or do if she came out of his office and found him like this. With that thought came a rush of lust so strong he couldn't hold back his climax any longer. He let go and a low groan escaped his throat as stream after stream of his own seed spurted onto his chest and belly.

For a few moments, he simply lay there trying to catch his breath. It had been a long time since the mere image of a woman going down on him had brought about such a powerful orgasm.

Fuck! He had to keep his wits about him and quit thinking with his dick. The Coalition was counting on him to figure out how to bond this ship, and Nadira was his best hope.

Taking a deep breath, Mikiel sat up. He touched his hand to his chest. It came away sticky and he winced. He needed to clean up, and a bath sounded really good.

In the bathing chamber, he took a long, hot bath to wash the semen from his torso and collect his thoughts. Well, at least it was done. He wouldn't have to worry about his wayward cock rearing its pesky head for a while.

Then he walked into his study.

She stood in the center of the room, her arms outstretched, her face tilted upward as if looking to the sky, but her eyes were closed. There was a look of utter concentration on her face. She looked like she was listening to something. No sooner had the door whooshed shut than she lowered her arms and took a step back away from him, the spell broken.

"What were you doing?" He regarded her with wariness. He'd bet his life she'd done it already. Bonded with his ship.

"I -- nothing."

"Don't lie to me, Nadira." He didn't raise his voice, but he made his tone as sharp as he could. If she'd linked with the ship, he needed to know. "Have you bonded with *Sword Breaker*?"

"No." She took a step backwards, then held her ground, raising her chin. "But I might have if you hadn't broken my concentration."

Mikiel took a few deep, calming breaths. Even still, his heart was racing. Just like that. For twenty-one Asalian sun cycles they had tried to figure out how to access the organic parts of the computer brain in this ship and she had done it in less than five standard hours.

"How?"

"I'm slightly empathic, but only with closely related family members. Somehow, this ship reached out to me on an emotional level."

Mikiel thought hard about his next question. If the *Black Star* had indeed linked with the *Sword Breaker*, Nadira would likely know *Sword Breaker* was not bonded and maybe even that they didn't know how to form a bond with their bloody cyborg ship. If she hadn't picked up that information, he didn't want to volunteer it. That was information that could potentially damaging if Nadira were to escape. He tried to phrase it as carefully as possible.

"Do your people have to be empathic to bond with a cyborg vessel?"

When she didn't answer right away, Mikiel knew she was measuring her response as well. "We believe so, yes," she finally answered.

Mikiel huffed an exasperated sigh. This was going to get them nowhere. If they were going to figure this out, they had to work together. He wasn't going to let her go, anyway. Why not simply tell her? Maybe she could solve their problem for him.

"We thought telepathic enhancers for the neurological conductor pathways in the synthetic brain would be enough."

Nadira shrugged and turned away. Apparently she wasn't going to volunteer information. While he admired her for it, it also made him angry. They had one of the most technologically advanced vessels in space and they couldn't fucking figure out how to use it.

He crossed the distance between them in three long strides, grabbed her arm, and jerked her around to face him. Her body landed flush against his.

"You're not going anywhere, Nadira." He gritted the statement out through clenched teeth. "Even if by some miracle your government decided it gave a damn because you've bonded with one of their ships, I absolutely *will not* let you go." He shook her slightly to emphasize his resolve, and she cried out. "I need you to tell me how to create a human-to-ship bond."

"You don't understand!" she yelled back at him. "I don't know how! This ship reached out to me, not the other way around." She paused for a moment, her breathing shallow and her cheeks flushed. "I didn't even bond with the *Black Star*."

For a moment, Mikiel was too stunned to say anything. He simply gaped at her, trying to decide if she was telling the truth. Her silver-blue eyes were wide in shock and fear. When he had pulled her to him, he hadn't realized the arm not holding onto her upper arm had snaked around her waist, but now he used the leverage to pull her closer.

He wasn't sure why he did it, but when her mouth parted in surprise, he couldn't help but taste what she'd inadvertently offered. He didn't take her gently -- quite the opposite -- he swooped down like he meant to conquer. He pulled at her lips with his teeth and plunged his tongue inside to explore.

When she moaned and tilted her head back, something inside him snapped. His other arm went around her to grasp her ass, and he pulled her pelvis into him. His cock had gone rock hard, and he ground it into the soft flesh of her belly. The form-fitting outfit offered only a scant barrier between them. The heat from her flesh seared him.

After a brief hesitation, Nadira kissed him back. Her touch was tentative at first, but before long she kissed him with as much vigor as he kissed her. Wrapping one leg around his hip, she struggled to find a position that gave her some relief. Mikiel knew what she wanted and pressed his thigh between her legs. When Nadira made contact with him, she cried out yet again and began to ride him rapidly. She ground herself onto his leg, obviously hitting her clit with the friction she needed.

It wasn't long before her breathing became erratic and her cries louder and more frantic. Within moments, she tore her mouth away from his, threw her head back, and screamed out her climax. When she fused her mouth to his once again, Mikiel was startled when she bit him, actually drawing blood. He pulled her back with a fist clenched tightly in her hair close to her scalp. The fierceness in her eyes, the unadulterated lust, called to his own baser nature. She might be a virgin, but she certainly knew what she wanted and went after it as aggressively as she flew ships.

With that thought, a realization of what he was about to do came crashing down on him. He shoved Nadira away from him a little harder than he should have, and she stumbled and fell. Her face hit the edge of his desk. Mikiel resisted the almost overpowering urge to help her to her feet, but he was afraid that if he touched her just then, he'd rip the uniform from her delectable body and fuck her until they both collapsed. Even so, when she turned back to him, tears trickling down her face -- he could see from the look in her eyes it was from the shock of the blow as much as from the pain -- he almost went to her, anyway.

Nadira touched the injury gingerly with her fingertips. "I guess I'll have matching bruises." She gave him a deprecating smile. "I supposed I deserved that."

Mikiel wiped a trail of blood from his chin where it had dripped from his lip. "No woman deserves that, Nadira. We don't treat our woman like that, slaves or not."

"So you said once before." She got shakily to her feet and almost fell. Mikiel couldn't stop himself this time. He did reach out to her. When she flinched, he thought he'd throw up. He wanted -- needed -- to keep his distance from her emotionally, but he didn't want her to fear for her safety. She was needed as a pilot. Anything else would have to be her choice and not like this. She had to make a rational decision, not one made as a result of stress and sexual tension. Mikiel had never taken advantage of a slave -- or any other woman for that matter. He didn't intend to start now.

"Nadira --"

"No." She held up a hand and looked away from him, as if she couldn't bear the sight of him. "I don't want to hear how sorry you are, or how 'if only we'd met in another lifetime' or some other shit. You don't want me. That's all I need to know. I'll never do that again."

That statement enraged him and he wasn't really sure why. It was what he wanted, wasn't it? Why did he feel so strongly for this woman out of the blue? The thought that she would never seek him out was almost as troubling as the thought that she believed he didn't want her. He took a few deep breaths, hoping it might slow his pounding heart and get the blood flowing to his brain instead of his cock.

When he had better control of himself, he spoke with more conviction than he had ever felt about anything in his life -- up to this point. "You *will* do that again. Once you've bonded with this ship and learned her as you knew the *Black Star*, you will come to me on your own."

"What makes you so sure of that? What makes you think I won't escape and spill all your secrets to the Coalition once I learn them?"

"Because I don't believe you can share that kind of bond with this ship only to betray her in such a manner."

She looked helpless and afraid for a moment before she schooled her emotions and blanked her face. "I will not pursue a man who does not want me. I won't lower myself."

He advanced on her again and almost pulled her into his arms to show her how very wrong she was. "There's a difference in not wanting a woman and not wanting to take her before she's ready." He pointed his finger at her, bringing it inches from her face. "You need to learn the difference. When you do, then you'll come to me."

Mikiel watched Nadira for a few moments, purposefully letting his lust for her show on his face. She would come to him, and when she did he would prove to her how very much he wanted her. Nadira gasped and would have taken a step back if she had been a lesser woman. She might look young and fragile, but she had the heart of a warrior.

Satisfied he'd gotten his point across, Mikiel turned and left the room. His life was going to be hell for a good long while.

Chapter Six

Nadira thought about his words as the days turned to weeks and weeks turned to months. She never did get her own cabin, and the one time she asked about it Mikiel snapped at her, "I'll get to it when I have time!" She got the impression he wasn't one to yell, but he seemed to have no patience where she was concerned.

Their time together grew more and more strained, and it confused Nadira as much as it hurt her. To make matters worse, the sexual tension between them was almost palpable. He never touched her -- he'd promised he wouldn't -- but that didn't stop the smoldering looks he gave her. Unfortunately, with all the time that had passed, she wasn't sure if those looks were looks of lust or anger and resentment. In her quest to master the *Sword Breaker*, she had done her best to ignore him and even though this was what he expected her to do, she was afraid he had grown to hate her for it.

For her part, she'd gotten to the point where she couldn't concentrate when he was around. Any link she might have been able to form went out the window every time Mikiel walked into the room. She could sense the ship's impatience with her, which was also frustrating, but it wasn't a sensation new to her. Nadira had often sensed the same emotion from the *Black Star*. That combined with her constant sexual awareness of Mikiel made concentration impossible.

Now she sat at the pilot's station performing one mindless hyperspace maneuver after another. Mikiel sat behind her and to the left. She could almost feel the burning sensation at the back of her neck, knowing he was as focused on her as she was on him.

Without warning, there was a tremendous lurch. The ship made an emergency rapid descent into normal space. The only possible cause for that kind of immediate descent was a near collision with something that wasn't supposed to be there. Claxons blared, lights flashed, and she expected pandemonium to engulf her. But all noise from the other officers in the control room ceased and everyone concentrated on their respective panels. A stream of information flooded her console.

Immediately, she began to process, as a stream of data was force-fed into her brain. It was uncomfortable, and totally unexpected, but she managed and was amazed when she realized she actually understood most of what was being given to her -- information that would have taken her several minutes at best to process in any other manner.

"It's the *Black Star*, Sir." Hers was the only voice all around them. "And it's directly in our path."

"I'm aware of that," he snapped, and waved her to silence. Apparently she had made some breach in protocol but she'd be damned if she knew what it was. Her face heated and she knew it must be as red as a Drazilian Firebush.

Without another word, she turned to the information streaming into her head. The *Black Star* seemed unaware of their presence, but Nadira had no doubt they were looking for her. Apparently her father wasn't willing to let her go so easily. Not only were the *Black Star*'s defenses on minimal only, but there was no indication she was ready to fire, which meant they had time to capture her old ship without firing a shot.

Her heart raced. What should she do? This was her one chance to get out of this, but if she did anything to give them away, she might lose any possibility of linking with a cyborg intelligent ship.

And she might get them all killed.

Nadira sat motionless at her console. Apparently, the rest of the crew were communicating by some means other than what she was used to, so she concentrated on processing the data stream. The only clear order she could make out from the conversation within *Sword Breaker*'s master internal comm system was to stand down and not make a move. There was simply too much information for her to pick out anything else.

Are you ever going to let go and let me have control?

The voice was male, deep, and very soft. It was almost buried underneath the torrent of information flowing inside her brain and seemed almost to be an afterthought. As if the voice didn't expect her to hear it, anyway.

So. You've finally decided to pay attention. Took you long enough. The voice was stronger now, but still very non-obtrusive. *Are you ready to do this?*

Nadira was stunned. The *Sword Breaker* had made first contact with her, not the other way around. She didn't know what the ship meant, but the only answer that popped into her head was, *I'm not taking advantage of the vulnerability of the* Black Star *to catch Mikiel an interstellar prize.*

Do you really think that's what he wants?

Do you really think he doesn't? I haven't learned much, but I do know the Asalians don't have any more of a clue about cyborg intelligent ships than the Vok'nair do. He knows I couldn't link up with the Black Star, *but his government doesn't believe him and wasn't happy he let her go in the first place. They still want the* Black Star *and if he can take advantage of this situation, he might still get back in their good graces.*

Do you think the opinion of anyone matters so much

to him that he would endanger the lives of so many people?

If not for that, then what? Why engage the Black Star *at all?*

Have you not been listening to anything going on around you? The ship was annoyed now and Nadira could tell he thought her daft.

They haven't said a word.

Have you not used your psycom?

My what?

Psycom. Everyone aboard this ship is fitted with one to avoid confusion during battle.

Well, not me. I guess that's something my benevolent master *forgot to see to. I get all the data entered into your data banks at once, and what little I can glean from your master comm, but nothing else. And the information coming to you is simply too much for me to catch more than bits and pieces.*

There was a sigh and a very long pause.

No wonder you're confused and frightened. The last thing Mikiel wants right now is a confrontation with the Black Star.

If that's true, then why did we come out of hyperspace?

Did they teach you nothing when they trained you to fly space ships? The voice was more than just impatient now, it was condescending. *You came out of hyperspace because there was another ship directly in your path. Had I not pulled us out, we would have hit the* Black Star *at a speed faster than light. What do you suppose would have happened then?*

I know that. But one order from him and a minor course correction, and our flight is not disturbed at all.

Not if the Black Star *was also in hyperspace.*

Nadira blinked, startled. *Oh. I didn't think of that.*

You weren't thinking about anything. And I'd appreciate having your full attention when you attempt *to fly me. You might have a grand reputation in the Vok'nair Empire --* the tone in his voice said he believed otherwise *-- but I've yet to see any of it here.*

Goddess! Are all the male members of this society so exasperating?

Only with females who are acting stupid. You are far too intelligent and far too adept at flying ships to be so careless.

I can't concentrate! That infernal beast behind me keeps me in a state of constant arousal and I can't think when he's around! Make him stop and I'll be more careful!

I see. In a flash, all the annoyance and condescension was gone, replaced by understanding. Nadira could almost believe the ship had experienced it first hand.

I could be off the mark as I can't connect with the good captain's thoughts and feelings as I can yours, but I think he is experiencing much the same thing. His actions indicate he wants you near, yet is unwilling or unable to satisfy himself. His argument with you shortly after you arrived seems to have prevented him from, shall I say, making the first move.

We're wasting time with useless nonsense. How am I supposed to communicate? He's either unaware I haven't been fitted with their communication devices or doesn't want me to know what's going on now with the Black Star.

Just be ready. When I tell you, push the sublight engines to maximum to a point one thousand meters off the starboard side of the Black Star. *They haven't detected us and you should be able to engage a tractor beam and capture her without firing a shot.*

I don't understand. Any second in command worth his pay will see us coming.

Not if he's not linked and the Black Star *doesn't want him to see.*

Nadira sat in stunned silence, barely able to input the instructions she was preparing to execute.

There was a bigger picture here she wasn't seeing.

Only because you haven't tried, my dear. Sword Breaker sounded more like a fatherly figure now than a cyborg entity.

The claxons had long since quieted, and the silence was deafening as Nadira waited. Sweat trickled down the back of her neck and between her breasts, and the clingy uniform stuck to her damp skin. She reached out with all she was to the *Sword Breaker*, trying her best to get a feel for what was happening. All she sensed was a building sense of excitement. *Black Star* would finally take her place beside him. *After all these decades.*

Now, Nadira! Now!

Nadira pressed the button to execute the commands she had already entered. It worked like a charm, just like *Sword Breaker* had said it would. The *Black Star* seemed to be caught completely off guard, except Nadira knew better. The information *had* been there. She could sense it in the back of her mind. The link with the *Black Star* she had tried so hard to form all those months ago was grossly incomplete, but a link nonetheless.

The command team let out a collective breath. One young man a little less disciplined than the others pumped a fist in the air in celebration. Mikiel's expression was blank. He gave nothing away, but his eyes were focused squarely on her. She tried to hold his gaze, but it wasn't long before she dropped her eyes. He knew something had happened.

"Even though we have every right to bring the *Black Star* back to Homeworld, I gave my word to let her go. We can hardly fault her captain for attempting to rescue a valued crewmember. Tow the *Black Star* back to Vok'nair space and disable her weaponry. If she tries to follow us, disable her engines. Then set a course back to Asalian space with all possible speed. I'll be in my quarters." When Nadira turned to obey his command, he grabbed her arm and dragged her from the pilot's station to the door. She cried out as his fingers bit into her arm, but he didn't loosen his grip. He hissed in her ear. "Not a word until we're alone."

You cannot let him make Black Star *go away.* The ship sounded almost frantic, not the smug, self-assured entity of only a few moments ago. *Convince him to bring her with us and try to get her to join forces with the Asalian Coalition.*

He doesn't care about my opinion. What makes you think he'll listen to me?

Just be honest with the questions he asks you. Answer everything. *Tell him what you feel.*

Why? Why is this so important to you?

Sword Breaker answered her with silence.

Before she could question the ship further, Mikiel opened the door to their quarters and yanked her inside. "How did you know what maneuver I was planning? I know for a fact you haven't been implanted with a psycom unit, yet you executed my exact command the instant I opened my mouth to give you the instructions."

Nadira swallowed. She was so confused and disoriented she didn't know what she should do. If she did as the *Sword Breaker* instructed, the goal would be to capture and turn the *Black Star* into an Asalian ship. If she didn't, they would tow her old ship to safety. Only a few months ago, she would have kept her mouth shut. Now, well, she missed the *Black Star*. She might not want her old ship turned into an Asalian vessel, but she wanted to walk her decks again. Besides, Nadira realized there was something else going on. Something she was missing, but thought she ought to be able to see clearly. "I've made a tentative link with *Sword Breaker*. He told me what I should do."

Mikiel studied her intently. "What else did it tell you?"

"That you should take the *Black Star* with you and convince her to join us." Goddess, Nadira hoped she'd done the right thing. If not, even her father wouldn't be able to get her out of this one should he succeed in rescuing her.

Mikiel paced the room twice before sitting down on the bed and scrubbing a hand over his face. "The ship told you this." He made it a statement instead of a question. He looked wearier than Nadira had yet seen him. Usually he wore a mask over his emotions. This sudden lapse in control meant he was either weary indeed, or he was simply becoming used to her. She rather liked the latter.

"What would you have me do? I doubt your *friend* Damon will join an enemy force without a very good reason. The longer we stay in Asalian space, the greater the likelihood of us being discovered by another vessel more concerned with bettering their career than the good of the Coalition. Your precious *Black Star* might end up stardust."

"Then take us to neutral space."

Good idea! Thank you, my dear. Thank you. The *Sword Breaker* now expressed his relief with an almost human inflection to his words.

Mikiel raised an eyebrow. "Neutral space." He considered it for a moment. "Do you think you can convince Damon to defect?"

"I honestly don't know."

"Is there anyone there who has linked with her?"

"I don't know." Nadira found she enjoyed this

simple information exchange with Mikiel. He wasn't yelling at her, and she wasn't avoiding him. They simply talked. It was a pleasant experience. "I do know that there is something going on between the *Black Star* and the *Sword Breaker*. I just don't know what it is, and this stubborn ship of yours hasn't seen fit to tell me."

Yet. Not yet. Soon, my dear.

Nadira wasn't sure why she suddenly felt bold enough to openly study Mikiel, but she did so now. His black uniform, lined in gold, fit his large, firm body snugly, hugging the contours of his muscles. From strong arms and powerful thighs to a massive chest and rock hard abdomen, Mikiel was the perfect specimen of manhood as far as she was concerned. The intense features of his face only accentuated his masculinity and rugged maleness. Nadira didn't think of herself as having a very creative imagination, but the things she had done to this man in her dreams and daydreams made her wonder at that assessment of her character. Even now, she was wondering if he would stop her if she simply shrugged out of her clothing and draped her body over his.

"We'll try it your way. If you can't convince Damon to join us, we can always part ways without fear of a Vok'nair ambush." His statement startled her. She had been sinking fast into a sexual haze. When she realized he was actually listening to her input, she almost had to shake her head to make sure she'd heard him right. Before she could comment on his last statement, he opened communications with the command room. "Central Command, this is the commander. Change our course to the Sclactian sector. Best possible speed."

"As you command. Sir, the *Black Star* is demanding to know our intentions."

Mikiel stood and walked to Nadira until her breasts would surely touch him if she took a deep breath. She had to tilt her head back to keep his gaze. Never taking his eyes from hers, he gave instructions to the officer. "Inform the *Black Star* we will be discussing a possible alliance between our two ships. Make sure you word it exactly like that. Don't embellish."

"It will be as you command, Sir."

Nadira couldn't stop herself. Her hands rested lightly on his chest before she realized she'd moved them. Her palms burned where they touched him and she could feel the ridges and valleys of his muscular frame. His chest moved in and out deeply and rapidly with his breathing and desire sparkled in his eyes.

"I understand what you tried to tell me when I first came aboard. What I don't understand is why it mattered to you that I make a conscious decision to come to you."

"I want no regrets, Nadira, and I don't believe in taking advantage of a woman for sex. But you --" He brought a hand to her face to stroke her cheek and chin. "-- I knew from the moment I saw you I wanted you. Now I'm beginning to think I'll do anything I have to in order to keep you."

Her breath caught in her throat. Goddess, the man knew the way through a woman's defenses. Especially ones as flimsy as hers. "Then why have things been so awful between us? I thought you might hate me and I didn't know why."

He smiled then and pulled her to him in a tender embrace. "It is difficult to keep a civil tongue when one is sexually frustrated beyond belief and the object of that frustration lies only a few feet away each night."

"You could have given me the separate living

space you said I'd have that first day."

"And give someone else the privilege of joining you there? I think not." He held her to him tightly, sending a thrill through her that was almost overwhelming. "Besides, there's no one on this ship who would be as gentle with you as me."

Nadira snorted. "Forgive me, but you aren't the first person I think of when I picture a tender lover. You're more the type to swoop down and conquer."

"You don't think I can be gentle?"

"I think -- oh!" She cried out in surprise when he scooped her up and threw her onto his bed, following her down to cover her body with his. He lay sprawled out between her legs and rested his weight on his forearms. Nadira's breath came in little gasps of excitement. This was it. This was really it.

"I can be gentle." He lowered his head to hers and whispered once more, "I can be gentle." And he kissed her.

Chapter Seven

Mikiel had never felt such a tremendous sense of relief in all his life. She was finally his. He might have made the first move, but she had made the decisions she needed to make. Yes, he had kept her in his chambers when he should have given her solitude, but he just hadn't been able to let her out of his sight. He'd had a need to keep her as close as he could. There was something about her that called to something inside him and he couldn't fight it anymore. A hardass he might be, but he was putty in her hands. He wasn't sure how he felt about that.

Right now, all he felt was an overwhelming need to be inside her, to fill her with his cock and his seed. To claim her as his. She was right. He wasn't a gentle lover, and he was very much afraid he wouldn't be able to control himself this time. The woman beneath him was lush, full-figured. Just looking at her enticed him. She was unlike any other woman he had ever known. He had always held himself back for fear of hurting the delicately built women he usually bedded. With Nadira, he knew already from their previous encounter she was as aggressive as he was, and he had a feeling she wouldn't be impressed by a gentle lover any more than he was.

She wrapped her legs around him and pulled him to her more firmly, her hands pulling at his clothing. Their kiss was an explosion of pent up lust. There was nothing as important at that moment as getting their clothes off and joining to their mutual satisfaction.

Mikiel wasn't sure how he managed it, but he got his uniform off and simply ripped Nadira's from her body. Her wide, lust filled eyes told him he'd shocked her, but she approved. Greatly. He knew he needed to take his time, he knew he had to be as careful as he could so as not to hurt her, but all he could do was reach between them with one trembling hand to ensure she was slick with readiness before guiding his cock to her entrance. With one mighty thrust, he pushed past her barrier. They both cried out. He in ecstasy, she in a combination of pleasure and pain. He did pause then, needing to make sure she was OK.

"Nadira?" To her, it sounded like Mikiel's voice was coming from the other end of a dimensional gateway. Her ears rang and she was light-headed -- probably from hyperventilating -- and she couldn't decide if the sensations coming from her cunt were the ultimate in painful pleasure or just plain painful. She burned and felt full to bursting, but she also had an almost overwhelming need to make him do it all over again. Her pussy tingled and throbbed where they were joined. Her clit was in firm contact with his body and she was stimulated beyond anything she'd ever dreamed of every time either of them moved.

"Don't stop." She forced the words out as best she could, but they sounded hoarse and raw, far from the commanding tone she would have preferred. She used her legs to pull him into her again when he retreated.

After a few strokes, he finally began a fierce, almost violent rhythm. He grunted with each powerful surge forward and their bodies slapped together loudly. Satisfied he wouldn't stop, Nadira spread her legs wide, allowing him to drive just a little bit deeper. She pulled her knees as close to her shoulders as she could and forced them open as wide as she could possibly manage. The new sensations blew her mind.

Never had she imagined anything could strip away all self-control and make her crave the harsh, raw fucking Mikiel was introducing her to. She had to have more.

Mikiel covered her body with his, only the retreat of his hips and her spread legs separating their bodies. His forehead rested on the bed beside her head, supporting some of his weight, his breathing harsh in her ear. His arms were wrapped tightly around her, holding her to him as if afraid she'd try to flee. Nadira knew how he felt. She had the same fear, afraid he'd push away from her and leave her in this awful state of needful lust.

"You like it rough, don't you?" he growled, his own need abundantly clear in the husky timbre of his voice. At least she wasn't alone in that area.

"Goddess, yes!"

"You love being fucked by me. Say it!"

"Yes! Fuck me! Goddess, please! Fuck me harder! Now!"

And he did. Unbelievably, harder and deeper than before. Nadira wrapped her legs around him once again and lifted herself to him, meeting him thrust for thrust. Her head thrashed from side to side as the pleasure built and built and threatened to overwhelm her. Just as her orgasm began to wash over her, her lips accidentally collided with his neck. She didn't know why she did it, but she latched on to his flesh and bit down as she came. Hard. On both counts.

Mikiel was so surprised by Nadira's unexpected and aggressive bite that he lost what was left of his control. When her pussy contracted around his cock, his seed spurted so explosively from him he wondered if he might have actually blown the head off of his dick. It was so violent, a heady combination of pleasure and pain. Never in all his adult years had he had such a ferocious, complete orgasm. Never had he held a woman so tightly, or wanted to continue holding her to prevent her from leaving him and denying him such astounding pleasure whenever he chose. But he found that, deep in his mind and heart, he had a driving need to see she was pleased, too. He would have delayed his own release indefinitely, no matter the pain to himself, if it meant she would find even one more ounce of pleasure. He didn't know why. Only that it was so.

Still clutching Nadira, he tried desperately to catch his breath. In a few short minutes, his life had changed completely. Utterly. Keeping his distance from her both physically and emotionally would be next to impossible now. With her on his ship, there was absolutely no way he could pretend none of this had happened. And he wouldn't try. It might take everything in him; he might eventually lose himself in her. It was totally opposite from the way he was as commander of the *Sword Breaker*, but he would make sure everyone on this ship and every other they encountered knew she was off limits.

The Black Star Princess belonged to him.

* * *

Nadira opened her eyes. She was still in Mikiel's bed, but he was no longer with her. When she sat up, her body protested greatly. Every muscle in her body ached, to say nothing of how she felt between her legs. Perhaps she shouldn't have participated so enthusiastically. The most amazing part was she could actually feel the *Sword Breaker* going through his routine programs as the ship sped through space toward their destination. There was a tension in him, but she attributed that to the impending meeting with the *Black Star*. She had the same feeling of anxiety, so she didn't think twice about it. Swinging her legs over the side, Nadira sat there a few moments, trying not to whimper. She needed a hot soak in that bathing pool again. Thinking of that, she couldn't help the silly grin on her face.

When she trusted her legs enough to hold her, she carefully made her way to the bathing chamber. There she found Mikiel leaning over the sink with his head hanging down as if he thought he was about to be sick. He must have heard her because he raised his head and caught her gaze in the mirror. What she saw there made her take a couple of steps back, and caused a sick feeling in the pit of her stomach.

Anger.

Hurt.

Despair.

"When were you planning on telling me?"

Oh, Goddess! He knows. "It's not something I think about on a daily basis."

He pushed away from the vanity and whirled on her. "How can you *not* think about it? It's who you are!"

That rankled a bit. "Who I am has nothing to do with who my father is. Who I am is what I've chosen to be."

"Don't play games with me!" The explosion shouldn't have been unexpected. Still, his shout made her jump. "You knew all along they'd come for you, didn't you?" When she didn't answer immediately, he repeated his question in such an awful, angry yell Nadira actually cringed and raised her hands as if to protect herself. "Didn't you!"

"I had no reason to think my father would treat my capture differently than he would the disappearance of any other Vok'nair soldier. Our parting wasn't exactly --"

"You didn't think the king of the mighty Vok'nair Empire would send a rescue team after his only daughter?"

"He didn't exactly approve of my career choice. We've barely spoken in a couple of years. It's so bad, we yell at each other most of the time when we're forced into a meeting. No. I didn't think he'd send anyone after me. I figured most likely he'd be glad to be rid of such an embarrassment."

"You're not stupid, Nadira. You knew. You had to know."

She didn't know what to say to that. The only thing she could think of to say was, "How did you find out?"

Mikiel pushed past her back into the bedchamber and began to dress. "Your friend Damon Singh enlightened me when I contacted the *Black Star* to gauge his mood. I like to know my chances of a successful negotiation before I enter into one. He informed me he was instructed to bring you back at any and all cost. The penalty for him if he fails will be death."

Nadira felt like her world was crashing down around her. "I can't go back, Mikiel. I can't. I've learned so much, and leaving the *Sword Breaker* would be like leaving home. Your people, this ship. You." She pushed a hand through her thick tresses. When one lock fell over her right breast, she was suddenly self-conscious about being nude. Crossing her arms over her breasts, she scanned the room for something to cover herself. A tunic she often donned after her duties were finished for the day was draped on a chair in the far corner of the room. She crossed quickly to it and slipped it on. When she pushed her head through the opening, she found Mikiel regarding her with a mixture of interest and outrage.

"What do you expect me to do? Take on the whole Vok'nair Empire?"

"No." She managed to get the word out through the lump in her throat. "I don't expect that." Pulling herself together and clearing her throat, she asked him, "When do you meet the *Black Star*?"

"One standard hour. Be ready to leave." Without another word, Mikiel finished dressing and left their cabin.

Nadira stood there a moment, unable to move. She felt hot tears trickle down her cheeks. She'd finally accomplished what she'd set out to do -- bond with a cyborg ship -- and accidentally found a man who could spin the stars in a thousand galaxies when he took her to bed. Now she was going to lose them both and she didn't know what, if anything, she could do about it.

Chapter Eight

When Mikiel left his quarters, he wasn't sure where he was going. He needed to think. He needed to get Nadira back aboard the *Black Star* and run like hell back to Asalian space. If he had any sense, he'd simply stop and shuttle her over. But damn it, he didn't want to. Never mind she would seriously compromise Asalian security -- he simply didn't want to let her go.

The more he thought about it, the faster he walked until he was jogging, then running, then sprinting as fast as he could down the corridors. People scrambled to get out of his way, but he hardly noticed. He was losing her. She'd stumbled into his life with the force of a thousand gigaton neutron plasma cannon, blown his world to bits, and nothing would be the same again. Ever. Even if they hadn't just shared the most explosive and satisfying sex in the entire universe -- several entire universes -- he knew he'd never be able to simply let her walk out of his life. There was something about her that felt like...

Home.

He couldn't imagine going back to a life without her.

Before he realized it, he found himself back at his cabin door. What was he going to do now? He'd just tell her how he felt. He didn't give a damn if an entire fleet of Vok'nair ships pursued them, she was staying here and that was final. If she didn't want him, too bad. She was a security risk. Mikiel was certain he could get backing from his government on that fact alone. He could probably make a good case on her being a prisoner of war, or some peacetime equivalent.

Pressing his hand to the entry pad, he stormed inside, but Nadira was nowhere to be found. He only had a few minutes before they arrived in the designated sector. *Damn it!*

With an exasperated -- and desperate -- huff, he stomped out of the room and made the trek to the command center. There, at the pilot's station where she belonged, sat Nadira. Her back was ramrod straight, her face pale except for a delicate flush to her nose, and he noticed her hands trembled slightly as she made minute course corrections. Mikiel watched her trail a hand lovingly over the console as if it were something precious to her. The sight was heartbreaking to him, and for the first time in his adult life, the stress of the situation was enough to make him need to vomit. He was so torn apart inside he wasn't altogether sure he could make it through without embarrassing himself in front of the crew.

"Status report," he barked.

"We're here, Commander," Ranier reported. "All's clear for twenty parsecs."

Mikiel punched a few buttons on his console, then addressed the *Black Star*. "Commander Singh. We will speak."

"There is nothing to speak about. You will return Nadira to me, or we will take any and all measures to take her from you."

"So you've said." Mikiel's heart pounded. He couldn't breathe. He had faith his ship could outfly the *Black Star* with anyone other than Nadira at the helm of the *Black Star*, but he had to try to convince Damon to join with them before he left. He knew it was important to Nadira. "However, I find myself in an awkward situation. Nadira has been studying this ship in an effort to adjust herself to life aboard the *Sword Breaker*. Simply letting her return to you would be a security risk of the greatest kind."

"I will not leave here without her, Commander Anjoom. I cannot."

"And I will not part with her, Singh. I'd say we have a big problem."

Out of the corner of his eye, he saw Nadira's head whip around in his direction. He couldn't see her expression, and he refused to look at her for fear of seeing something in her face he didn't want to see. Instead he gripped the armrest of his seat and kept his attention focused on the display screen in front of him that monitored the *Black Star*.

"Mikiel." Nadira's voice was soft, hesitant. Goddess, he didn't want to look at her! He didn't want to see rejection in her lovely eyes. This woman had made him soft, turned him into putty in her hands, and though he hated how weak it made him, he couldn't condemn her for it.

"I've made my decision, Nadira. You know too much about our ships and their capabilities."

"That's exactly why my father wants me. He truly might stop at nothing to get me back." The desolation in her voice was easy to hear. She hadn't figured out how to hide her emotions yet, thank the Goddess.

He met her timid gaze head on and knew the emotion on his own face must have been fierce because she wasn't the only one who cringed. "And I will stop at nothing to keep you. You're *mine*, Nadira. Nothing and no one will take you from me."

The look of hope that graced Nadira's features was worth the slight snicker he heard from Ranier. The man might have been young, but he knew Mikiel better than anyone. He also knew this was so out of character for Mikiel, Ranier most likely couldn't stop himself showing his mirth. Seeing his commander and friend fall so completely for a woman would, no doubt, amuse him for months. Well, that was all right. This particular woman was worth it. She was worth anything.

"Keeping her is a death sentence. Do you realize that?"

"If I only had a credit chip for every time I've heard *that* line. I'm confident I can overcome anything the Vok'nair Empire throws at me."

There was a pause, and Mikiel could imagine the older man considering his words. "Coming from anyone else, I'd say you were simply overconfident. But somehow, I think you just might be able to back up your claim. I should tell you, however, that I am just as committed to freeing Nadira from you as you are to keeping her. Not because her father told me to, but because I love her as if she were my own daughter. So, it would seem we've reached an impasse."

"Not necessarily." If he was going to be able to persuade Damon to join the *Black Star* with the *Sword Breaker*, this was his only chance. "The only question is, did you really mean you love Nadira like a daughter, or are you bluffing?"

"He's not bluffing, Mikiel." Nadira had turned almost completely around to face him now. "He raised me from when I was a very small girl. In fact, the reason I wanted to become a pilot was because of his influence." She must have guessed where he was headed. The excitement and hope in her face made his heart ache. How could she have gotten under his skin so completely?

"What do you want from me?" Mikiel could hear a wariness in his voice, but also resignation. He had him. It was time to explain everything.

"Nadira has formed a bond with the *Sword*

Breaker. She believes the *Black Star* has a part in that bond, though she doesn't know the nature of it. We'd like you to give her the chance to explore it."

"Interesting. How much of a role does this ship play in that bond?"

Mikiel looked at Nadira and nodded, giving her the go ahead to explain.

"It's not so much that I've bonded with the *Black Star*, though I did have a very small connection with her before I left. It's more like the *Sword Breaker* has bonded with her. Don't ask me how, but it's the only way I know how to describe it."

"Wait a minute. Did I understand you to say you believe the *Sword Breaker* has bonded with the *Black Star*?"

"I think so, yes." Damon seemed to be very interested in Nadira's mild reply.

"Has the ship said anything in particular about the *Black Star*? Has it told you why it has this bond?"

"He, Damon. The *Sword Breaker* is unquestionably male, just as the *Black Star* is female."

"Did he *say* anything, Nadira? Please! It's important!"

"What's going on?" Mikiel interrupted them, not because he was curious -- though he *was* curious -- but because Nadira cringed when Damon yelled at her. He got the feeling it hadn't happened often, and it upset Nadira.

"Quiet! Nadira. What did the ship tell you?"

"When we were knocked out of hyperspace, he said 'after all these years.' I got the feeling he meant the *Black Star*."

"Of course he did." The reply was no more than a whisper and a deep, resigned breath. "OK. I'll join you. But you have to give my crew a safe way back to

Vok'nair space."

Mikiel wasn't surprised. There was something going on with these ships only Damon knew. He wasn't pleased to be left out of the loop. "I assume you'll fill the rest of us in on this?" He couldn't keep the sarcasm out of his reply.

"Just promise my crew won't be harmed."

"I'll give them one of my best ships to return to Vok'nair. I have no interest in harming anyone. I only want the ship."

"The ship has a name! *Black Star*!" The intercom screeched both from the ship's speakers and all internal psycom units. Crewmembers screamed and covered their ears, though it didn't do any good.

"*Sword Breaker*! Please stop!" Nadira screamed her protest. Mikiel wanted to go to her, help her, though his head throbbed with the sudden burst of sound inside it.

"I'm tired of both of us being treated like inanimate objects. We are people. Not things." The volume was considerably less, but the voice still came from both sources.

"What's he mean, 'we'?" Mikiel was losing the thread of the conversation. He knew he had missed something somewhere, but things were moving too fast for him to keep up.

"He means the *Black Star* and the *Sword Breaker*. Do you know how cyborg vessels and cyborg androids are made?" Damon's voice from the intercom sounded wary, as if he was trying to measure his responses. Nadira wished she could have seen his face to gauge the situation a little better.

"A synthetic brain is grown from manufactured neurological cells. It is then implanted into the central computer. I don't know which parts, but it's the brain that allows the computer to free think, and more importantly, to allow a living human to link with it."

"Didn't you ever wonder what would happen if a *non*-synthetic brain from a living person was housed in the central computer? The Vok'nair have been linking with synthetic cyborg vessels for several years now. The Asalians only built one. Me. They could never find anyone to link with me and never tried an alternate method. The Vok'nair solution was simply too costly, not to mention slightly immoral from the Asalian viewpoint.

"Now, we have little Nadira. She's linked with me and I just bet you don't have a clue as to why." *Sword Breaker* was impatient by the sound of him. Like he was dealing with a bunch of lack wits.

Mikiel shook his head. It was like hearing an echo. The voice in his head was a split second faster than the voice from the speakers. It was distracting, but not so much he didn't understand what *Sword Breaker* was saying.

"So, you're saying you have a brain from a human donor housed inside your computer?"

The voice responded with contained fury. "No. I'm saying they paralyzed my voluntary muscles, shaved my head, and cut my skull open. They then connected my brain to the master computer, which was later connected to the lesser computers running this ship. Once that was done, my brain was severed from my body, which died immediately. And here is where I've been for the past twenty-three years. I'm not saying I have the brain of a human donor. I'm saying I *am* the brain. I *am* the human donor." No one spoke for several moments as the *Sword Breaker* let the image sink in. "Worse, I was very much alive and conscious during the entire grotesque procedure. So was the

Black Star. It was the only thing in a hundred years the Vok'nair and Asalian governments did together."

"But --" Mikiel could see Nadira's hands shake as she fiddled with her console. "-- the *Black Star* was only commissioned in the last six months. If the Vok'nair government had her all this time, why keep her a secret?"

"Because no one has been able to bond with her. It is the same with me, only the Asalian Coalition saw fit to use my other talents and change crews every so often in case someone was actually able to bond with me."

"You sound as if you know what the problem is." Mikiel was incensed. What the ship was describing was nothing short of torture.

"Asalians have very few true telepaths, or empaths for that matter. You can enhance my telepathic and empathic abilities all you want, but if the person trying to form a link with me isn't capable of telepathic communication, a bond will not be formed." *Great Sword* made perfect sense. It would explain why they hadn't figured out the key to bonding with the ship.

"What about enhancers to the one who is to be bonded?"

"Enhance all you want. You can multiply zero by a hundred million and you still get zero. If you don't have the gene that enables telepathic ability, enhancing a gene that's not there isn't going to make a hell of a lot of difference."

"But what about me?" Nadira looked at Mikiel then. He could see she was confused. "I was never enhanced. My telepathic ability extends only to close members of my family. I've never had contact with anyone else."

"Then --" *Great Sword* made his statement without holding anything back, without softening the blow one little bit. "-- it is quite likely that you would never share a telepathic link with anyone outside your family."

Mikiel thought he might be sick, and from the look on Nadira's face, she felt the same way. He could see there was no way she could force the words out, so he said them for her.

"How are you related?"

There was an awful silence. His command crew had identical looks of sympathy directed at Nadira, but she didn't seem to be aware of it.

"Damon?" Her voice was small, like a child going to a beloved parent for answers to life's questions.

"The essence within the *Sword Breaker* is your father." Damon's whisper was almost lost as it came through the speakers.

"Wait a minute." Mikiel had stood and was now beside Nadira with a hand squeezing her shoulder in support. "You told me Vok'nair's king was Nadira's father."

"So I did. And I'm probably the only other living person who could say otherwise. Her mother was in love with a star pilot named Darian, but she was forced into a marriage with Samair, Vok'nair's king. Even still, Nani kept seeing her lover. When she became pregnant, the king had the six-month-old fetus tested and found out the child wasn't his. He knew immediately who the father was, and had Darian arrested and condemned him to death.

"Instead of carrying out the sentence, however, Samair was persuaded to turn Darian over to the science division of the Empire, where they were working with the Asalian Coalition to develop cyborg vessels such as the *Black Star* and the *Sword Breaker*.

"As for Nani, she was allowed to deliver the baby and the same fate was bestowed upon her. Six months after Nadira was born, her parents' brains were transferred into the ships you see now. And here they'll stay until the organic parts wear out. When that happens, the ships go back to being ships. When everyone failed -- and I mean many, many people tried and failed -- Samair figured the only other alternative was to allow you to try. *Black Star* was altered yet again. This time, blocks were created within her telepathic matrix to keep her from relaying any information that would compromise the secrecy of this project. He needed you to bond with this ship, but he didn't want you to know who she really was."

"Why did he keep me in the first place?" Nadira asked. "I-I mean, you raised me and he's not had much to do with me, but still."

"That I couldn't say."

"Well --" Nadira stood. "-- what do we do now?"

Mikiel needed to bring this to a close and get Nadira back to their quarters. She needed time to process this. "We send the crew of the *Black Star* on their way and get back to Asalian space." He turned to Ranier. "How long will it take *Morning Star* to rendezvous with us?"

"Not long, Sir. Two standards hours maybe."

"Very well. Damon, ready your people for transfer. Anyone who wishes to stay aboard the *Black Star* may do so -- the rest will be transferred to the *Morning Star*. That ship is scheduled for sale and has been stripped of all nonessential equipment. It will get them safely back home without giving away too many secrets."

"I'll make the necessary arrangements. Nadira -- " Damon's voice changed. Mikiel could hear the sadness there. "-- I'm so very sorry you had to find out like this. Your father was -- is -- a good man. He didn't deserve his punishment, but since it's done, you couldn't be in safer hands. As long as you're aboard that ship, you'll have the best guardian angel anyone could ever have."

Mikiel saw a tear trickle down Nadira's cheek and decided that was enough. "I'll be in my quarters, Ranier. Alert me when the *Morning Star* is ready for departure with its new crew." Then he took Nadira by the arm and led her down the corridor to their dwelling. She didn't even try to resist.

Chapter Nine

It was all too much for Nadira, though it did explain a great many things. Her father's indifference to her at times for one thing, his adamant refusal to give her permission to learn to pilot a space ship for another. Still, it was hard to imagine the man who had ordered such horrible fates for his wife and her lover had allowed his wife's bastard child to be born and then taken on the responsibility of caring for that child himself. True, he hadn't had much of a hand in raising her, but he had given her the protection of his name and had never denied the privileges that went with that name.

Mikiel didn't say a word on the way to the privacy of their quarters. He held her arm firmly, but gently, in his grasp. Over the time of her stay with him, she had started to see a whole new side of him. He might not have said the words, but she had no doubt this man loved her.

When the door finally slid closed behind them, shutting out the rest of the universe, Mikiel wrapped his arms around her and held her tightly to him. There was no sexual implication, only affection, support, and comfort.

Nadira couldn't help herself. Silently, she let her tears flow. When her vision blurred from the moisture in her eyes, she simply buried her face in Mikiel's chest. He scooped her up into his strong arms and carried her to the bed.

"Are you all right?" His voice was more tender than she could ever remember hearing from him.

"I will be. There are so many unanswered questions."

"There always are, Nadira. You were born into a

world where there will always be more questions than answers."

She smiled. "I know. It doesn't mean I have to like it."

Mikiel dipped his head to kiss her and she accepted willingly. After the mental beating she'd just taken, she needed a soothing balm and Mikiel was exactly that. His tongue lapped gently at her, demanding neither her response nor participation. It was a kiss meant totally for her pleasure, and she loved him for it.

After long moments, Mikiel ended the kiss and pulled her close to him, fitting her easily into the curve of his body. "What am I going to do with you, Nadira?"

"What you're doing now seems pretty nice."

His slight chuckle warmed her to her toes. "It does, but I was thinking in longer terms."

"Why should things have to change? We've managed to find a comfortable way to coexist with each other. And the sex wasn't bad either."

"Very funny." No sooner were the words out of his mouth than he flipped her onto her back and covered her body with his. "But things *do* have to change. As a Vok'nair, you could never be anything other than my mistress."

Nadira felt the blood rush to her face and wasn't sure she could breathe as the meaning of what he was saying sunk in. "Mikiel?"

"I sent a request for asylum and citizenship for you several weeks ago and today I got the approval. I thought you should at least have the choice if you wanted it. It's up to you."

She was so excited her heart felt like it might pound out of her chest. With a swift move and a hard shove, she flipped Mikiel to his back and straddled his hips. "Mikiel, is this your roundabout way of asking me to join my life to yours?"

He looked a little annoyed, but Nadira could see the vulnerability in his eyes. "Yes. That's what I want, Nadira, more than anything."

"Then I accept."

She leaned down to kiss him and he wrapped his arms around her to hug her close. The emotion she felt from the touch of his mouth and arms brought tears to her eyes. When he ended the kiss, she smiled at him. "Who said you couldn't be gentle?"

Mikiel laughed. He had never felt so good in all his life. For the first time, he felt complete. Whole. There wasn't anything he wouldn't do to keep her with him.

"I love you, Nadira. With all that I am, I love you."

"I know." She giggled when a look of male suffering came across his face. "You're pretty good at hiding your feelings, but I figured it out."

"And you? I took you, kept you here against your will, and made your life miserable for several months. Can you find it in you to love me back?"

Nadira grew serious, all kidding and joking pushed aside while she spoke what was in her heart. "I'm not exactly sure when I realized I loved you, but I've known it for a while now. I think it was your decision to keep me here rather than give me my own place that started me down that path. I lived with you -- difficult as you were sometimes -- saw you in a way no one else ever could, and managed to see through the gruff exterior you present to everyone else." She cupped his face in one of her hands. "You're a good man, Mikiel. You've always done right by me, even if you did trade me for the *Black Star*'s freedom." She chuckled at that. "Which, by the way, turned out better than I could have hoped. Not only do I have my freedom, but I have a wonderful man and a father I never knew. I'd say things turned out for the best. You even got the *Black Star*."

"Yeah, well. I think it might be wise to keep that a secret for a while. I don't want these ships separated until I can figure out what to do. What happened to them simply wasn't right. I won't compound that injustice by running back to Homeworld with a war prize."

Nadira's heart swelled. He truly was a remarkable man. "Just one more reason why I love you, Mikiel."

She wrapped her arms around him as he took her mouth again. This time, he demanded her participation. His hands shaped the curves of her body. If he lived an eternity, he would never grow tired of how womanly she felt in his arms. Every curve, every contour, was created with him in mind. She was the perfect woman for him, both in body and in spirit.

He rolled off her so he could rid himself of his clothes and she did the same. When she bent her knees and spread her legs, Mikiel situated himself in the cradle of her body. With one forward surge of his hips, he filled her. Nothing felt so good as Nadira's tender flesh surrounding him.

She arched her back, and he took the offering of her breasts. One hand supported her back while the other squeezed and fondled one large mound. His mouth latched on to the other and he knew he had reached the glory of the afterlife. Surely there could never be a place or time as wonderful as the moment he was in right now.

Nadira met him thrust for thrust, her pussy hot and becoming wetter with each pull of his mouth and each surge of his hips. Her breath came in short gasps, and when he lifted his head to take her mouth once again, he noticed sweat dotting her forehead and upper lip. Her cunt clenched and unclenched and Mikiel knew it wouldn't be long before she came.

"I love you, Nadira. I always will." He managed to get the words out as he pumped himself into her faster yet until he felt the spasming of her pussy growing out of control. When she threw back her head and screamed her pleasure, he let himself go. Stream after stream of his cum bathed her inside. With any luck, he had planted the seed of his child inside her.

Time would tell.

Time would tell.

Epilogue

Black Star had never felt so empty. Damon had just put the last crewmember aboard the ship that would take them back to Vok'nair. He had no doubt a bounty would be issued for him as soon as his crew arrived. The king would not be forgiving in this betrayal.

But that was OK. If he had stood up for his friend all those years ago, none of this would be happening. Anything the king saw fit to do to him, he probably deserved.

Only a handful of the *Black Star*'s crew remained -- those who were loyal to him and not the Empire -- but he needed a pilot. When he'd requested assistance from the *Sword Breaker*, they had sent a man only slightly older than Nadira named Ranier. In only a couple of hours, he was handling the helm as if he belonged there. His easygoing manner put the rest of the command crew at ease, and they soon settled into their regular routine. Confident everything was under control, Damon headed back to his quarters to lie down. It had been an exhausting day.

When the door swished open and the lights didn't automatically come on, Damon went into full battle mode. Something wasn't right. He stepped carefully around the room, letting his eyes adjust to the dim light, the only illumination coming from starshine through the window. That was when he noticed the oddly shaped lump on his bed.

"Lights," he barked. The computer complied, and the lump shrieked and sat straight up. In the middle of his bed sat an incredibly thin woman dressed in nothing more than tattered rags. Her long white hair tumbled around her face in a frizzy tangle.

Dirt and grease smudged her skin. And she stank.

She must have snuck aboard at the last outpost they'd visited to pick up supplies. Wherever she had come from, she was here now. Probably after a better life for herself.

Well, time would tell if she had made a wise decision. For now, he'd clean her up and feed her. Then they could figure out what came next. Damon had the feeling life was about to get interesting.

He'd just acquired a stowaway.

Black Star Stowaway
A Sci-Fi Futuristic Alien Adventure
Marteeka Karland

Phoebe Lightheart is on the run from the Hand of God, a sectarian religious group known for their ruthless rule over the space stations they control. For the last ten years, she's functioned as little more than a slave. She vows no man will ever have that kind of power over her again.

Stowing away on the *Black Star*, she's discovered by Damon Singh. Although he knows Phoebe doesn't want a man in her life, Damon is drawn to her with a passion that frightens him. And Phoebe can't deny the attraction she feels for Damon. He's the most gentle, sincere man she's ever met. And the sexiest creature in the universe.

Unfortunately, she forgot one important thing about the Hand of God. There is no leaving them, and even the legendary *Black Star* may be hard-pressed to keep Phoebe safe.

Chapter One

Lights from the entryway to hangar thirty-five flooded the vast, open "visitor" area of Graves Station, deserted in the wake of the strict curfew. Every footfall, every whisper was magnified in the severe silence. Phoebe Lightheart shivered in her hiding place in the deep shadows of one of the many ventilation ducts, an iron grate the only barrier between freedom and continued life as a slave to every man on the station.

She had sat in the place for many days and nights, working loose the iron screws in order to be ready for the slightest chance of escape. Phoebe was risking her life on the hope she could sneak aboard a ship and leave this accursed place forever. If she were caught, her death would not be swift. Even now, she had reached the point of no return. She had been gone for too long. Even one day was too long. There was no doubt she had already been missed. It would still take several days for the Hand to search the lower decks. In their arrogance, they would assume she was simply hiding to avoid her "chores." It would take time for them to realize she had betrayed their holy community and was attempting escape.

No one escaped from the Hand of God. No one.

Phoebe intended to be the first.

When the legendary ship *Black Star* had docked there the day before, Phoebe's heart had soared. This was her chance. Her *only* chance. If this didn't work, she doubted she'd live long enough to wait for another ship to dock in this remote area of the station. She had only been able to smuggle out a couple days' worth of food -- which was long gone -- and she couldn't go back. Trying this in a more populated area was as out of the question as going back to the Hand.

No one had been in or out of this hangar for hours now. It was time to move. Silently, she pushed open the heavy grate centimeter by centimeter. Crawling carefully from her hiding place, Phoebe stayed close to the bulkheads and shadows, making her moves slow and patient. She hadn't come all this way, waited all this time, only to be discovered because of impatience.

The gangplank was down, but that was likely to be guarded from the inside. She circled the ship until she found what she was looking for. The solid waste outlet. During flight, the small hatch was locked tight, but when the ship landed, the change in air pressure released it for easy garbage disposal by the station's personnel.

And it was the perfect inlet for her.

The chute was small, and it was a very tight fit, but she managed to crawl inside. The smell of rotten food and stinking trash was strong, but not unfamiliar. While the men of the Hand enjoyed all the clean comforts of the station, women who hadn't been chosen as wives or house maids were often forced to live in places that smelled similar. The farther down in the station one lived, the stronger the stench. Compared to a whole community's waste, this was only a mild odor.

Once she reached the main garbage hold, it was just a matter of being quiet and choosing carefully. Pausing to catch her breath and muster her failing strength, she looked carefully at each hatch door. She chose one of the smaller hatches, as those should lead to a less populated area of the ship. An exhausting ten-minute crawl later, she reached another small hatch. This time, when she opened it, the smell of clean, fresh air assaulted her almost as much as the stench of garbage would have someone else. Her nose tingled with the sensation, and she had the almost uncontrollable urge to sneeze.

After days of being in almost total darkness, the dim lights of the corridor hurt her eyes. She wasn't exactly sure what she was going to do, but she knew she needed to find a seldom-used closet or vacant crew quarters and find a place to hide. With any luck, she wouldn't get caught, or if she were they would be so far away from Graves Station they wouldn't insist on taking her back.

The thought no sooner crossed her mind than she heard two sets of heavy footfalls coming nearer. Her heart slammed in her chest as she looked around. There wasn't anywhere to hide. Every door she'd tried since she exited the trash chute had been locked. Looking frantically, she spotted a nook in the wall with two steps leading down to a closed door panel. It was probably locked, too, but with the dim lighting, if she crouched as low as she could on the landing in front of the door, they might not see her.

Quickly darting across the corridor, she made the two steps and huddled as tightly against the wall as she could, trying to keep her body in the shadows as much as possible. They were getting closer. She could hear them talking. She was sure they'd be able to hear her heart thudding. Her breath came in rapid gasps as fear assailed her. She felt like a rat caught in a trap.

Just as the men were about to round the corner, the door behind her slid open silently. Phoebe jumped, startled at first, but she'd never been one to question good fortune when it came her way. She ducked inside, and the door slid shut behind her.

The spacious cabin filled with a soft, dim light as soon as the door closed. She just stood there a few moments, letting her eyes adjust and waiting to see if the men had noticed her. If so, she expected they'd follow. They had been so close, there was no way she'd have time to hide even if she'd seen a good place right off.

She didn't. The room was so Spartan, she was sure no one occupied it. Only a desk and a large bed graced the interior. Phoebe let out a sigh of relief. If she were careful, maybe she wouldn't be noticed.

First, she looked around for some kind of food replicator. She had heard some of the Imperial ships had them, though it was rumored the Coalition preferred actual cooking to synthetic nourishment. She was terribly hungry and a trek to find food outside her new haven would have to wait until she figured out the ship's schedules. The last thing she wanted was to get caught in a morning rush.

Nothing. There was nothing she could eat. Disappointment hit her harder than she expected. She was hungrier than she could ever remember being. It had taken every ounce of energy she had left to get this far. Many more days without food and she wouldn't be able to walk across the room, much less sneak around an unfamiliar ship.

At the moment, however, there wasn't much she could do about it. She needed sleep almost as badly as she needed food, and the bed on the far end of the chamber, next to a blackened window panel, looked particularly inviting. She knew she shouldn't sleep there, out in the open. She knew it was dangerous. But she wanted so much to sleep in a real bed and not a cold floor padded with only one of the two blankets each woman was allowed. It was a temptation she simply couldn't resist.

Decision made, she crawled into the middle of

the bed. As soon as her head hit the pillow, she took one deep breath, sighed happily, and fell promptly asleep.

* * *

"Lights." A husky, male voice barked out the order. Phoebe sat straight up in the bed and realized, too late, her mistake. She had fallen asleep. Now she was well and truly caught. She had no idea how long she'd been out, but she was fairly certain her escape had just been cut short.

"Well, well. A stowaway." His nose twitched. "From the smell of you, I'd say I need to look into putting security at the solid waste outlet hatch."

"I'm sorry to ruffle your delicate sensibilities, but it was the only way inside." Phoebe had never backed down from anyone. It was the reason she'd spent so much time in the bowels of the station instead of being snatched up as a man's wife or concubine, or even a maid. She tended to speak her mind. Still, this time she cringed inwardly. This wasn't the time to piss off this particular man.

His only response was a raised eyebrow. "Indeed. And now what? You expect free passage to wherever you see fit?"

"I don't suppose you'd let that happen, would you?"

"Not if I want anything to get done. Everyone on the *Black Star* has to earn his keep. If you want to stay here, you'll have to do the same."

There was no inflection in the man's gravelly voice, but the steel in his gray eyes told her exactly how serious he was. If she didn't do what he told her, he'd likely space her.

"B-but no one knows I'm here." Phoebe stammered her response. A sense of dread was slowly but surely closing in on her. She hated being on the defensive, but she didn't really have a way to combat him. She *was* a stowaway aboard his ship. If he chose to make her pay his passage, there wasn't much she could do about it. Her only hope was to get him to agree to something she could live with.

"Just how long do you think that will last? How will you get food? If I bring rations back to you, everyone is going to wonder why I get double, and why I bring it back to my quarters. They'll soon figure it out." He crossed his arms over the massive expanse of his chest. "Hiding you isn't an option. You want passage? You'll have to work for it."

Briefly, Phoebe thought about bolting for the door, but this wasn't a small man. He stood there, feet slightly apart. As spacious as the room was, he dominated it. She might be able to get around him, but she was willing to bet she'd not get far.

Phoebe crossed her legs and sat up a little straighter. "I don't have many skills, I'll warn you. But I'm smart, and I'm willing to learn."

For the longest time, the man simply looked at her as if sizing her up. Phoebe had to stick her hands underneath her to keep from fidgeting. His gaze was too intense. He saw too much.

Finally, he spoke. "Later. If I'm going to have to put up with you for any length of time, I'll have to be able to stand being around you." He pointed to a room on the far side of his quarters. "Shower's in there. Have you ever used an ultrasonic shower?"

Phoebe hated looking like she wasn't wise to the universe around her, but if she said yes, she'd used one, he'd undoubtedly leave her to it by herself. "I'm afraid not. Just show me how to operate it, and I'll manage on my own."

Again, he raised an eyebrow, as if the whole thing was amusing to him, but he didn't say anything. He stepped ahead of her and into the small bathing chamber. Entering a combination of numbers on a keypad outside a booth that looked barely big enough for one person, he handed her two small, spongy disc-shaped objects.

"Put these in your ears."

"What are they for?" Phoebe looked curiously at the things. They were pliable, but rather stiff, as if they wanted to hold their shape no matter what form they were squeezed into.

"The ultra high frequency of the shower will damage your hearing if you don't protect your ears."

Her gaze snapped to his. "Then why not just use water? I don't want to get in that thing."

"You don't have a choice." He leaned against the wall and crossed his arms over his chest. In the small room, Phoebe got a stark visual on exactly how big he was, and how tiny she was in comparison. He wore a black formfitting uniform that should have looked silly. But on this man, it outlined every powerful curve of his body. The muscles in his arms, legs, chest and chiseled abdomen stood out underneath the material as if a master sculptor had carved them. Phoebe had to force herself to look at his face. That wasn't any better, though. He wasn't pretty or handsome as some men were, but his features held a wealth of wisdom and promises of something she couldn't quite put her finger on.

Judging by the way his nose twitched, he also didn't want to be near her much longer. That was acutely embarrassing, because she could have stood there and looked at him all day.

"No. I don't suppose I do." She fiddled with the

earplugs in her hand. "So, I stick these in my ears. Then what?"

"Then you get in and let the ultrasonics do the rest."

Phoebe stuffed the spongy things in her ears and gasped when they expanded. She immediately started to dig in her ears, trying to get them out. It felt like they were going to burst through her inner ear into her brain.

The man's strong hands grabbed her wrists. He mouthed the word "no," but she couldn't hear anything. He held her gaze captive, looking intently at her, watching. Waiting.

In a few seconds, the sensations in her ears eased, but all sound was gone. The only thing she could hear was the sound of her own heart beating wildly, and air moving through her sinus passages as she sucked in breath after breath. She made an effort to slow her breathing, knowing that hyperventilating would only cause her to pass out.

He nodded his head and moved his hands from her wrists to her shoulders, squeezing them reassuringly, then let go of her. When he inserted two of the same discs into his own ears, she realized he meant to shower with her. Immediately, her breathing and heart rate shot up again. She shook her head and pushed at him, trying to shove him out the door so she could do this on her own. The last thing she wanted to do was to undress in front of this perfect specimen of a man.

He gripped her shoulders again and shook her slightly. Phoebe was beginning to panic now. What if he intended for her to earn her keep with her body? She fought madly now. His mouth moved, but she couldn't hear anything. She pushed him into the wall, and knocked over a few small bottles and a cup from the tiny vanity stand, but no sound reached her. The whole thing was so surreal, she would have laughed if she hadn't been so terrified.

Phoebe fought like a mad woman, kicking and clawing. He managed to spin her around and wrap one arm above her breasts, and the other just under her chin. Without even flinching, she bit him, all the while digging at her ears, trying to free them of the shit she'd put in them. She whipped around to face him and one well-placed kick caught him in the knee, and he grimaced. She hoped he yelped in pain, but she didn't hear it. Apparently, that was all he was going to take.

The man backhanded Phoebe. Hard. Her head spun and she would have sunk to the floor if he hadn't caught her. Eyes blazing, obviously angry, his look said she was in big trouble. She wanted to fight him, but she couldn't get her legs underneath her. She still reeled from the blow he'd delivered.

He pulled her into his hard body and maneuvered them into the impossibly tiny stall. Her back was pressed against one wall and she was sure he was in a similar position. Phoebe watched as he pressed a few buttons to her left before reaching above them and sticking two eye shields over her eyes, then his own. She could still see, but it was like looking through dark glasses. He pressed another combination of buttons, and very bright light flooded her vision. Even with the shields, it made her wince.

Phoebe's skin tingled and her scalp itched. She happened to catch a glimpse of her hair where it hung down her arm. No longer was it a tangled, stinking mass. It was long, silvery white, and soft as down against her shoulders. The shock and amazement combined with the recent blow to her head made her head spin, and her knees buckled. The man's strong arms tightened around her, and she gratefully, passively, let him hold her. Her head fell against the hard muscles of his chest. His musky, masculine scent filled her nostrils. She blamed the sudden lightheaded feeling on the blow he'd given her, but she suspected it was her damned woman's hormones making her drunk. She didn't believe everything the Hand of God taught, but maybe they were right about this one thing. Maybe women were weak when it came to sex. She should hate this man, or at the very least be terrified of him. After all, he held her life in his hands.

Instead, at this very moment, she wished with all her heart her first impression of this scenario had played out. She wanted to be naked with him. OK, so mostly she just wanted *him* naked. She wanted to feel his skin against her cheek. Would it be smooth, or roughened with hair? The scent of him would be much stronger, of that she was sure. What would he taste like? Would he groan if she reached out with her tongue and laved the pebbled nipple even now stabbing the material of his uniform?

She shivered. When his arms tightened around her, she looked up at him. Gentle compassion shone in his eyes, but there was something else there as well. When Phoebe shifted her position, trying to stand more fully on her own, she realized what that "something else" was.

Lust. Need.

She tried not to cling to him, but the evidence of that lust and need poked her soundly in the belly. Her legs turned to mush yet again and she balled her hands into fists to keep from clutching his broad shoulders and caressing those bulky muscles.

Seconds later, the light faded and he guided her

out of the stall. Taking an instrument from the vanity, he raised it to her ear. Phoebe didn't protest, but let him do what he would. He removed first one earplug, then the other, before removing his own.

"Now," he crossed his arms over that chest again, "do you think you can make it back to the main room without trying to kill me?"

Chapter Two

Damon honestly couldn't blame the tiny woman for being scared. The first time he stuck those accursed earpieces in his ears, he'd nearly come unglued. He'd paid for his thoughtless mistake, though. The little hellcat had almost taken his leg off. His knee still throbbed, and he limped slightly, gingerly.

He was getting too old for this.

She couldn't have been much older than Nadira, the girl he'd practically raised. He had to remember that. If he didn't, he'd likely do things to this girl that would surely send him to the Seventh Level of Hell. Even before the ultrasonics got her clean, she'd stirred something primitive inside him. The second he'd taken her into his arms, even fighting as she was, his cock had gone rock hard.

He would have never taken her by force, ever. He wouldn't take her, period, until he was sure she wanted him as well. She was just too damned young. Anyway, a girl as lovely as she was would never be interested in an old goat like him.

Damon retreated to the far side of the room to give her some space. He watched her as she stared in amazement at her reflection. The transformation was astounding. She was still way too thin for his liking, like she had been starved, but she was absolutely stunning.

Her hair was the most pronounced change. Before, it had been a frizzy mass of tangles and dirt. He had initially wondered if it was a platinum blond, but once it had been blasted clean of grime, it shone a lustrous, brilliant silver-white. High cheekbones were made more prominent because she was so thin, but it gave her an exotic look that called to his baser nature.

The tattered clothes she wore were still in very bad condition, but at least they were clean now. She needed new garments, but he'd be damned if he didn't like looking at her in what she was wearing. There were bits of creamy flesh visible in the most tantalizing places. The fine muscle of one thigh, the curve of a breast, and an amazingly sexy belly button were just taunting him like no woman ever had before.

He wanted her. Badly.

"So," he began, clearing his throat when his voice came out more husky than normal, "what are we to do with you? What task can you do to earn your keep aboard this ship?"

She turned to him then and wrapped her arms around her, as if she felt too exposed, which she was. "If you're thinking of anything… indecent… forget it. I'd rather be spaced than sell my body to anyone." Her chin came up a notch or two in defiance, but Damon didn't miss the tremor in her chin.

"From what I observed on Graves Station -- and I know that's where you came from because it's the only place we've stopped in three standard months -- I would have thought you'd done that already." He was fishing. He knew she'd been through a lot just by looking at her. It wasn't only her initial appearance. There was a haunted look in her eyes he couldn't ignore.

"There's a reason I looked and smelled so badly, and it wasn't only your garbage hold. I did my best to stay below the station to escape notice. The nastier I was, the less likely someone would decide he wanted me for a wife or housemaid. Those women have a harder time deciding how their bodies are used, and that's just not something I wanted to be a part of."

"Is that why you're here? To protect your body

against invasion?"

"That, and because I'm tired of being a slave to every man on the station. I should be able to work to help myself, not in order to live." Again, that haughty, defiant expression graced her face. She looked more like an avenging angel than a slave.

"Then you won't mind working here." He turned to a computer panel on the wall and began tapping keys. He accessed the areas where help was needed on the ship, but he didn't need to. Damon knew the *Black Star* and her crew inside and out. It was more a reason to focus his attention somewhere other than the bare curve of that one breast. His cock twitched at the thought of exposing it fully and taking it into his mouth and…

"I won't work for passage only. I need some way to make money for when you drop me off."

Damon smiled. She was a feisty little thing. "Who said you had to? I pay fair wages and anyone may leave at any time. All you have to do is perform a useful service in a necessary area and you can stay until we get to wherever you want to go, or until you've saved enough to start a life of your own."

They looked at each other for a moment, and Damon could have sworn he saw his own hunger mirrored in her eyes. Then she looked away and admitted, "I can't do much. All I ever did on the station was cook, and only for the women and girls below decks. We didn't have much, so I had to be creative."

Damon raised an eyebrow. This might work better than he'd thought. "Are you any good?"

"Well, I never had any complaints, and the kids said they loved it when I cooked."

"We'll give it a try. If the crew approves, you've

got yourself a job."

When she smiled, Damon knew he was in real trouble. Her whole face lit up. Fear was replaced with hope, and she looked at him like he was somebody special. Important to her. Denying her anything was going to be almost as hard as it had been to leave Nadira aboard *Sword Breaker* several months earlier, and that was saying something.

"By the way." She gave him a quizzical look. "What's your name?"

Damon could have groaned out loud. It wasn't possible he could actually do this twice in less than one standard month. Of all the stupid things. "My apologies. It seems I still lack the necessary diplomatic skills to even exchange names before I get deep into negotiations. I'm Damon Singh. Captain of the *Black Star.*"

She approached him hesitatingly, but extended her hand in greeting. "Phoebe Lightheart…"

Anything else she might have said was totally lost on Damon. The second he had her hand in his, it was like an electric charge shot up his arm and straight to his groin. His fingers tingled, and as he looked into her eyes, he had the sensation of falling into their silvery green depths. She was hypnotizing him with her subtle sexuality as effortlessly as one of the highly skilled courtesans of the Asalian people.

The two of them stood there for what seemed like forever -- at least it did to Damon. Finally, Phoebe pulled her hand free and averted her gaze.

"I won't, Captain," she whispered. "I won't sell my body, even for my life."

It took Damon a moment to find his voice because his throat was so dry. "I would never ask it of you. I apologize for my weakness." It was hard for

Damon to admit this to a stranger, but he'd never been one to be dishonest. It was the only way he knew how to gain the trust of his crew. Honesty. He waited until her gaze returned to his. "I would never force myself on someone who didn't want me, Phoebe. And I would never use my position aboard this ship to influence anyone into my bed."

She seemed to consider this before finally nodding her head. "Well, if I'm going to do this, I suppose you should show me the kitchen. I'd like to know what I have to work with."

"Of course." Damon was grateful for the chance to focus on something else, but then he remembered her state of dress. Or rather undress. "Perhaps --" He almost blurted out something that might sound insulting but caught himself. "Let me get you a uniform. That way everyone will know you're a part of the crew."

She blinked a couple of times before looking back down at her garments. "I'd almost forgotten how inadequate they are." She crossed her arms over her breasts. "I suppose I look horrible."

She looked so dejected, Damon didn't even try to measure his response. "On the contrary, Phoebe. You look like an angelic fairy. The only thing missing is your wings."

Phoebe hadn't known what to say. She hoped it was a compliment, but she really didn't want to think about it. If she did, this was a man she could easily surrender herself to, and that could be disastrous for her. She didn't know Damon. She didn't know what he was capable of, and she certainly didn't know what his plan for her was. It had been her experience that every man had an agenda. She'd just have to figure out what his was.

Once she was dressed in the black, form-fitting uniform of the *Black Star*, Damon took her to the kitchen area. It was larger than anything she'd ever seen, and she was a bit intimidated. What had she gotten herself into? Not that it mattered. She didn't have much choice but to learn.

"How many do I have to feed?" she asked, dreading the answer. The sheer size of the kitchen was answer enough.

"At present? Twenty. Assuming we pick up more from *Sword Breaker* when we rendezvous with him, you could have as many as thirty-three."

Phoebe's jaw dropped. She had had to feed more than two hundred women and girls with about half the space and equipment the *Black Star* afforded.

"Is that going to be a problem?"

She almost laughed. "Are you kidding? With all this? Unless you simply have no food, I think I can come up with something." For the first time since sneaking aboard the *Black Star*, Phoebe was excited about the prospects for her future. Perhaps she had won this impossible gamble after all.

The grand tour was just that to her. Wonderfully grand! There was enough food stored on this ship to feed everyone in the below decks of Graves Station for months. All this food for a maximum of thirty-three people? It was unimaginable.

"I don't think there will be a problem," she said when he'd finished. "I might require someone to show me how to work some of the equipment, but I think I can figure out most of it." She hesitated before asking, "There isn't anything in here that could blow me up, is there?"

He chuckled. She got the impression he didn't

laugh much, but his eyes sparkled when he did. It nearly took her breath. This man affected her like nothing she was prepared for. She was about to thank him for being so nice to her when a claxon sounded and Captain Singh was requested in the command center.

"Do you remember the way back to my quarters?" The smile she'd thought so engaging disappeared, and the stoic captain returned.

"I can find it," she said. "Go on. I'll be fine."

He nodded smartly and spun around to leave. Once he was out the door, she heard his heavy footfalls quicken. Phoebe left the spacious kitchen and headed in the opposite direction of Captain Singh. She'd do what he asked of her. In the years she'd spent under the rule of the men of the Hand of God, she'd learned to assess people quickly. She got the impression he was a man of his word. She wasn't sure why she thought that, but the sense was so strong, she was willing to bet her life.

Chapter Three

"Captain, unknown vessels exiting hyperspace on the starboard bow." The second in command didn't so much say the words as hiss them. Everything he said sounded so menacing, it prickled the hair on the back of Damon's neck. Viktor scared the shit out of him, but he was one hell of a Second. "They look like they've been cobbled from every class of vessel in the known universe. Heavily armed, but not very well armored. One solid hit, and we'd punch through their hull."

"Have they tried to contact us?" Damon studied the strange looking ships and their formations, and tried to get a concept of how they moved and what they were capable of.

"Negative, Sir. They've apparently been mirroring our course through a series of hyperspace jumps just out of range of our sensors. I only found them by accident." The Second swung his chair around to face Damon. "My guess would be…"

"They're waiting for reinforcements." Damon finished the sentence for Viktor with a sinking feeling in his stomach. "Any idea who they are?"

"They're too small to go far without a mother ship, and anything that big, I'd be able to locate as long as it stayed within the range of those fighters. The only place they could have come from was that border station we just left."

Damon raised an eyebrow. "Interesting." Why did he have the impression this had something to do with his new crewmember? "How far away is *Sword Breaker*?"

"Assuming they're already at the rendezvous point, five standard hours. However, it could be as many as eight if they were delayed as Captain Anjoom feared they might be."

"Perhaps you should let him know it would be in our best interest to have some backup."

"As you command, Sir." If Damon knew Viktor - - and he prided himself in knowing his crew inside and out -- the cybernetically enhanced vampire loathed the idea of asking for help. It grated him to think there was a situation he couldn't handle by himself. It was Viktor's only fault. He had to learn to be part of the crew, to rely on his shipmates as they relied on him.

"Try to talk to them. See if they'll tell us what they want."

"I've been trying, Sir." Viktor sounded annoyed. "They either aren't capable of communication or they're ignoring me."

Damon tried to control the smile playing at his lips. "I see."

"I don't like being ignored, Captain." The big man was definitely annoyed. Of all the people aboard the *Black Star*, of all the people Damon had met, period, Viktor was the last person he would want annoyed at him.

"Just don't get an itchy trigger finger, Viktor. Not until I tell you to." The Second only grunted. "Keep an eye on them. If they make any sudden moves, I want to know about it."

"As you command."

Damon knew he needed to remain at the command center, but he had to get his new crewmember settled. For some reason, he didn't want to make it widely known she was here. He felt like the longer he kept Phoebe to himself, the longer she'd be his. The girl had gotten under his skin but good, and he'd only spent a few minutes in her presence. He was too old to be acting like a teenager with a crush.

He rose, making eye contact with Viktor as he did. "You're in command. Notify me at the slightest change in their behavior."

His Second didn't speak, only raised an eyebrow. Damon turned on his heel and headed out the door. Back to his cabin.

He found it empty. Phoebe had been back -- her uniform jacket lay on the bed -- but she had apparently left.

Damon's heart raced. Where was she? Had she left him already? He felt like a little boy. Insecure. Scared. And for what? A woman? A woman he didn't even know. He was obsessed with her. Ridiculous!

Heading back to the bridge would be the best plan, but he knew he wouldn't. After an hour of searching, Damon punched a bulkhead. No Phoebe. Where was she?

Actually, where was *everyone*? The ship was deserted. And what was that smell? It wafted through the halls, growing stronger and more delicious as he went.

"Captain!" Damon spun around. Connor. He was a junior officer in engineering. "I don't know where you picked up the new cook, but thank the stars you did. I thought I'd die eating that freeze-dried shit they pack for us." The man gave him a "thumbs up" as he passed him.

He headed to the galley, the aroma of food growing ever stronger. It was the most delicious thing he'd ever smelled. Coming from the kitchen. Hurrying to the crew mess, Damon found the answer to his missing crew. Every last man not on duty was eating. Not that he could blame them. His mouth was watering.

Every man in the mess raised his glass and cheered when Damon walked in. He couldn't help the crooked smile that came to his lips. "I guess this means the new cook is a hit?"

They all laughed and gave their assent before returning to their meals. He was just about to go in search of his own plate when one was set in front of him. The food was unbelievably tempting, but not so much as the sleek arm extending his plate. He gulped. What had he gotten himself into?

"I take it you had no trouble figuring out how to use the kitchen?" It was the lamest thing in the universe to say, but he couldn't seem to find any other words.

"Yes. I knew I could. You've got quite an assortment stockpiled. Making good meals for your crew for the next month shouldn't be hard."

"Month?"

"I can probably stretch it farther, but somehow, I don't think that would be a very popular decision. I'll try it if you need me to."

"No. A month will be fine. Actually, I didn't think it would last nearly that long." She slipped into the seat across from him, and he couldn't take his eyes from her. She mesmerized him.

When he continued to stare at her, she cleared her throat. "Um, are you going to eat? It's not the best in the universe, but it's filling."

"Oh! I'm sorry," he stammered as he stirred the contents of his plate around with his fork. Steam rose from the concoction consisting of meat, noodles, and some kind of sauce. Scooping up a forkful, he stuffed it into his mouth. The instant his lips closed around it, a burst of rich, meaty flavor exploded on his tongue.

His brain shut down. If ambrosia truly existed,

this had to be it. A groan escaped him somehow, and he began to chew. Then he took bite after bite, eating like a starving man at a banquet table until he scraped the last bit of sauce from his plate. When he finally looked up at her, she was grinning like she was the happiest person in the world.

"I've always loved to see people eat like they really enjoyed it. I take it you approve?"

"Absolutely! Where did you learn to make such wonderful meals?"

"For the girls. They won't eat if it's not tasty. We got the things the men didn't want. Most of the time it was either spoiled or just not fit to eat. I learned to improvise to keep everyone alive."

The instant she responded, Damon regretted asking the question. Her eyes went from happy to haunted, and she paled visibly. Whatever she'd gone through at her previous home, it hadn't been pleasant.

"You don't have to worry about it now. You're here. With me. You'll never have to be hungry again."

"I know." She smiled. "I'm not sure why, but you have that look about you. If you give your word, you're the type of man to keep it. I'm just worried about the girls and other women. I'm thinking maybe the god the men of the Hand worship meant for me to stay where I was so all the forgotten females would have at least one thing to look forward to. I abandoned them."

"I don't know what kind of life you lived before, Phoebe, but judging by the state you showed up here in, I seriously doubt you'd have lived a very long one. No one could in those conditions. You left to save your own life."

"Perhaps. But who's going to save the lives of everyone else?"

When she stood, he didn't try to stop her leaving. There was a lot he had to think about. Like how he was going to convince Viktor going after Phoebe's friends wasn't a suicide mission.

Chapter Four

Trust a man to ruin a perfectly good mood. Phoebe's movements were crisp and jerky in her anger as she cleaned her kitchen. Still, a smile tugged at her lips when she thought about it. *Her kitchen!* Maybe not in reality, but no one else seemed to even try to invade her domain. She'd had several offers of help with the clean up, but she'd refused. If she was going to earn her keep, she'd do just that. Everyone here had their own area they were responsible for. The kitchen was hers.

When she finished cleaning, she set things up for the next meal -- in the morning -- and left. Her choices of where to go were limited. The only place she knew how to get back to was Damon's -- Captain Singh's -- quarters, but that didn't seem proper. They hadn't had time to discuss living arrangements, and she wasn't sure she was comfortable living with a man she didn't know. But, with a certain amount of trepidation, Phoebe headed toward the captain's rooms. As uncomfortable as she was going back there, it was worse to think she'd accidentally wander into someplace she wasn't supposed to if she explored on her own.

The door slid silently open when she pressed her hand to the entry pad, which surprised her. She figured Damon would have reprogrammed the thing by now so that it wouldn't admit her so easily. Damon sat at a small desk, staring intently at a computer screen. A fierce looking man spoke from the screen and the two of them seemed to be having an intense discussion.

"I don't have any choice in the matter, Mikiel."

"You always have a choice, Damon."

"Right. The same choices you'd have in the same damned situation."

Mikiel chuckled. "I didn't say you had much of a choice, just that you had one. We should be in the sector within eight standard hours if we take the scenic route."

"That should work. Just make sure you've got at least one ship that can get there in the event these guys are more persistent than I think they'll be."

"Shouldn't be a problem." The man on the screen grinned. "Good luck, my friend. I have the feeling you'll need it."

Damon growled when he punched a button disconnecting the interface. He sighed and rested his head in his hands. "Stars, I'm too old for this."

"Too old for what?" It was as good a way as any to announce her presence.

He spun around in his chair. "Phoebe. I didn't hear you come in."

"I'm sorry. I shouldn't have just come in."

There was an awkward silence. Phoebe fidgeted, shifting her weight from one foot to the other. Damon didn't take his eyes from her. Phoebe couldn't help but return his gaze. The man was scrumptious. She would have no problem simply staring at him all day, but she'd prefer he not catch her at it. The heat she saw in his eyes, the lust shining bright, shot straight through her. Had he been just a little closer, she'd have tackled him to the ground and forced herself on him. Not that she'd have had to force very hard. If the look in his eyes was any indication, he was as close to desperation as she was.

He cleared his throat. "Well, I apologize about not getting you your own rooms. Unfortunately, the only private quarters we have are for the senior officers, of which we have a full complement. Junior officers share one large bunk area. Considering they're all male, I didn't think you'd be comfortable." He waved a hand around the room. "At least here, you only have to worry about one man pawing at you."

Phoebe giggled. She was nervous, but she recognized a joke when she heard one. Though, honestly, she didn't think she'd mind if this man pawed her a bit. "Somehow, I'm sure you'll be able to restrain yourself."

Damon stood and crossed the space separating them. Phoebe could see the war he waged with himself clearly on his face. "Don't bet your life on it." His normally husky, soft-spoken voice sounded strained and on the verge of being out of control.

With no further warning, he swooped down and fused his mouth to hers. Phoebe felt like she was flying. Her head spun and her whole world existed where his tongue delved into her mouth to find hers. His kiss wasn't sweet or tender, but conquering and demanding. There was no way she could do anything other than respond to such blatant sexuality.

She gripped his powerful, muscular shoulders and held on. His arms snaked around her waist, and she felt herself being pulled against an impossibly hard male chest. His cock trapped between them was hard and unyielding, and she wouldn't have it any other way.

There was a brief flash of fear when she got her wits about her enough to realize what she was doing and she shivered, pushing away from him slightly. Immediately, Damon stopped his onslaught of her body, if not her senses.

"I -- I'm sorry. I didn't mean --"

"No! It's OK. I just -- I mean -- if we'd been

caught doing that on the Outpost, they'd have…" She trailed off, not wanting to relive what she'd witnessed many times in her life there. She took a deep breath. "They give women of questionable morals to the unattached men on the station. Not just within the community, but to the men visiting the station. They pay a fee to the proprietor, and the women are given to them for a time. It's the worst life imaginable for a woman on the Outpost. The men who frequent that establishment aren't very… nice."

"I didn't mean to make you uncomfortable, Phoebe. You're a member of my crew now, and contrary to my actions a moment ago, I don't fraternize with my crew in this manner." He seemed to think about that a moment and added, "Even if there were any women on board. I mean, I personally prefer women to men and --"

She felt that giggle bubbling up inside her again. This man was even more uncomfortable with the attraction between them than she was.

"What's so funny?"

Phoebe quit fighting the laughter. She let it go in a joyful surge as she wrapped her arms around Damon's neck. When he tightened his arms around her waist, Phoebe sighed in contentment. Never in her wildest dreams would she have guessed she'd want a man in her life. Now, she found herself wondering what it would be like to have such sinfully wonderful physical contact with such a powerful man every day.

"You. Me." She buried her face in his neck and kissed the bit of flesh she found exposed by his uniform. "We're both so afraid of what's happening, we're liable to miss out on something great and beautiful. Something many people wait their whole lives to find and never do."

"The great Damon Singh fears nothing."

"Right." She snorted. Then they both held each other and laughed. A good, warm, healing laugh.

Damon scooped her up in his arms and carried her to his bed. Following her down, he spread her thighs with his knees and settled atop her, his weight resting on his forearms as he gently stroked her hair with his fingers. "You're the most beautiful woman I've ever seen. With the most tender heart. I'm not sure why I'm doing this, but I've worked out a strategy with my commander and his ships. We're going after your friends."

She felt like she'd had the wind knocked out of her. This was the last thing she expected. "What?"

"We all knew there was something wrong at Graves Station. One of my men commented on the conditions at the only brothel on the station -- it has to be the one you were referring to. That, combined with the bits I've learned from you, decided my course of action. I can't stand by and know people are suffering."

Tears came to her eyes. She couldn't stop them. But she also couldn't let him do this. "They'll kill you, Damon. If you try to take something they see as theirs, or worse, threaten their entire way of life, they'll fight to the death."

"They're no match for the *Black Star*. We've seen their ships. They've taken the best of what they could scavenge, but they're still vastly inferior to us."

"But are you willing to risk your lives to achieve your goal?" She struggled until he let her rise up onto her elbows. "Those men will do anything they have to, including sacrifice themselves, to keep their community intact."

"Let me worry about that, Phoebe. I'm smarter than you give me credit for." He grinned. "If all goes according to plan, we'll have the women and girls in the lower decks out of there and be long gone before anyone even knows they're not where they're supposed to be."

"Just promise me one thing, Damon." She took his face in her hands, caressing his cheek with her thumb. This was so surreal. The lust shining in this man's eyes was matched only by the tenderness she saw there.

"Anything."

"Don't do anything that would get you taken away from me."

His smile was full of promise, and something Phoebe was afraid to name. She wanted it to be love, but if it wasn't, she didn't want to know about it. She wanted this illusion as long as she could have it, because she was very much afraid she'd fallen in love with him when he'd first found her in his cabin.

Damon descended on her once again, kissing her until she no longer feared anything that might happen. The only thing that mattered was the here and now. This man's arms, lips, and body loving hers so completely she felt like the most treasured woman in the universe. He broke their kiss only long enough to unzip her uniform and help her out of it, and loosen his pants to free his cock.

"Have you done this before? I don't want to hurt you." He probed her pussy with his fingers, stroking her deep, testing what he found.

"I'm not a virgin. You won't hurt me unless you stop."

As he stroked her cunt, his thumb brushed her clit lightly, and Phoebe arched her back. Her whole world centered around what Damon was doing between her legs. She cried out and spread her legs farther, inviting him inside, needing him as she needed to breathe. Never in her life had anything compared to this.

The man in her arms trembled as he readied his powerful body to enter her. "By the stars! I've never wanted a woman more." Damon guided his cock to her entrance before resting over her once again.

"Damon, wait." Phoebe couldn't believe she'd been so stupid. "I don't have a contraception or disease prevention implant. I don't think I'm infected, but I can't be sure."

He kissed her nose. "I have both, sweet. I'll protect you until we can get any implant you want."

She smiled. "Then love me, Damon. I need you."

He needed no further encouragement. With one smooth, slow stroke, he entered her. Phoebe was stretched, full. The sensation was so erotic it was almost unbearable. She wrapped her legs around him, pulling him closer. His body was flush with hers, his hair-roughened skin abrading her tender flesh exquisitely.

Both of them gasped for breath as their movements became more erratic. Sweat slickened their skin. The sweet smell of sex hung heavily in the air, combining with their own musky personal scents. Phoebe's tongue tingled when she tasted Damon's skin and lips. It was an experience unlike anything she'd been prepared for.

Damon surged into her faster and harder with each stroke. The slight burning sensation in her cunt only added to the intensity of the moment. It wasn't long before a tingling sensation started where their bodies joined. She gripped him with her arms and legs ever tighter. Her breath caught, and she struggled to look Damon in the eye. "Oh, sun and stars!" Her voice barely worked.

"Push, Phoebe. Reach for it and push through it." Damon buried his fingers in her hair and locked his gaze with hers. "Now, Phoebe. Come for me. Now!"

Phoebe screamed. And screamed and screamed. Her whole body convulsed. She wasn't alone. Damon's own shout of release shook the walls.

Eventually they both came down from the orgasmic high they'd taken each other on. Damon collapsed on top of her and rolled them to their sides.

"By the moons of Solum." Damon pulled Phoebe close. Her naked body felt so good against his, he didn't ever want to let her go.

"I second that." She sounded about as content as a woman could possibly be. And she might have stayed that way for a long, long while.

Gods. Just looking at her made him hard all over again. Damon wanted nothing more than to sink his cock into Phoebe's sweet, hot cunt over and over again till she screamed out his name with her every breath. Unfortunately, Viktor -- and a couple of security guards -- chose that exact moment to barge in.

Chapter Five

Damon groaned. Phoebe squealed and would have jumped away from him had Damon not held her fast. How many more ways could he look like an idiot? He snatched at the cover to shield Phoebe from the eyes of his unwanted guests.

"What the holy *fuck* are you doing, Viktor?" Mortified didn't begin to describe Damon's feelings right now.

"We heard a disturbance. It sounded like you were in trouble."

Ranier -- the *Black Star*'s pilot and a man Damon liked and respected above anyone else in his crew -- snickered. "Oh, he was in trouble all right. It sounded like he blew his tonsils out his --"

"That's enough!" Damon knew his face was as red as a Tamarian Blood Ruby. "If I need help, I'll ask for it."

"What exactly would you like us to wait for?" Viktor crossed massive arms over an equally massive chest. "We could hear your screams from the corridor."

"We're aboard the *Black Star*, Viktor! Nothing can happen to me here." Why wouldn't they just *leave*?

Ranier's continued amusement grated on Damon's nerves. "Yeah, well, I didn't think it was possible to pick up a stowaway either. Yet, here she is." Ranier winked at Phoebe. If he hadn't been butt naked, Damon would have crossed the room and cheerfully punched the man. "My apologies, miss. I sincerely hope you won't hold such a barbaric intrusion against me and withhold my rations. My friend, on the other hand --" he nodded toward Viktor, "-- doesn't need his rations anyway. Keep me in mind if you have extra, will you?"

The soft, muffled giggling next to him drew his attention. Phoebe had the sheet pulled up to her nose -- her enormous silvery-green eyes and mass of silver-white hair were all that was visible. Damon rolled his eyes. Why was he the only one so acutely embarrassed?

Viktor turned to leave. "*Black Star* should reactivate your security protocol once we leave. And just so you know, the ship is as amused as the rest of us."

"Just because you've managed a tentative link with the ship doesn't mean you can stand there and make fun of me and Phoebe."

Viktor whipped around and raised a hand against further protest. "No, my link with the *Black Star* doesn't give me the right to have a chuckle at your expense -- being your friend does. As to the young Miss Phoebe, if such a beautiful, passionate woman were mine, I would love her as thoroughly as you just did. I'd hold nothing back."

The man hardly ever spoke more than a couple of sentences at a time. The mere fact Viktor considered himself Damon's friend shocked, but also flattered, Damon. The big vampire wasn't *anyone's* friend.

Viktor slowly turned and left the room. As soon as he did, Phoebe burst out into gales of laughter. Did everyone on the entire bloody ship -- including the bloody ship -- need to have a good laugh at his expense?

When Phoebe's arms snaked around his neck, and she kissed his shoulder in between giggles, the humor of the situation finally hit him. He could only imagine the look on his face when Viktor and Ranier had come rushing in on them.

"Oh my, but I don't see how any of them kept a

straight face." Phoebe wiped tears from her eyes and pulled Damon back down on top of her. "I never thought I'd find humor in that kind of an entrance, considering what it would have meant in another lifetime, but I've never laughed so hard in my life."

Looking down at the smiling woman with laughter in her eyes as bright as the tears, it struck Damon exactly how deep he was in. Up to his eyeballs.

Damon Singh was head over heels in love with Phoebe Lightheart.

* * *

Phoebe finished cleaning up after the morning meal. The men had scarfed down everything she'd fixed. There wasn't even a drop of gravy left. More, one of the younger men had insisted he help her with the dishes. The work had been done in half the time and she'd finished preparing for the midday meal early enough to explore a bit.

Her new home was wonderfully spacious, if a bit plain. The floors were covered by a thin padded runner down the center, and computer linkups were the only thing that marred the smooth surface of the metal walls. Even the doors didn't break the continuity. The only entryways she found that did break the illusion of a never-ending hallway were the captain's, the one leading to the engineering section, and the one leading to the command section. Command was a very formidable place to be if you didn't know your way around.

She wondered again how she'd managed to end up where she had. She could just as easily have wandered into the detention area and gotten herself locked up. Still, she rather liked it here. It was clean. Almost painfully so.

At the moment, however, something was wrong.

She wasn't well versed in navigation, but she could have sworn they were going in the wrong direction. More than all that, though, the place was empty. There were no sounds other than the normal mechanical sounds everything made when not planet side. No one was in the recreation area, or the mess hall. The one person she did see was in a big hurry and looked a bit strained. He didn't even acknowledge her as he passed. Strange.

Phoebe turned to head back to the kitchen when the ship gave a tremendous lurch. Claxons blared, and the ship continued to shudder for several minutes. Phoebe stumbled to her feet. Staggering down the corridor, she finally made it to the mess hall where she ducked under a table and braced herself. There wasn't much in the area to fall, but if anything did, she didn't like the idea of it falling on her head.

Used to a space station that made a continuous orbit around a dead planet, Phoebe felt every move the *Black Star* made. They pitched from side to side, up and down, every movement quick and precise. Phoebe had the sinking suspicion they were avoiding something, dodging a battle.

"Phoebe."

The mechanical, but ultra-feminine voice coming from the comm startled Phoebe so badly, she bumped her head on the table. Stars danced in front of her eyes and she had to shake her head to clear it.

"Phoebe, can you make it to Damon's quarters?"

"Who said that?"

"There's no time to explain. You need to go to the captain's quarters and lock yourself in until either he or I tell you it's safe."

"What's going on?" Phoebe knew this conversation was real and not the result of head trauma only because the voice had precipitated her head trauma to begin with.

"Don't be difficult! Just do as you're told before you're taken!"

An explosion rocked the ship this time. There was a sound suspiciously like that of a hull breach. Phoebe had heard it only once. Three women on Graves Station lost their lives that time. "Was that a hull breach?"

"Yes! Get to Damon's quarters and hurry. We're being boarded!"

Phoebe didn't waste any more time contemplating the wheres and whys of the disembodied voice. Things were happening fast, and she very much didn't want to get caught in the middle of them.

She ran down the hall, colliding with two crewmembers wearing the remnants of tattered space suits -- Toshie and Brenner. Toshie looked like half his face had been burned off, and Brenner was half carrying, half dragging him toward the medical unit.

Phoebe immediately grabbed Toshie's other arm and put it over her shoulder. "What happened?"

"We were ambushed." Brenner grunted as he shifted Toshie's weight to allow for Phoebe's assistance. "Damned cultists waited until we had everyone on board here or *Sword Breaker*, then attacked."

Phoebe was betting they were after not only their "stolen" people, but the *Black Star* herself for salvage. It was how they made their "fleet." They captured the ship that had the parts they wanted and incorporated the technology into whatever vessel they needed it on. As a result, no two ships of the Hand were alike, and that made it difficult for anyone to identify a lone ship as belonging to the Hand.

"Captain Singh is trying to fight them off, but he's going to need the vampire's help." Brenner said that like asking a vampire for help was worse than being taken by the Hand.

"The vampire. Viktor?"

"Hell, yes, Viktor! If the captain lets that man loose, blood will flow like a river. Not only that, but it will be hard to get him back under control."

Brenner carefully lifted Toshie and laid him on an exam table. The doctor, whom Phoebe had met only briefly at the last meal, examined Toshie carefully. "Leave him to me. I'll start the grafts and see if I can stop the burn's progression. If I don't, he won't be fit for anything other than cybernetic recycling."

With nothing more to do, Phoebe and Brenner left the unit. Brenner scrubbed a hand over his face. He looked worried, and scared.

"I'm sure the doctor will help him, Brenner. What happened?"

"Plasma burn. He got caught in the flash fire when the bulkhead gave way."

A sickening feeling washed over Phoebe. "Damon?" she whispered. "Is Captain Singh all right?"

"He was burned, but not badly. Thank the stars he and most of the others managed to get atmospheric suits on before the inner bulkhead failed. Right now, they're fighting those thrice-damned fanatics. With that section of the hull exposed, it's not easy." The young man looked nervously back the way he came. "I've got to go. The captain will need all the help he can get. Excuse me, ma'am."

Phoebe thought she might be sick. Damon needed her, but if she was captured, she was as good as dead. She started back to the cabin, but stopped after a couple of steps. No. If Damon lost, they'd find her wherever she was. If it was meant for her to die, it would be at Damon's side.

Chapter Six

"Keep heavy fire on that ramp! It's the only way in or out!" Damon fought through the pain. His right leg and hip hurt, but he'd live. If he didn't lead his men in this fight, they'd all very likely die. They were a great crew, but they weren't terribly experienced.

Except for Viktor. And he had to keep the cyborg vampire out of this or he would die. That wasn't acceptable to Damon.

The men of the *Black Star* fought fiercely, but they couldn't afford to lose another man. The *Black Star* was vastly outmanned, but they still held the advantage in firepower.

"Why haven't the temporary bulkheads automatically engaged, Captain?" Juanas, a young man from *Sword Breaker*, fired off several shots, his automatic comm unit keying up when he spoke inside his airtight suit. "If that hole was sealed, we could move away and blast those bastards into oblivion. Not to mention fighting with no atmosphere and no gravity ranks up there with eating *yassat* turds."

"Because they've stationed two men directly under the breach. The computer won't engage until they move. A safety feature I could do without right now." Damon repositioned himself, braced against a support beam and fired again. Juanas was right. Damon thought he'd rather eat the *yassat* turds.

"Did the women all make it?"

"All but one. Last I saw of her, she had on a mask, but I don't know if she got a suit."

Both men fired at the gaping hole in the side of the *Black Star*. They scored direct hits on the two men, but the energy bolts were absorbed by some kind of force field. Damon didn't think it surrounded them.

The energy the shield couldn't absorb was bouncing off, sometimes behind the second guy where his shield couldn't reach. The odds were, they were frontal shield only. Those would be less difficult to maintain.

"What do we do?" Juanas looked at him like Damon remembered looking at his commanding officer when he was Juanas's age. "They've made our numbers. Any attempt to rush them from the flank would be instantly recognized."

"I know." Damon looked around him, desperately needing something to give them an edge.

Viktor laid a hand on his shoulder. The look in his eyes said he was ready to sacrifice himself. The thought chilled Damon to the bone.

A female voice with a strange accent commed in. "Lay me some cover fire." It wasn't one he recognized. "I can make it behind them through that blow hatch." Damon looked around to see the one woman he hadn't accounted for. She had indeed managed to get her suit on and she moved with the grace and efficiency of someone who had worn a suit just like it many times.

"I take it you've fought in deep space before?"

"A time or two. The name's Diamond. Cover me, and I'll see what I can do to help."

"That's suicide," Viktor hissed. "If they catch you, you'll be a sitting duck."

She turned to Viktor. "You have a better idea, vampire?"

Damon saw the tiny tic in Viktor's cheek. Most likely, it wasn't that she'd called him "vampire" like he was a bug she'd like to squash, but the fact that he *didn't* have a better plan.

The woman nodded her head smartly. "Good. Just keep them focused on you. I'll do the rest."

Damon wasn't sure Viktor didn't have the right

of it, but he didn't have a better idea, either. Damon threw everything he had into their defense. Three enemy soldiers dropped almost instantly -- another followed a few seconds later. Still, they kept coming.

"Viktor, we need to know how many people they have. Can the *Black Star* give you any idea of their troop strength?"

"She estimates eighty to one hundred, but there's another carrier on the edge of sensor range that's capable of carrying at least a thousand more."

"If they're looking for us, that's a bit of overkill, don't you think? A thousand men to take one ship?"

"If that ship is looking for us, my guess is their intention is to capture the *Black Star*. The carrier is designed to transport ships as well as troops. It's empty."

Damon winced. "How close?"

"If they follow their present course, they'll be here in forty-seven standard minutes."

"Damn." Damon thought for a second, trying to figure out the best way to help the woman currently saving their asses. "Everyone. Concentrate your fire at the top of the bulkhead. If we can get it hot enough, the laser fire should melt the titanium alloy and give them something else to worry about."

It didn't take long for bits of hot metal to start falling on top of the two underneath it. One of them jumped back with a yelp, but another took his place. The new man extended his shield to cover his head, but it left his feet and ankles exposed. Damon fired several shots at the guy's boots, causing him to jump, but otherwise did little damage.

"Damon." Viktor gripped his arm. "Have you noticed the firing isn't as thick from their end?"

"Now that you mention it, yes."

"Something's happening outside." Viktor shook his head slightly. "*Black Star* says there's more than one female outside. The second one's Phoebe."

Ranier snorted. "Figures."

Damon gave the young man a sharp look. "I doubt she knows how to put on a suit, much less walk outside a space vessel."

"Are you really sure about that, my friend?" Viktor said quietly. "Do you really know anything about her at all? I've learned to trust *Black Star*. If her sensors tell her it's Phoebe, then it is."

Damon couldn't respond. He *didn't* know Phoebe. Not like he should have before falling in love. Of course, in matters of the heart, one couldn't always help the little things. None of it could be helped. At the moment, the only thing he could do was try to protect her as much as he could.

He was about to tell Viktor it didn't matter -- all that mattered was getting out of this mess and back to Asalian space -- when the ship was rocked by a nearby explosion. Grabbing an open panel door, Damon reached for Ranier but missed. The man would sail straight to the gaping hole in the ship if someone didn't catch him. Either way -- into enemy hands, or into open space -- would be a death sentence. Damon craned his neck to find Viktor. The vampire had used his cybernetic enhancements to drive his hand into the inner bulkhead and hold on tight as he snagged Ranier before he sailed by.

Once they all regained their equilibrium, the firing continued until one of the men behind the shield, under the bulkhead breach, was yanked off his feet. His tether apparently cut or otherwise disengaged from its anchor, he floated through space, flailing his arms and legs. The second simply slumped over and bumped into the shield from the back. It wasn't long before he, too, floated off into space.

Damon called a cease-fire and waited. "What's happening, Viktor? The women? The rest of the attackers?"

Viktor held up a hand while he processed the information. Viktor's link with the ship wasn't very strong yet, and it took time to understand what the ship was trying to tell him.

"The explosion was on the enemy vessel. It seems one of our girls planted an explosive device on the outer hull. There's only a handful of them left, and their ship's completely disabled."

"What about the women, Viktor?" Damon gritted the words out. He could give a flying fuck about anything else at this point. He'd deal with it later.

"They're both alive --" Viktor moved to the compartment beside the hatch where the woman had exited and grabbed two short tether lines, "-- but they're both injured. Phoebe not so bad as the other woman, but they both need help."

"I'll go with you." Damon moved toward the gaping hole in his ship. "Just let me shut down those force shields and let *Black Star* make temporary repairs. Has *Sword Breaker* gotten here yet?"

"Just pulling alongside us now, Sir." Viktor tossed him a tether when he pushed off in his direction. "*Black Star* has apprised them of the situation. They're awaiting your instructions."

"Have them ready their medical unit. They're better equipped than we are."

Viktor nodded. "Understood."

"Let's go."

"You concentrate on finding the women. I'll keep

us attached to the ship."

With Viktor's strength, Damon didn't doubt for a moment he could keep them both from floating off into space. "Keep me posted on their condition."

"Will do."

Once they got around the hull breach, Damon had a chance to look at the vastness surrounding them. He didn't like being so exposed on the threshold of something that empty. It was strangely peaceful, though. The only thing keeping him grounded with reality was Viktor's slight tug on the tether every now and then as they moved together.

"There's one of them!" Damon had to restrain himself from shoving off from the ship in the direction of the body gently tumbling in space. Instead, he gave the gentlest of pushes, floating out to the end of his tether.

"That should be the other woman," Viktor commed. "Phoebe is near the hull breach just outside the temporary barrier. She's fine, but running out of oxygen. Tie on to this one quickly and let's get Phoebe."

Viktor pulled them back and they went after Phoebe. She had just enough oxygen to keep her conscious until they got back to a pressurized area.

Damon hurried to get everyone to the medical unit and checked out. He was worried about Phoebe -- so much he felt like his heart was going to explode -- but there were many more who had been injured in this attack. All of his crew were important to him.

"*Sword Breaker* is opening her aft cargo bay doors for us." The smaller ship had pulled dangerously close, but the two ships seemed to move like dancers who had anticipated each other's movements for a very long time.

The four of them floated into the bay and into an airlock. A few seconds later, the airlock pressurized and the crew of *Sword Breaker* helped carry the two women to the medical unit. Damon lost his grip on Phoebe. He yelled her name, desperate to get to her, but Viktor held him back. She made eye contact with him and gave him a weak smile as they whisked her off. It would have to do for now.

Damon stood there with Viktor. Just the two of them remained. Damon sank to the deck, his knees unable to support him any longer. "I think I'm going to be sick."

"I know, my friend. You love her."

"Yes, Viktor, more than I'm comfortable admitting to just anyone, but it's not only that. How many did we lose? I don't even know. In all my years, I've never lost a crewman before."

Viktor reached his hand to Damon. "That's why you're a good commander, Damon. Men the Empire has in command now don't care about the lives lost, only the power gained." He pulled Damon to his feet. "We've got to get back to the *Black Star*. I think something's happening."

"Like what?" Damon had a sinking feeling he knew. He also had an even worse feeling he knew why. It was the only explanation.

"That carrier is now on an intercept course and will be here in less than ten standard minutes. We've got no time to spare."

The two men got permission to take a shuttle and headed back to the *Black Star*. It was time for the most feared ship in the known universe to earn her reputation.

Chapter Seven

The medical unit on this new ship was smaller than that of the *Black Star*, but it was a great deal more comfortable. This was a ship built with her crew's comfort in mind. For all the technology she saw, and all the comforts afforded the patients here, Phoebe didn't see nearly enough staff. From what she could gather, there was one doctor and three nurses. Compared with *Black Star*'s one doctor, she supposed it was a lot, but there were at least eight men injured in the fight, not to mention Diamond, who was by far the most critically injured.

Everyone's time was taken up with the care of Diamond, the woman who had initiated the daring assault, and the men were left to wait until someone was free to tend them. Phoebe's injuries were minor. She'd been hurt worse on the station and managed to treat herself.

Looking around, she saw things she could do. The man sitting next to her was burned from his knee down, the flesh red and covered with blisters, but not charred and blackened. It probably hurt like a son of a bitch. If she put some clean cloths over it and found clean cool water, she could at least give him some temporary relief. It wasn't anything she hadn't done before for the females in the lower part of Graves Station.

No one was paying any of them any attention, so Phoebe took a quick look at everyone around her. Some of the patients had burns as severe -- or worse -- than the first man she'd looked at, but most were minor burns, cuts, and bumps. Phoebe then pilfered every cabinet and drawer she found for bandages and basins. This ship seemed to have plenty of water, thankfully, so treating the burns was relatively easy.

Caring for these men wasn't the burden she had felt back on the station. She had only been with them a day, but already she got the impression they embraced her as one of their own. As she started her rounds, treating them as best she could, they thanked her. With hopeful looks when she passed, hoping for a little relief, maybe just a kind smile, they all looked at her like she was someone important. She didn't see the insulting or suggestive looks she often did from men on the station. These men expected she knew what to do and would take care of them. Even more, she didn't want to let them down.

By the time the unit staff returned from their critical patient, Phoebe had done all she could. Many of the wounded would require more than she was capable of giving, but she had eased their pain and gotten to know all of them in the process.

"Will she make it?" Phoebe was as anxious about the one person in the group she didn't know as she was about the men she now considered friends.

"I honestly don't know," the doctor stated frankly. "Time will tell. She's strong, and fighting hard." He glanced in the direction of his patient. "With rest and strength of will, she's got a good chance."

"I don't mean to sound ungrateful for the hospitality, doctor, but how soon can we return to the *Black Star*? They only have one physician on board and no staff. I'm sure they could use any help they can get. These men are roughly half his crew. I'm sure he needs them."

The man glanced around the room once, did a double take and walked to one of the men from the *Black Star*. After examining the wound Phoebe had dressed, he asked, "Is there anyone who still needs attention?"

"Well --" she cleared her throat, "-- Josiah has some pretty bad burns. He's comfortable, but he'll need something more than my pitiful efforts. Cain has a pretty deep gash on his right thigh. It's bandaged and the bleeding's stopped, but it will need to be sealed. I think Evan has a broken wrist, but the rest aren't so bad. They can tell you more about what they need than I can."

"Don't let her fool you, Doc." Cain, who was sitting next to where Phoebe was standing, clapped her on the back hard enough to make her stagger forward. "She's had experience with patching people up."

"It definitely looks like it." Doc made a quick examination of every man in the room. "As much as I'd love to let you get back to your ship, I can't." Everyone in the room protested at once. Doc held up his hand for silence. "I'm sorry! There's nothing we can do. There's a carrier ship just out of hyperspace in the sector. Captain Anjoom has given orders for closed quarters. No off duty personnel is to be roaming the ship. We all have to stay put for safety reasons."

Outrage spread across the men. Some of them jumped up from their beds and would have advanced on the poor doctor if Phoebe hadn't stepped smoothly in between them.

"Just wait," she hissed at Josiah. The tall, lean redhead backed down, but not willingly. "Just wait, Josiah."

"The captain needs us, Phoebe. He's running on less than a skeleton crew."

"I know, but the doctor can't countermand an order from his own captain." She needed to keep them calm if her plan was going to work.

"So what do you suggest we do? Leave Captain

Singh to defend himself?"

Phoebe grabbed his face in her hands and made him look her in the eye. "Yes, Josiah. That's exactly what I'm suggesting."

There was silence while Phoebe willed the young man to trust her. She hadn't survived the wrath of the Hand of God by being stupid. You tell the powers that be what they want to hear, then you do what you have to. Fortunately, the doctor on *Sword Breaker* wasn't a member of the Hand.

"Good." The old doctor clapped his hands together. "I'll get back to my patient. Just stay put, and as soon as the crisis is over, I'm sure the captain will see to it you're returned to your ship with all possible speed."

It was obvious the doctor wasn't interested in staying around to confront anyone. When he left to go back to his patient, Phoebe let Josiah go and went to a computer display. A graphic of the ship's interior was displayed prominently, most likely for ease of movement in the case of an emergency.

"Look." Phoebe pointed at the image. "The shuttle bay is only a few hundred meters away. It shouldn't take long to get there."

"I just looked out the door, Phoebe." Evan jerked a thumb over his shoulder. "There aren't many people out there, but I seriously doubt they're going to let us just roam around the ship at will."

"Who said anything about going out the door?" Phoebe raised an eyebrow and grinned.

* * *

It only took them ten minutes of crawling through the ventilation and maintenance crawl spaces, but it was six minutes too long for Phoebe. Unfortunately, those shafts weren't made for solidly built, really *big* soldiers, especially with each dragging a suit through the shafts. There was more pushing and shoving from the men in the ducts than feeding time in a herd full of starved *yassats*. More than one of the men got stuck, but everyone managed to make it.

Phoebe crouched behind a crate in the main hangar area, assessing their options. They weren't good.

"Somehow, I doubt we'd make it to the shuttle and manage to take off before anyone notices it missing," one of the older men -- Lammet -- observed. "Besides, with all the fighting going on, I'm not so sure a shuttle is a good idea. We'd be blown to bits."

"True," Phoebe agreed absently. She was thinking. The shuttle was definitely out of the question. "But, what if we didn't take the shuttle?"

Eight pairs of eyes looked at her with a combination of disbelief, dread, and that you've-got-to-be-kidding look only men could produce.

* * *

Laser fire streaked through space at horrifying intensity and concentration. Explosions flashed on all three ships engaged in the battle as lasers bounced off deflector shields, but no sound reached Phoebe's ears inside the airtight helmet. It was like watching a film with the sound switched off.

For space to be so empty, Phoebe would have thought she and her companions would have had more room to maneuver, but instead it just made the laser bolts seem that much bigger. They were designed to bring down a destroyer class warship, after all. This close to them, one bolt looked three times as big as a shuttle bay outer door. Perhaps a space walk from ship to ship using the portable tractor beam they'd "borrowed" as propulsion wasn't as great an idea as she'd first thought. Especially not during a battle. Hell, it would have sucked *yassat* turds in the best of conditions. This was not the best of conditions. There was nothing like floating through the vast emptiness of space to prove exactly how tiny you were in the great universe. As it was, Phoebe was getting a panicky feeling from being in such an open area.

"We're sitting ducks out here," Evan commed. At the end of the line, he double-checked everyone's tether for the fifth time as they were pulled along. "Not to mention the risk of losing the tractor lock if they do too many extreme maneuvers."

"I know, but would you rather wait until this is all over to get back to your ship?" Phoebe couldn't agree more with Evan, but they'd come over halfway. Turning around now wasn't an option. They didn't have enough oxygen to get back.

"I didn't say that. I'm just saying there had to be a better way than this."

"You had your chance to come up with a better idea. No one said anything."

"Well, this seemed like a good idea at the time. I revised my opinion the first time the heat of a near miss made my hair sizzle though."

"We're almost there. Only a few hundred more yards and we'll be inside the *Black Star*'s shields. That should give us enough protection until we get inside."

"Are you sure we can penetrate those shields?"

"Sure," Phoebe lied through her teeth. She wasn't at all sure. "The basic design of a standard deflector shield is to prevent super heated or fast moving material from penetrating. Since we're neither, we should have no problems getting in."

No one said anything. Phoebe knew the principle was sound, but she had no idea if *Black Star* used a standard shield or not. All she knew was Damon needed manpower, and if these men were willing to follow her, willing to try, she'd do anything she had to in order to get them there. They knew the risks -- probably better than she did. Besides, another few seconds would tell the tale.

"Phoebe, what the hell are you doing?!" The voice that squawked over the comm unit was Damon's. He wasn't a bit happy. In fact, he sounded furious. If she'd known she could have communicated with the *Black Star*, she'd have given them a heads up before they got caught in the laser fire.

"We're approaching your deflector shield. Can we get through or will we bounce off?"

"I have your location. I'll deactivate that section. Get through as fast as you can and get your ass aboard this ship. Out."

Phoebe winced. This might not have been the smartest thing she'd ever done.

The rest of the trip didn't take long, and it was made in silence. By the time they entered through the same blow hatch Phoebe had used during the first skirmish, the battle was over and Captain Singh was waiting for them. There was no mistaking he was indeed *Captain Singh* -- the tender, loving Damon Phoebe had fallen in love with was nowhere to be found.

"You risked not only your life, but the lives of eight members of my crew with that little stunt. What exactly did you think you were going to accomplish?" Damon's features were hard, and his eyes flashed in unmistakable anger. Pissed didn't begin to cover it.

"You were fighting with so few men aboard the ship, I thought you could use some extra hands."

Damon slammed his fist into a nearby crate.

"And how did you help us? The fighting's over! You took *my* men into the middle of a firefight -- without even the protection of the most rudimentary of ships -- for no reason! That was the craziest thing I've ever seen, not to mention the stupidest! The way you were tied together, if one of you had been hit, the force would have sent the rest of you hurling off into deep space!" He had to lean down because he was so much taller than Phoebe, but he got in her face, almost nose to nose. "Consider yourself relieved of duty." He turned his back on her and stalked away. As he did, he gave one final order. "Viktor, Phoebe Lightheart is charged with intentionally and recklessly endangering the lives of eight members of this crew -- possibly the entire ship as well. Place her under arrest and put her in a holding cell."

Phoebe's heart pounded. What had just happened? "Damon?"

"You'd do well to address him as 'Captain Singh' or 'Sir,' Miss." Viktor gave her the creeps from the first moment she'd met him. Now, he looked more terrifying than anything from her worst nightmare.

Tears formed, but she refused to let them fall. She looked back at the eight men who'd come with her on that crazy stunt. They stood smartly at attention. None of them met her gaze. "I don't understand. I was only trying to help."

Viktor ignored her. "You will come with me now." He didn't give her a chance to comply. He simply took her by the upper arm and practically dragged her to her cell, shoved her in, and turned on the force field. Before he left, he growled at her, "You've betrayed this ship and her crew, but more importantly you've betrayed a man who loved you more than you'll ever know. That man is the best friend I've ever had, and I take this very personally. You may not have figured it out yet, but I'm not someone you want for an enemy." The smile he gave her was positively evil. "Sleep well, my dear. If you dare."

This was all of Phoebe's fears come true. She could have still been on Graves Station. Locked up without understanding why and unsure of what her future might be, Phoebe sat on the slim cot and folded her hands in her lap. She would sit there until they came for her. When they did, she would do what she was told and accept her fate as it came to her. Most importantly, she would not let them see her cry.

She would *not* let them see her cry.

The tears came, anyway.

Chapter Eight

"Is there even the slightest possibility you're wrong about this, Viktor?"

Damon was not only trying to salvage what was left of his heart, but his pride as well. During the battle, Viktor and Ranier had figured out how the Hand of God ships had managed to keep course with them from such a distance. They hadn't locked onto them -- they'd been following a beacon set to beam a high intensity burst to a special receiver on the other ship. The problem was finding it. When the enemy had started firing on *Sword Breaker*, Viktor put it together and had *Black Star* comb the area for that transmitter. When Phoebe had isolated herself outside the ship, finding the thing had been easy. It was on Phoebe herself.

"It's there, Captain. Planted deep within her brain. *Black Star* found it, but she says the probabilities of removing it are not good. Well, not without killing -- or severely damaging at best -- the host. When this was done, it was done with the intention of it staying there forever."

"So, she sneaks on board with a tracking device implanted in her brain. Why? The one time we were in danger, she and that other woman saved our asses. And when we caught her, it was because she removed herself from the presence of too many people." Damon scrubbed a hand over his face. "What was she out to accomplish?"

"Maybe the idea was to get us away from witnesses, or to catch us by surprise to give them a greater advantage. They had to know they were no match for us on an even field." Viktor shrugged. "I suppose you'd have to ask her. I'd ask the men who followed her, but they fled as soon as they were able."

"Well, whatever the reason, they'll always be able to find us as long as that chip is in her head, or as long as she's with us." Damon felt tired. Old and tired. "Damn."

"If you'll pardon me for interrupting, there's something you should know before you go making rash decisions." The silky feminine voice startled Damon, but Viktor didn't seem a bit surprised.

"I take it you've kept something from me? Again?" When Viktor was angry, things like this only enflamed him. "How am I supposed to be your link to the human world if you won't give me information I need?"

"I'm trying to, dear, but you're a tad hard-headed. You tend to hear what you want to hear and not what you need to hear."

If Damon hadn't been in such a bad mood, he probably would have laughed. The ship sounded like his own mother.

"Well, enlighten us, *dear*. I'm sure we're just dying to know." Viktor looked angry enough to punch something.

"First of all, if you'd care to look, you'll notice not one, but two beacons. One of them is coming from somewhere on *Sword Breaker*."

"So?" Viktor was probably getting himself in deeper and deeper. If he was going to continue his relationship with this ship, he was going to have to learn not to argue with a woman who had all the facts when he didn't.

"So, dear, who is still aboard *Sword Breaker* who came from the same place little Phoebe did?"

"OK, so she and the other woman are both spies." Now Viktor was being stubborn. Truth be told, he had been stubborn the whole time because the man hated being wrong even more than he hated asking for help.

"Or they don't know they're being followed. Have you even researched your enemy at all, Viktor?"

"I --"

"Of course you haven't." *Black Star* was as smug as any woman Damon had ever met. He continued to believe his policy of keeping silent was a good thing. "If you had, you'd have discovered that no one has ever left their community. Those who tried were always hunted down and killed. Now, I know I'm just a hunk of metal thrown together with a human brain, but you add that to the very specific type of transmitter imbedded so deep inside the brain of these women and you realize the Hand was looking for the escaped women, not you or myself."

For the first time since Damon had met the man, Viktor was speechless. He stood there, a murderous look on his face and a vein in his temple prominent in his anger. "Damned ship."

"Best you not forget it either, Viktor. I've been damned since the day I was transferred to this hunk of metal. Naturally, I have no patience for people who refuse to see what's right in front of them because they're too proud to admit they're wrong."

"OK." Damon figured they'd work out their differences eventually -- they had to if they were going to survive together and function as the symbiotic beings they needed to be. Perhaps if he had Nadira explain how she and *Sword Breaker* managed to find peace together it would help him. He looked at Viktor's normally fierce controlled features. The pure rage and impotent fury shining there made him think there was probably nothing that would help. The man would have to find the answers on his own. For now, however, there were more important things to worry about. Damon knew the woman the *Black Star* had been, and she hadn't changed much at all except maybe to be less tolerant. He knew Viktor, too. The man could only be pushed so far. Pushing him any more was unhealthy for everyone around him. And futile. "They were after Phoebe and her friend, but the question is did they know and simply refuse to tell us?"

"That I couldn't say, Captain. All I know is you have a young woman in a cell who's frightened and hurt. Perhaps you should have asked her that before you treated her like the very men she was running from."

Yep. Just like his mother. And just like his mother, she was right.

"What I don't understand is why she risked the lives of those eight men, taking them on a crazy space walk like she did. The only way that makes sense is if she knew she would be detected and was trying to draw the Hand back to the ship she was supposed to be on in the first place. She hadn't intended to be taken to *Sword Breaker*."

"And her mad dash outside to help Diamond? The two of them single-handedly saved this ship and everyone aboard. Does that sound like someone who wanted to intentionally hurt those men?"

"No matter what Viktor thinks, Nani, you are a very wise woman. You always were."

"Nani is dead, Damon." The sarcastic know-it-all persona was gone in an instant. The *Black Star* now sounded angry, bitter, and very much alone.

The only relief from her tortured existence was when she was allowed to link up with *Sword Breaker*, who had been her lover in another life when both of them had been human. Mikiel, the captain of *Sword Breaker*, and Damon both tried to allow them a continuous link, but distance sometimes interfered. As a result, they tried not to separate the ships unless it was absolutely necessary.

"All that's left of Nani is her love for Darian. The rest of her died the day the *Black Star* was born."

"I'm sorry. Things might have been different if I'd spoken up or tried to stop the madness Samair precipitated."

"Certainly things would have been different. You'd have been executed, or worse, stuck in a hulk of twisted metal and computer chips."

None of them spoke for a while. The silence was deafening and very uncomfortable.

"There's something both of you should know," *Black Star* continued in a more controlled tone. "These two women may well be the key to the salvation of both the Vok'nair Empire and the Asalian Coalition. I can't say why, but there's something tickling my sensors about this whole situation. I just can't figure it out yet."

Damon looked at Viktor. He'd hoped to have the man offer some insight, but Viktor's eyes were glazed over and pure fury covered his face. "You just love making a fool out of me don't you, bitch?" Viktor was almost frothing at the mouth, he was so angry. "Why didn't you tell me before? Better still, why didn't you let me in on your little secret when we last practiced our link?"

"I hid nothing from you, vampire. Anything you didn't pick up is your own limitation."

Damon held his breath. The strain on Viktor the last few months had been tremendous. The link he had established with the ship caught him completely by surprise. Combine that with the fact that he'd had to alter his survival methods drastically since taking on the assignment aboard the *Black Star*, and he had pushed himself to the breaking point. No one would serve on a ship with a vampire who fed from anything other than synthetic blood, so it had been necessary, but very uncomfortable. Add a frustrating female into the mix and it was a wonder the vampire had lasted this long.

"Viktor, what do you need?"

"You *know* what I need! Find me a willing female and let me drain her while I fuck her senseless, and I might be sane for a few minutes." He wasn't lying. That was exactly what it would take. Unfortunately, there was no one outside of a woman from his own race who could tolerate what Viktor needed to dish out. Damon *had* to find a way to get them to the vampire home world. Fast.

"You're confined to quarters for the remainder of the journey. We'll use best possible speed to get you home. Until then, you'll understand if I place security fields on your residence."

A moment of sanity returned to Viktor's eyes. "I'm afraid it might be too late, Damon. Double and triple secure everything. I don't want to hurt anyone. Please."

It was a horrible thing to see a man Damon considered the most controlled person he'd ever met slipping into a madness of violence and lust. It was like watching the most gifted of minds degrade with the ravages of age, only much, much worse. The violence about to be unleashed could kill them all.

"I'll see to it personally." It pained Damon to watch as three guards escorted his friend away, but he didn't have a choice. A vampire on the rampage was a horrifying prospect.

But not nearly as horrifying as the possibility of either learning Phoebe was a spy for the Hand of God, or losing her because he had treated her like the very people she was running from.

* * *

Phoebe was numb. She had come to terms with the possibility she'd lost her freedom. What she was having trouble with was why. There was no way she could have completely misjudged Damon. He simply wasn't that type of person. So the question remained -- why?

Her tears dried soon after they fell, and she vowed she'd not waste them on a man who didn't love her. She'd been strong her whole life. She'd fight her way through this, too. She hadn't survived this long only to let a man strip her of her pride. If she was to be a captive the rest of her life, however short that might be, she'd meet the challenge as she had every other -- with her head held high.

Lying on the small cot -- the only furniture in her cell -- Phoebe faced the wall, pulled her knees to her chest, and tried to calm her mind enough to rest. The stars only knew what lay in store for her over the next few days. Or months. Or…

She cringed. She'd deal with that when the future was more certain.

She'd just about dozed off when the door to the holding area whooshed open. She didn't have to look to know who it was.

"Leave us." Damon's gruff, husky voice held a deadly note of command. Phoebe sat up and took a deep breath. She didn't want the guard there any more than Damon did, but she needed someone there to make her keep her resolve. Breaking down in front of anyone other than Damon wasn't an option.

The guard, Chaz, stood at attention, but made no move to leave. "I'm sorry, Sir, but I can't do that."

Damon looked a little startled. "I beg your pardon?"

"The rumor ship-side is you and Viktor believe she's responsible for the attacks against us and *Sword Breaker*." The young man swallowed. "We respectfully suggest that your logic is flawed in that line of thinking, Sir." The poor man obviously didn't like going against his captain.

Damon smiled. "Relax, Chaz. We've already seen the error of our ways." Damon turned to Phoebe. "I still have some questions, but rest assured --" he turned back to Chaz, "-- she's perfectly safe with me."

Chaz -- bless his soul -- looked to Phoebe. "Miss?" It was obvious the young man didn't take going against his superior's orders lightly, but having done so, he wasn't about to back down.

Phoebe stood. "I'll be fine, Chaz. Thanks for your help. You and everyone."

"We know what you did during the first battle, and the others told us how you got them back to the *Black Star* during the second one. That was the most creative and bravest thing any of us have ever heard of. We figure we owe you for that." He grinned then. "Not to mention the food."

Phoebe's heart lifted. "Thanks for standing up for me." She glanced at Damon, and bitterness filled her heart. She wanted to say so much. No one had ever had the courage to take her side in anything. No one had ever cared enough. No matter how much she'd done, no matter how many times she put her life on the line for others, no one had ever returned the favor.

"You'll never know how much it means."

Neither Damon nor Phoebe said anything until Chaz got to the door. "I don't want to be disturbed. See to it no one enters, no matter what anyone hears this time." Apparently the entire ship had heard about Viktor and Ranier's breach of Damon's cabin door security, because Chaz snickered quietly as he exited.

They were alone. Phoebe drank in the sight of him. Even though she was hurt and angry, he still looked good enough to eat. His reference to the last time they'd made love took her breath as the memory washed over her. Nothing in her life had prepared her for the pleasure she had found in the arms of this man. She doubted if anything in the universe would ever give her as much pleasure ever again. He was everything she had ever wanted in a lover. He could be so gentle, yet his passion for her had matched hers for him. When he had experienced his own pleasure, he had held nothing back from her.

"You have every right to hate me, Phoebe."

"What makes you think I don't?" She couldn't breathe. It wasn't right that the perfect man for her had to be an asshole.

"The way you're looking at me." He started walking toward her, a predator stalking his prey. "The lust shining in your eyes tells me you still want me, and I don't think you're the type of woman to want a man you hate."

Phoebe refused to retreat. Instead of backing up in the face of his advancement, she planted her feet and raised her chin to look him in the eye. "Just because I still want to *fuck* you doesn't mean I want *you*."

Her words seemed to make something snap inside him. He crossed the remaining distance between them in a rush, fisted a hand in her hair and pulled her to him none too gently.

"I can definitely fuck you." He kissed her, plunging his tongue into her and, in the process, taking her soul as completely as he took her mouth. "Nothing in my life has ever compared to the way I feel when you're in my arms, Phoebe. And I'm not leaving you this time until I make you feel the same way."

Chapter Nine

Oh, sweet universe, she *had* to love him as much as he loved her. Damon tangled both hands in the snowy silk of her long tresses, turning her head to the perfect angle to plunder her mouth with his tongue. Phoebe whimpered, and it was only a few seconds before she was kissing him back.

She hooked a leg around his hip and pulled herself into him, grinding her clit against the ridge of his engorged cock. Damon was lost. Nothing mattered -- not the ship, not the Hand of God floating out there somewhere picking up a signal from her brain, nothing. Only this woman. This place. This moment.

He was filled with her sweet essence, a scent that was uniquely hers. Rose petals and lotus blossoms danced with a musky feminine scent only Phoebe carried. There was a sweet, minty flavor lingering on her lips Damon was only too glad to lap at.

Until she bit him.

A sharp intake of air was all he was able to manage. He tasted blood leaking from the wound on his tongue as he pulled back. She didn't let him go far.

"That's for being an asshole. Whether you deserve more is something I'll figure out later." She was breathing hard, and her breasts underneath the form-fitting uniform heaved with the exertion. "Now, fuck me."

That did it. Any semblance of control Damon might have had went right out the air lock. With a growl, he grabbed her suit at the neck and tore until she was exposed to the waist. He wanted to see all of her, but those wonderful, rounded globes of flesh beckoned him like a plasma string calls to an *arnat* entity. There was no force in the universe that could have stopped him from diving face-first between her breasts.

Kissing the valley between them, he grunted when her hands found his head and pulled him to her. He licked a path to each peak, sucking the nipples into his mouth before releasing them with an audible pop. She cried out when he nipped one with his teeth, so he did the other one.

"Sweet sun and stars, Damon, that's good! So very good. Oh, yes! Like that! Bite my nipples!"

Sweat slicked her skin, and he felt flushed, himself. His cock ached with the need to be inside her, to fuck them both into oblivion. Going back between her breasts, he licked her sternum and the inner curve of each breast until they were slick with his saliva. Once he was satisfied, he freed himself.

"On your knees, Phoebe. I want you to suck me."

She sank to her knees, a wicked grin playing across her face. "What happens if I don't?"

Damon knew she was playing. All might not be forgiven yet -- and he was sure there would be hell to pay before it was over -- but she loved this as much as he did. "You'll force me to punish you."

She raised an eyebrow, but the smile stayed in place. "Oh, really? And how would you go about that?"

"I'd bare that sweet little ass of yours, turn you over my knee, and spank you until you begged to be fucked." He was only half joking. The image he'd just conjured was almost his undoing.

"Is that supposed to be an incentive to suck you off? 'Cause it's only making me want to defy you all the more." She opened her mouth and took the head of his dick inside her mouth, but let it slide free after only a couple of strokes.

Damon had to grit his teeth to keep back the moan. "You truly want a spanking? Your cries and the sound of my hand smacking your ass would only cause Viktor to break out of his cell. What if he caught you in that position?"

If Damon had once thought Phoebe an innocent of any kind, her next words shot that image all to hell and back. "Then maybe he'd like to join us."

That was it. Damon yanked her to her feet and threw her on the cot. She landed on her back with her legs hanging over the side. Before she made a move to get up, Damon braced his knees on the edge of the bed and lowered his pelvis to her chest. His cock rode between her breasts, and she squeezed them around his cock with her hands. He was helpless to do anything but thrust against her chest as he would thrust into her cunt. The fleshy mounds hugged him as snugly as she had the first time they'd made love.

"You like this, don't you, Damon." It wasn't a question. He was sure the sweat popping out all over him was a good indication he was enjoying himself.

She raised her head up slightly and licked the end of his shaft. Her saliva, the pre-cum oozing from the tip of his cock, and her sweat increased the lubrication deliciously. Several times she licked him, the sensation teasing him unmercifully. He could no longer keep the grunts of his efforts at bay.

"That's it, Damon. Fuck my tits. Come on my face and chest, and I might let you spank me while Viktor watches. Would you like that?"

Damon couldn't seem to form a coherent thought. Of course he didn't want Viktor to watch! But he couldn't make himself say it. Just the thought of the big vampire leaning against the wall behind them, his arms crossed over his chest, his fangs bare and ready to drink from one or both of them was enough to push him past the point of no return.

"Moon and stars! I'm coming, Phoebe!" That hoarse croak couldn't have been his voice, could it?

Phoebe lifted her head again, sticking her tongue out and licking the head of his cock as it thrust madly up at her. "That's it, that's it," she panted. "Give it to me, Damon. Show Viktor I'm yours and no one else's. Mark me with your seed."

When his orgasm hit, it did so with the force of a thermonuclear detonation. He couldn't have stopped the shout of utter ecstasy if he'd tried. Cum erupted from his cock. He sprayed her with spurt after spurt of thick, white semen. Phoebe opened her mouth and caught some of it. She let it dribble down her chin to mingle with what she hadn't caught, and Damon was hard all over again. She was the sexiest woman he'd ever seen. The look of ecstasy on her face was worth any price Damon had to pay. She hadn't come herself, but she had enjoyed what she'd done to him. Most likely, she enjoyed the power it gave her to be in total control of his pleasure.

When he'd had a chance to catch a couple of breaths, Damon stood. "All right, you little temptress. You asked for it -- you're going to get it."

Damon yanked her up from the bed by one arm. She yelped, but made no move to get away. In fact, when he split her uniform the rest of the way down, she helped him by kicking off her shoes and stepping out of the tattered remains of her clothing.

Once she was naked, he sat on the bunk and pulled her face down across his lap, her bottom raised perfectly atop his thighs. Phoebe looked back at him over her shoulder. The look in her eyes dared him, begged him to do this. His hand rested on her rounded bottom, rubbing her cheeks, kneading them.

He waited until her breathing grew deep and rapid, until he knew she was as hot as he was. When she trembled beneath his hands, he smacked one cheek sharply. Phoebe hissed. He swatted her again, and again, never in the same spot. When she whimpered, he stopped and caressed her reddened bottom.

"That lovely ass blushes prettily when I give it attention." He smacked it again. "I love that sound. Especially when I wonder if you deserve it." He had to bring up the transmitter in her brain, but he didn't want to do it in an accusing way. He felt her tense at his words. He had to be very careful. "*Black Star* says it's not her or *Sword Breaker* the Hand is after. She says it's you and your friends."

Phoebe's eyes narrowed. "That's not a surprise. They don't let anyone walk away from them."

"It's more than that, Phoebe." When she opened her mouth, most likely to either protest or add something to her previous statement, Damon swatted her ass smartly. She squealed but didn't say anything else. "You have a transmitter on you. It's sending your location straight to the Hand. No matter where you go, they'll know exactly where you are." Damon measured her response. "Did you know that?"

As he talked, her eyes widened, then a look of horror washed over her. "Sweet sun and stars!" Phoebe made a move to get up, but Damon stopped her with a stinging swat across her backside, as well as a hand on her upper back.

"I didn't say you could get up yet." He swatted her a few more times, careful about placing his smacks on a part of her bottom he had yet to hit. "Let's try this again. Did you know you had a tracking device on you? Yes or no?"

"I --" His hand connected with her flesh three times in rapid succession. "No! I didn't know!"

"Good girl." He rubbed her bottom again. "What are the chances that Diamond knows?"

"Damon, let me up -- oh!" Her ass was bright pink now from the small of her back to the tops of her thighs. Despite her demand, she didn't really try to get up, and she wiggled her butt so enticingly, Damon couldn't bring himself to stop. For several more strokes, he continued until the heat from her skin burned his hand.

She had spread her legs, and now she trembled with the effort of keeping them that way. Her ass was as high in the air as she could get it, which left her pussy open to him if he wanted it.

He wanted it.

When his fingers came in contact with her slit he wasn't surprised to find her dripping wet. "I'll let you up when I'm good and ready. Now, answer the damn question."

"No. No, I don't think she knows. Oh, stars, Damon! Stick your fingers in me. Neither of us knew. We're innocent. I swear it!"

Damon dipped his fingers into her once, and she cried out sharply. "Do you know why you and Diamond would be fitted with transmitters while the other women weren't?" It was a long shot, but Phoebe knew these people better than he did. If anyone had an insight into their thinking, it would be her.

"I -- Damon, I need to think." Her words came out through panting breaths, her cheeks were almost as flushed as her backside, and her hair stuck to her face from the sweat.

"Then I'll remove my fingers."

"No!"

Damon chuckled before sliding his fingers in deeper and repeating his question. "Why were the two of you singled out? There has to be a reason none of the others have similar transmitters."

Phoebe was sure her eyes rolled back in her head when Damon plunged his fingers back inside her grasping cunt. She couldn't remember her own name, much less come up with a reason why she and Diamond had been singled out. All she knew was she didn't want Damon to stop anything he was doing.

"Look," she stammered, "maybe everyone has one and you just can't find it. I find it hard to believe they'd put tracking devices on some and not all of us. In their whole existence, no one has ever escaped from them for long. It's part of the stigma of who they are. You know when you're brought there, you're not getting out." She would have arched her back and raised her ass higher if she could have. Anything to get him to take the hint. She wanted more.

"No. *Black Star* and *Sword Breaker* both checked everyone thoroughly. The two of you have very sophisticated tracking devices implanted in your brains. We didn't notice them at first, but *Black Star* doesn't give up easily. It took her a while, but she found it."

Phoebe froze. In her *brain*? "Sweet stars." OK, now she was officially freaked out. Sexual haze or not, that was just too weird. Damon must have been prepared for her mood change because he immediately withdrew his fingers and urged her to turn over.

"*Black Star* has isolated it and done a full diagnostic. She knows exactly how it works, just not how to block it. Yet." He kissed her forehead, then her nose.

"Is it a transmitter only? I mean, they can't blow my head off or anything, can they?"

"Absolutely not. It's a tracking device only. Like I said, *Black Star* has mapped this thing down to its last nanotransister. Once she figures out how to block the signal, we can use it to our advantage. Until then, we just have to stay a step ahead of them. Having *Sword Breaker* around will help too." His smile was genuine, the compassion in his eyes almost as great as the lust. Phoebe also saw a vulnerability there she'd never expected to see. He was genuinely sorry for what had happened. "Phoebe…"

"Shhh." She covered his mouth with the tips of three fingers. "It's OK. You did what you had to do. I didn't enjoy it, and I'll remind you of it often, but I do understand." She smiled. "At least, I understand you have to protect your ship. I'm not so sure you had to throw me in the brig."

"Well…" Damon urged her to straddle his hips, "… here, we actually have a door that will lock."

"Right. We had that before. And I'm sure you planned it exactly this way, too."

"Just shut up and fuck me, Phoebe."

Phoebe was more than ready. She reached between them and found his cock, hot, hard and ready. After a few experimental pumps, Phoebe rose up on her knees and impaled herself on it.

Both of them screamed. Phoebe loved the full feeling of having him inside her. She ground her pelvis into him to put much-needed friction on her clit. His hands gripped the deliciously punished flesh of her ass, and his grunts of exertion were music to her ears. He was just as affected as she was.

It wasn't long before Damon flipped Phoebe onto her back, never breaking their joining. He hooked her legs over his shoulders and began to thrust in earnest. Deeper and harder with each stroke, Damon plunged into her over and over again.

"Now, Phoebe. Come for me. Come on my cock and milk me dry!"

She wanted to comply, was about to comply, when she heard a small sound to her left. She turned her head, and the man she saw was familiar, but the vicious, lust-filled look was totally foreign.

"Focus on me, Phoebe." Damon gritted the words out. "Only me."

It wasn't hard. Even knowing Viktor watched, and was on the edge of his control by the looks of him, didn't bring Phoebe down from her sexual high. In fact, it escalated it. When her orgasm overtook her, she was sure she'd die from the intensity. Her ears roared as tingles and pleasurable spasms spread from her clit through her abdomen and legs. She screamed.

With one final thrust Damon followed, yelling loudly, and emptied himself inside her. He let her drop her legs, then collapsed on top of her. Phoebe looked to where Viktor still stood, the look on his face frightening to behold.

"You're supposed to be confined to quarters," Damon reprimanded.

"Ranier is waiting on me. I had to see…" He trailed off, shaking his head. "If I don't get relief soon, Damon, I am lost."

Damon's expression softened with worry. "Go back to your quarters. If you break out again, I'll have you shot, Viktor."

"You should, my friend."

Damon rolled to his side and pulled her close. "Someday, perhaps we'll be able to do that without getting interrupted."

"Only if you learn how to keep quiet." Ranier grinned at them from the open doorway.

"Shit." Damon scrubbed a hand over his face. "Not again."

"Sorry, Sir, but I thought you'd like to know all enemy ships have retreated. They don't seem too concerned with us since we kicked their asses."

"It couldn't have waited?" Damon was annoyed, but Phoebe knew he could see the humor in it.

"Well, yes. It could have. But that wouldn't have been any fun." The younger man chuckled as he ducked out of the doorway.

"One of these days, I'll kick his ass on sheer principle."

They both laughed.

"So, now what?" Phoebe snuggled into him. She loved the clean smell of this particular man. She could just lie there and let his scent wash over her all day.

"*Black Star* believes whatever is inside your head is essential to the grander scheme of things. I agree with her, but one thing still bothers me. Why were only you and Diamond bugged?"

"From what you said, I'd assume those little devices weren't cheap. Maybe they only had a limited number and just ran out."

"Or they planted them on those most likely to run."

"That's a thought," Phoebe mused. "How do we keep them away from us?"

"Let the ships worry about that. They seem to be the only ones around with a clue as to what's going on. I swear, if one more sentient ship starts talking to me like I'm an idiot, I'll unplug the whole lot of them."

"I heard that, Damon," *Black Star*'s voice squawked from the intercom. "There's more going on here than is obvious. Right now, the two of you need to get dressed and, more importantly, get Diamond aboard this ship ASAP."

Damon raised an eyebrow. "Diamond?"

"Just do it. The lives of everyone on this ship could well depend on it."

"Am I the captain, or are you?"

Phoebe laughed and turned Damon toward her for a kiss. "You'll do well to remember, sweetheart, never to argue with a woman who has more facts than you do."

"I seem to remember thinking the same thing about Viktor. Well, not the woman part, the other part." Damon laughed. "It will be as you command, ma'am."

All was well with Phoebe now. This man completed her more than any person she'd ever known. But she was troubled. She could feel the tension in Damon even during their happiest moments. Something was wrong. She'd bet a week's wages that problem was Viktor.

Epilogue

Viktor's heart raced. Sweat soaked his body. He had to have blood. Preferably with a female of his own species to supply it, but at this point, he'd take what he could get. He knew the *Black Star* was worried about how to rid Phoebe and Diamond of their unwanted brain implants, but he had problems of his own just now. If he didn't get what he needed soon, he'd take it. By force. No one on this ship could stop him if it came to that. If he didn't give in to his baser nature soon, he'd lose all sanity, and that nature would take over forever. If that happened, the entire crew was at risk. Viktor would kill them all in his need for blood. He only hoped it wasn't already too late.

He stumbled into his quarters and locked the door. His head spun, and he pressed his fists against his temples and roared his frustration, need, and desperation.

"So, what does a vampire do when he can't get blood or sex, hmm?"

The female voice was deep, husky, and had the most exotic accent Viktor had ever heard. When he turned around, he knew he'd found his salvation.

Or maybe his damnation.

Black Star Diamond
A Sci-Fi Futuristic Alien Adventure
Marteeka Karland

Viktor, the second in command of the legendary *Black Star*, is in the grips of the Blood Burning. He's denied himself blood and the unbridled sex all vampires need to survive for far too long. When he finds Diamond in his cabin, all his hard fought self-control flies out the airlock. Diamond knows the danger she is in by offering herself, but she also knows she's the only hope Viktor has of regaining his sanity. And she craves what he offers her, more than she thought possible.

When he finds Diamond after her intense encounter with Viktor, Ranier, *Black Star*'s pilot, is ready to end the vampire's existence. He wants Diamond for himself, to give her a life of comfort and tenderness she deserves.

Diamond craves not only Ranier's tender touch, but also the rough, demanding touch of her vampire lover. She needs them both, and knows they need each other. But before they can work out their differences, the Hand of God makes a move that not only threatens to destroy Diamond, but another escapee from Graves Station -- Phoebe -- and the *Sword Breaker* and the *Black Star* as well.

Chapter One

"So, what does a vampire do when he can't get blood or sex, hum?"

Of all the situations Diamond expected to find herself in after escaping the Hand of God on Graves Station and the explosion outside the *Black Star*, being vampire fodder was the last. She should have expected it, but she'd done her best to steer clear of Viktor and hadn't realized how far gone he was. Now, it might be too late to salvage his sanity. Or his life. Still, she owed it to the people of the *Black Star* and the *Sword Breaker* -- including Viktor -- to do what she could. Without them, she'd still be on that hellhole of a space station. Or dead. Yes. She'd help Viktor even if it meant her very life. She owed it to him.

Viktor was apparently deep in a blood lust caused by denying himself all the pleasures of the flesh vampires were meant to indulge in. Diamond would bet her life he hadn't had blood or sex in many standard months, far longer than any vampire could safely endure.

"You have exactly two heartbeats to get the hell out of here." Viktor's voice was husky, gravelly. Deadly. His eyes glowed red in a blood rage she'd never seen the like of. If she didn't do as he asked -- even giving her the option of flight had to have represented the last of his control -- he would very likely kill her. A vampire in the grip of this kind of torture was never a gentle lover. They were as vicious in taking blood as they were in taking their pleasure. Often, their chosen prey didn't survive. It was why vampires rarely mated outside their own species. It was why Captain Singh was making all possible speed to Viktor's home world.

"I can't, Viktor." She gave him a smile she suspected looked suspiciously like a sneer. "If I don't help you, I'm damned to the seventh pit of hell."

"What makes you think a puny human like you could possibly help me?" Spit flew from his mouth as he barked his reply. His disgust was clear. It was obvious he wanted nothing to do with humans on this subject.

"Nothing. Only that you need blood and sex. If you don't, you're dead."

He hissed. "You know nothing!" He slashed a hand through the air in an animated gesture. "Not having blood or sex won't kill me, only drive me insane. I can't be sure it hasn't already. You should leave before I drain you dry, *human*." The last word was said with more contempt than even men with the Hand of God had ever used in reference to her. He said it like she was so far beneath him, he'd as soon squash her like a bug instead of have to converse with her.

She bared her teeth to him. A show of contempt, herself. "Perhaps being deprived of the two things vampires crave more than anything else won't actually be your death, but if you go mad and start killing, the captain will be forced to terminate you. I seriously doubt even a vampire of your stature could withstand the entire ship's complement, not to mention the *Black Star* herself."

He tilted his head, and the light in his eyes dimmed minutely. "What do you know of the *Black Star*?" Apparently, his curiosity stemmed the madness for a while.

"Only what Phoebe told me. That the ship is sentient, and that you've formed a link with her. I also know that Phoebe and I have some kind of tracking device implanted deep inside our brains that the *Black*

Star is trying to devise a way to remove."

Viktor's eyes flashed once before dimming again. "For someone facing either major brain surgery or more encounters with a cult group like the Hand of God, you don't sound too worried."

"Of course not." She sniffed. "I'd welcome the chance to kill more of those bastards. As to the other -- " She shrugged. "-- whatever is meant to be will be. It made my decision to confront you all the easier. If I'm going to die --" She got up on her knees on the bed where she'd been waiting for him and unzipped her uniform all the way down to a few inches below her navel and shrugged out of it completely. "-- I'll damned well choose how. And I guarantee it won't have anything to do with those sons of bitches in the Hand of God."

When Viktor's eyes glowed blood red with lust and the need for blood once more, Diamond sat back on the bed with her legs spread. She watched him carefully as his chest heaved and he clenched his fists with the effort to hold himself back. Picking up the tube of lubrigel lying on the table by the bed, she shoved the tip inside her cunt and squeezed. "Well? I'm not leaving. Come fuck me."

With a roar that made her ears ring, Viktor tackled her.

She bit back a yelp by sheer force of will and barely had time to feel a twinge of fear before he covered her body with his and plunged into her core. She did scream then. Not only was she not ready for such an invasion -- a mistake on her part as she'd known he wouldn't be in any shape for foreplay and she'd had only very few sexual encounters with men in the past -- but his cock was simply huge. The pain was so intense she saw stars, and would have passed out if she'd been in any other position besides flat on her back. She wouldn't be too damaged, but she'd definitely be very sore later. Not that she'd expected anything different.

Viktor pounded into her with deep, rapid strokes. Each stroke brought more pain, and she had to bite her lip to keep from crying out again. His grunts and snarls filled the room, providing a violent soundtrack for the primitive act. She caught sight of them in the reflection from the window, which overlooked a vast starfield. The sight of Viktor driving into her body over and over was suddenly the most erotic thing she'd ever seen.

What was once only pain became a pleasure in itself. Had the pain not been there, the pleasure wouldn't have been nearly as intense. She gripped his back and dug her nails into his flesh as she cried out, digging her heels into his ass and urging him on. It was totally insane.

Diamond was on the verge of a powerful climax when Viktor sank his fangs into her neck. She screamed again, this time in pain. There was nothing pleasurable about it now. She tried to push him away, but he held her fast. Diamond could feel the sucking pressure on her neck and knew he was drinking his fill. If she wasn't able to stop him, he would kill her. No matter how unintentional. At this point, Viktor was simply beyond realizing what he was doing.

Over and over he thrust into her while pulling at the life-giving blood he so desperately needed. He continued until, with one mighty thrust, he came deep inside her cunt. His seed was hot. Painfully so. It was probably the burning of his blood. She'd been told about the Blood Burning in vampires. The only other vampire she'd met said every body fluid, every piece of his flesh, would be at least six degrees above normal. To anyone but a vampire, that degree of body temp change could be deadly. Vampires, it merely drove insane.

With another shout of fury, Viktor pushed himself away from her slightly -- enough to be able to look her squarely in the face and gauge her reaction, but not far enough that she could escape him. Blood stained his mouth and chin, making him look incredibly grotesque. She could feel the blood trickling from her neck. The sleepy feeling trying to overwhelm her told her he'd taken more than she could afford to give.

"You're not quite human, little jewel." It was a growled accusation. Like it offended him -- not that she wasn't completely human, but because of what it took to make her that way. "Who has touched you?" he shouted at her, a manic, almost hysterical look in his eye.

The room spun, but she knew she had to respond. In this state, any resistance on her part, no matter how unintentional, would be met with deadly force. "I -- a vampire on Graves Station. He saved my life and made me swear I'd do the same to anyone of his kind if I were ever in the position to do so. In order for me to live, he had to change me. He made me a perfect vampire blood slave. I have enough vampire blood in me to keep me alive through almost any injury except extreme blood loss, and I never get sick, but I'm human enough to have enough nutrients in my blood to sustain a vampire in lieu of an actual kill. Unless, that is, you take too much."

"And you have aspirations of being my salvation?" His husky voice was calmer now, though she still could see the barely controlled hunger in his eyes.

"Honestly? I could give a damn about your salvation." She struggled to keep her voice neutral. He couldn't know the agony he'd caused her or he'd try to suppress himself again, and someone could get killed. "I'm fulfilling a promise I made to someone in exchange for my life. If I get you through this, I'll have paid my debt." He sagged, his eyes becoming droopy. Good. He had drunk his fill this time and not killed her. She might make it through this yet. It all depended on how long he had to keep it up before his Blood Burning passed.

She pushed him off her, and he rolled to his back on the bed. "Don't be here when I wake, Diamond." And he promptly fell asleep.

Diamond stood on wobbly legs, but one step and she collapsed, too weak to even make it to the door. He was right. She definitely shouldn't be here when he woke up. Crawling took so much effort, she had to stop and rest before she could even unlock the door for it to slide open. When she did, she was met by an alarmed-looking Ranier with a hand raised to hit the door chime.

"What the blue *fuck* is going on? Are you OK?"

She wanted to nod her head, but nothing seemed to work. "Med Unit," was all she managed to croak out before the room started spinning wildly. Everything became blurry around the edges, her ears rang, and she felt herself falling. Then blackness.

Chapter Two

The amount of blood and destruction in Viktor's cabin was unthinkable. When Rainer saw the vampire lying stretched out on the bed as if dead, blood smeared from his mouth down his neck and chest, he truly thought the tiny woman had managed to kill him. Then he saw the blood on Diamond's neck and chest. And her thighs. The woman looked like she had been tortured.

Bloody hell! If Viktor was dead, he probably deserved it.

Ranier scooped her up and rushed to Medical. Her head lolled against his shoulder, lifeless. Her skin was a sickly pale, her lips almost disappeared into her face with lack of color, and she was cold. Deathly cold.

"Doctor!" Ranier was beginning to panic. It looked like this woman was dying in his arms. "Help her!"

The ship's doctor, Mahat Zabin, took one look at Diamond and snatched her from Ranier's arms. He ducked into a surgical suite where four medical personnel swarmed around her, closing a med unit around her to give them a summary of her injuries.

"Her hemoglobin and hematocrit are critically low, Doctor," one nurse read from a display. "She needs blood badly, but she doesn't match anything we have on board. I'm not even sure we can synthesize it."

The doctor looked at the readout, and his brows knitted together. "I can do it manually."

"Manually?" The nurse gave him a look that said *you've got to be kidding.*

"Yes." He turned from the display and went to a computer terminal. "Seal her wounds and stabilize her other injuries. Take special care with the tears and slight burn to her vaginal wall and external genitalia or she'll form scar tissue, making it difficult for her to have pleasure during sex."

"Doctor --" The same nurse put a hand on her hip and looked at him like she couldn't believe what he was saying. "-- at this point, that's the least of her worries."

Doctor Zabin looked up from his work and gave the nurse a scathing look. "As a doctor -- or nurse -- our job is to not only save a life, but to ensure quality of life." He clenched his fists. "If it is at all possible to put her back together the way she was before this happened, I intend to do it. Can't you see how badly she's been used? Assuming she decides at some point she wants sexual pleasure, make damned sure she can. If you can't accept that challenge, I suggest you relieve yourself of duty." The nurse simply shrugged before turning back to the patient.

"You." Dr. Zabin turned to Ranier. "Find whoever did this and kill him."

Ranier nodded, but there was nothing he could do. The *Black Star* had told Captain Singh to bring the girl to Viktor in the first place. Once she had been told the gravity of the situation, she'd seemed to know exactly what to do. Unfortunately, it looked like she'd been wrong.

Ranier turned to go, but a muffled moan from Diamond made him whip around and rush to her side. She opened her eyes slowly and found his. "Don't approach him until he wakes. He'll kill you if you do."

"Looks like he just about killed *you*." Ranier found her hand under the med unit and grasped it tenderly. "We're too far from his home world and any relief he might find. I have to tell the captain how far gone he is. We may have no choice but to kill him before he kills someone or injures anyone else." Ranier felt a sharp pain in his heart. Viktor was a sadistic asshole, but he was a fine warrior, and an even better friend… in his own sadistic asshole kind of way. The thought of ending his life was unthinkable, yet he managed to actually say the words without choking.

Not only that, but Diamond tugged at his heart as well. She was a strong woman. A brave woman. Yet vulnerable beyond belief. She needed something. Ranier wasn't sure exactly what it was, but he had a feeling it had something to do with Viktor. It made him angry as hell. Viktor didn't deserve a woman like this after his treatment of her.

He winced. Diamond was so lovely. He'd had thoughts of trying to win her for himself, but how could he possibly hope to have her after her experience with the vampire? Even if they had to kill Viktor, he'd likely haunt Diamond for the rest of her life after something like this. Ranier would only serve as a reminder.

"He won't, Ranier." She squeezed his hand slightly, and he was sure it was meant to be reassuring. "He's in the *Komanyar*. The Sleep of Death. It's a state all vampires enter after a Blood Frenzy. He shouldn't wake for several hours."

"Will he be back to normal?" Whatever that was. Ranier had the feeling he was about half crazy most of the time.

"No, but he won't be as deeply in the Blood Burning as he was before. I'll have to go to him several more times before it passes, and he'll have to have his needs met regularly for a long time or he'll slip back into it more easily and with less warning." Her words were starting to slur now. "Just trust me. I can handle this." She looked at Ranier with large, luminous green-flecked violet eyes, and he couldn't deny her anything.

He sighed. "I'll tell the captain. The decision is ultimately up to him, but I'll put in a good word."

Diamond nodded and smiled. "Thank you." Ranier turned to leave, but her grip on his hand tightened. "You'll come back for a while, won't you?" There. That was the lost girl he'd suspected was inside the toughened, battle-hardened woman. "I mean, your presence is comforting. I like talking to you."

"Of course." He smiled, his heart breaking. "I won't be long." When her lip trembled, Ranier had to comfort her. Not caring that everyone in the suite was watching, he dipped his head to hers and kissed her lips tenderly, stroking her hair as gently as he could. "I promise."

He noticed how her eyes widened slightly, but finally she smiled and nodded her head. Closing her eyes, she took one final deep breath before she slept. Ranier lowered his head once more and placed a kiss on her forehead. Sweet gods above! He wanted this woman. And, stars help him, he wanted to kill Viktor for what he'd done to her.

* * *

Viktor *burned*. Sweat dripped off his eyelashes and ran down his face in rivulets. He shouldn't have watched the captain and his little stowaway fucking in her holding cell, but he couldn't help himself. He needed sex like they'd had, only…

More. More intense. More violent.

It was the nature of the vampire.

The urgency had been muted somewhat since his encounter with Diamond, but he still didn't trust himself. When he'd awakened to find her gone, he'd almost gone into a rage. How *dare* she leave him when he needed her like this! Then he remembered telling her to be gone when he woke. He knew he'd hurt her, but he also knew he needed to have her again. She was, quite possibly, the only person, man or woman, within a million light years who could take what he had to give and come out intact.

At least, he hoped she had. Even through the haze of the Blood Burning, her fate weighed heavily on his mind. She didn't deserve to be abused by a vampire. No woman did.

When the chime rang softly, he snapped, "Enter." Ranier stood outside his door, a furious expression on his face.

"She thought you'd sleep for several hours. Why are you awake?"

"She was gone. My body recognized it and came out of hibernation."

"You almost killed her, you know."

"I figured as much." Viktor tried to control his tone as much as possible, but he still heard a waver that shouldn't have been there. "She will survive, then?"

Ranier scowled and entered his cabin. The door *whooshed* closed behind him. "Barely. How could you possibly do that to her? She was trying to help you!"

"Ranier, do you know *anything* about vampires?"

He pushed a hand through his hair before answering. "I know more than I ever wanted to know, including what you're going through. I know I sound petulant, but even though you're quite possibly the best friend I've ever had, I still cringe when I think about what I walked in on earlier. Since I met you, I've always thought of you as completely in control. Even when we knew you were pushed beyond your endurance, I still never thought you were capable of anything like that."

Viktor had to sink his fangs into his lower lip to keep from losing the fragile hold he had on his control. "I know you don't understand, Ranier, but I did everything I was capable of doing, including giving her a way out. She refused to take it -- even taunted me with her willingness to let me fuck her into oblivion. I happen to believe she knew exactly what she was getting into. I regret it, but I can't change it."

The smaller man paced the room a couple of times before turning back to Viktor. "I was going to the captain to recommend we destroy you, no matter how much the thought sickened me, but Diamond made me promise I wouldn't. She said you'd be better after this." He raised an eyebrow. "Are you?"

"I am." Viktor could say that without hesitation. "But I'm far from past the crisis. If I'm lucky, I can hold out until we get to Draggoon. Once I'm on my home world, I can get the relief I need."

"Then maybe I can keep my promise and tell the captain you're getting better and do so with a straight face." He sighed and scrubbed a hand through his hair again. "I have to lock you in, Viktor. You understand?"

The hurt and confused young man stomped out of Viktor's cabin and Viktor heard the soft chime of the security locks enabling. He wasn't sure how far they were from Draggoon, but if it was too far, and Diamond was gone too long, Ranier might regret letting him live.

Chapter Three

"I understand you have personal issues with this, Ranier, but I need you to be objective." Captain Damon Singh stared at Ranier with hard eyes, completely the captain looking out for the welfare of his ship, not the man who considered Viktor his friend as well as second in command. Ranier admired him for his ability to separate the friend from the monster.

"I can't give you an objective opinion, Captain." Ranier scrubbed a hand over his face. "Everything military in me is screaming for someone to kill him, but I can't ask my men to do something I'm not willing to do myself. I think Diamond knows his condition better than anyone, and if she's willing to bet her life that he's more stable now, I have to take her word for it. I have to believe there is still hope of saving him."

Damon paused a moment before asking in a tired voice, "Is Diamond all right? Phoebe is very worried." Ranier hadn't been on the *Black Star* very long, but he'd been there long enough to have learned to read between the lines. Phoebe might very well be worried, but Damon was equally so.

"She's in Medical, and came through better than I thought she would when I first found her, but it's going to take several days at best for her to recover."

Damon sighed. "We need to get Viktor back to Draggoon, but we've got another problem."

"Why does there always seem to be a problem? Why can't things work out without incident just once? What's the crisis now?" Ranier sounded a tad bit snitty, but he really wanted to be done with this. The emotional strain was more than he could bear at the moment.

Damon raised an eyebrow, but ignored Ranier's

outburst. "We have bigger problems than one vampire run amok. We're being followed. The Hand of God, as well as several Vok'nair war ships."

"What do you think they're after?" Ranier puzzled.

"Most likely, the Hand exchanged information on the location of *Black Star* for help in regaining the women. No matter what, I'm afraid we're in for a rough time. We'll have no problem outrunning them, but if they pick up a fleet of Vok'nair ships, they may very well have a good chance of succeeding in taking back the *Black Star*."

"Unless the vampires help us. Is that likely?"

Damon snorted and stood from his desk. Stalking to the large viewscreen that served as a window to the immediate area outside his office, he grunted. "You see how much trouble we have with Viktor. Can you imagine a whole planet of vampires on the rampage? No. They won't help unless they're threatened. To be honest --" Damon turned back to face Ranier. "-- given the potential for disaster, it's probably best they don't." He smiled. "We'll worry about that when the time comes."

Ranier turned to go.

"I'd feel better with you back at the helm, Ranier. But I don't want her to be alone with him again until the worst has passed."

Ranier threw his hands up in the air. "You've *got* to be kidding me. Do you have any idea what the *fuck* you're asking?"

"Yes, but I won't sacrifice Diamond for Viktor, no matter how much I need him on this ship. I'm counting on you to save them both. Go back to Medical and see how she's doing. If she's stable, report back to Command until she's released."

Ranier left the captain's office and Command, heading to Medical. He fully expected to find Diamond still sleeping as the doctor continued to mend her wounds, but he was wrong. She was still on the med table, but fully awake and receiving her blood transfusion.

When he entered the suite, she turned her head and smiled at him. She definitely looked much better.

"This is a surprise." Ranier took the hand she offered when he approached her. "I didn't expect you to be awake so soon."

"Me, either." Dr. Zabin entered, making notations on a palm computer. "Yet here she is." He raised an eyebrow. "Is there something you need to tell me, my dear?"

Diamond tried to snatch her hand away, but Ranier held her fast. He was not letting her pull away from him. Not now.

"It's OK," he said softly. "If it will help the doctor, you need to tell him."

She scowled. "Look, I'm grateful for your help, Ranier." She glanced at the doctor before returning her attention back to Ranier. "Both of you. But I'm not a freak show. I know I'm different. Until now, I wasn't exactly sure how different, but there's nothing either of you can do about it, so just drop it. I want to get out of here and find a decent meal."

"Do I look like I care how different you are? If anything I'm grateful for your differences. They saved your life." Ranier tightened his grip on her hand. "Those differences aided your recovery. They can only be good things. If it helps the medical staff better care for you, then they need to know. *Spill it!*"

"I already know," Dr. Zabin sniffed arrogantly. He tapped a few buttons on his hand-held computer. "I just wanted to know if she was aware of it." He addressed Diamond. "Did you volunteer for this transformation?"

She balled her fist in the sheet covering the lower half of her body, but looked at Rainer squarely. "Somewhat. I was injured -- badly -- and given a choice. Live or die." She looked at the doctor. "Naturally, I chose the former. In return, swore to help out any of my 'savior's' kind in need if the occasion ever arose."

"Well, I don't know what this person intended, but you're the perfect sustenance for a vampire. You have a perfect balance of vampire and human properties in your blood to be able to keep a vampire alive for many months -- years, even, with the proper care -- if he or she is unable to make an actual kill. Your body will heal any damage five or six thousand times faster than that of a non-altered human." He smiled then. "Viktor was lucky you happened along."

"I didn't come here to save Viktor." She pulled her hand free of Ranier's and sat up on the table, disconnecting the blood tubing and stalking across the room to where a fresh uniform hung. Dressed only in her underwear, she seemed as comfortable as if she were fully clothed. Ranier, however, was acutely aware of her state of undress. "I came here to save myself. Do you have any idea what the Hand would have done to me if they'd discovered my dirty little secret?"

"Nothing good, I bet." Ranier held up a hand, blocking Zabin's way when the doctor tried to advance on her. He shook his head, and Dr. Zabin shrugged. Without a word of protest, the doctor left the room, and Ranier approached Diamond. He raised his wrist to his mouth and commed the captain. "Captain."

"Report."

"Diamond's up and about. I'll explain later. Out."

He fumbled with his comm unit as he watched her step into the uniform. Ranier heard the faint noise as she zipped it up the front. When she turned around, he was only two paces away from her.

It was a moment unlike any he'd spent with a woman before. Ranier could see her need of... something... in her eyes. Yet she refused to reach out to him. When Ranier thought she might, she balled her hands into fists and raised her chin a notch, too proud to ask for whatever it was she needed.

Then it hit him. She'd asked him to come back. Reached for him when he'd returned. He didn't know her relationship with Viktor, but she needed tenderness Ranier wasn't sure Viktor was capable of giving. Especially now. The brutality she'd endured couldn't have been anything but traumatizing.

Moving very slowly, Ranier closed the distance between them and pulled Diamond into his arms. At first, she stiffened. Then she melded into Ranier as if she knew she belonged there. Her arms snaked around his waist, and she rested her cheek on his chest. He thought he felt her body tremble, but the vibration was so slight, he couldn't be sure.

He could have stood there all day, but the door slid open, and Viktor entered the room looking almost as wild and out of control as Ranier imagined he might have when he'd taken Diamond the first time.

"What the fuck do you think you're doing with my woman, human?" His normally husky, quiet voice was loud in his rage.

Ranier turned, keeping a grip on Diamond's arm so he could keep her behind his back and stay between her and Viktor. "I thought I locked you in. Get back to your cabin. Now. Don't make me shoot you." He pulled out his gun.

"No!" Diamond twisted her arm free and bolted to Viktor. "I can help him." Viktor grabbed her arm and pulled her to him. Diamond didn't resist, but winced. The flesh of her arm where Viktor's fingers dented it was white. It only took a few seconds for her arm below his grip to begin to mottle. She'd definitely bruise.

"Who's going to help you? If the captain hadn't sent me to check on Viktor, you'd probably be dead."

"You heard what the doctor said. I wouldn't have died. This is what I'm made to do." She looked pleadingly at him. Ranier ground his teeth. Why did women always want to think they could save the world? "I don't expect you to understand, but I gave my word to a man who saved my life. That's not a promise I can break."

Viktor only grunted, his eyes hungrily devouring her as he half walked, half dragged her to the door. "Mine," he growled.

"Oh, no. Maybe you will be fine, but I'm not taking any chances. You're not taking her anywhere without me, Viktor."

"You wish to participate in our little game, human?"

"Oh, *hell* no!" Ranier cringed at the thought. While exploring Diamond together had its up sides, with Viktor in this awful, violent mood, it wasn't something he was willing to even contemplate. "I'm going to make sure you don't cross the line this time."

The vampire only scowled, but didn't say anything. Diamond blinked in surprise, then smiled faintly before Viktor yanked her out the door and down the hallway. Knowing he wouldn't like what he was about to witness, Ranier trotted after them. If nothing else good came out of this, he'd keep Diamond safe until she felt she'd done her bit to save Viktor from total madness. After that, maybe she'd let him hang around for a while longer.

Still, as he followed the couple to Viktor's cabin, a part of him he hadn't realized existed peeped out from behind his mask of civility. He knew enough about vampires to realize he was about to witness something few people ever got to see. Viktor was in a madness of sex and blood that threatened to take him over. If he chose, he could simply take what he needed with multiple partners of any sex he chose. By choosing Diamond over everyone else aboard the *Black Star*, he was giving her more power over him than he had over her.

The act of lust and violence Ranier knew he was about to witness was the most primitive form of mating alive in the galaxy. If Diamond chose, after this was over and Viktor regained his senses, she could remain as Viktor's Mated One for as long as she wished. It would give her almost absolute power over the big vampire in exchange for her body and blood during times such as these when he was in dire need.

Though it could become violent at times -- like the first time Diamond had submitted herself -- it was actually an act no vampire took lightly. Even in the grip of madness, they made the choice to hold to one person, or seek out others to aid them in climbing out of the Blood Burning. Though something few humans -- or any other species -- understood, choosing a partner for a Blood Burning time was the ultimate act of love on the parts of both participants.

The scary part was, Ranier wasn't entirely sure he'd spoken truthfully when he'd said he didn't want to join them. Also, Ranier knew he'd wonder what it meant that Viktor had asked if he wanted to participate in their little game. From what he knew about vampires, they always chose carefully to meet their needs during this time. It was very unlikely he'd choose Diamond as someone he was willing to join his life to and choose a second person to use, then toss away. If Viktor wanted to choose a second person to be involved in this, it would be as an equal to Diamond.

Stars help him! This was becoming a situation he wasn't sure he wanted to resist.

Chapter Four

Diamond was nervous.

She'd watched Ranier during her short stay. He always seemed fun-loving and light hearted, but Viktor always flanked him. It was as if the two were joined at the hip. Diamond tried to take courage from the fact Ranier was with her and Viktor this time, but she honestly wasn't sure she wanted Ranier to stop things if they went too far again. The first time had been brutal, but she had found pleasure. Part of her was eager to try it again. It was part of her she'd never known existed. She had actually craved the pain in the end. Had she thought, she would have realized he needed to bite her, take her blood, and she would have been prepared for it. It might even have been enough to push her over the edge into her own climax.

They reached Viktor's cabin, and he shoved Diamond inside. Viktor immediately undressed, ignoring Ranier altogether, and pulled Diamond's clothes off in a huff when she didn't follow suit.

Diamond glanced nervously at Ranier, hoping he wouldn't go all noble and try to stop Viktor. She wanted this. Not only to help Viktor, but because something perverse and deliciously wicked inside her needed the pain to mix with the pleasure at times. Viktor seemed not to notice. Or care. He shoved her onto the bed and crawled between her legs, obviously intending to simply spear her as he'd done before. This time, Diamond knew she wouldn't need the lubrigel. She was positively soaked just thinking about it.

"Wait a minute, wait a minute." Ranier held up his hands and shook his head. "You can't mean you intend to simply fuck her and be done with it."

Viktor growled and turned his head to the other

man. "It's all that's in me right now. You can try and stop me, but I guarantee you can't." Diamond felt that enormous cock of his probing her entrance and she closed her eyes, bracing herself for the pain of the invasion and craving it with every fiber of her being.

"Viktor! Stop!" Ranier hurried to the bed and crawled to them. Diamond felt Viktor's body shift as he prepared to surge forward.

Then he stopped.

Diamond opened her eyes and groaned. Ranier was on his knees, his legs spread. He and Viktor stared at each other, neither giving an inch.

Several seconds ticked by before Viktor's eyes sparkled red in his lust. "So, human." He bared his teeth, hissing slightly. "What do you intend to do now?"

Ranier seemed to push Viktor away from Diamond, though she didn't see how at first. She sat up and was about to tell Ranier how much she needed this when she saw Ranier had wrapped the fingers of one hand around Viktor's cock, effectively halting the vampire's movements. A thrill of excitement shot through her, releasing more cream from her pussy.

"If you're going to do this --" Ranier didn't release Viktor once he was away from Diamond. He still held Viktor's cock firmly in his grasp. Diamond stared, fascinated. "-- you're going to give her as much pleasure as possible. She's doing this to help you, not because she has to. You're damned well going to make it worth her time."

They stared at each other. Diamond held her breath, sure the flush creeping up her neck and face gave away how much just looking at Ranier holding Viktor's cock affected her. She'd seen, and participated in, sex involving two females -- it was the only sexual attention from another person most of the women in the bowels of the station got or wanted. But she'd never seen two men pleasure each other. She very much wanted to. The thought was intoxicating.

"What do you intend to do now, human?" Viktor hissed, his hands at his sides. He didn't seem in too big a hurry for Ranier to let his cock go. "She likes what she sees." He closed his eyes and inhaled deeply through his nose. "I can smell her cunt from here." When he opened his eyes again, they glowed red in his blood lust.

Ranier gave her a cocky grin and winked at her. He was trying to ease her fear, but she could tell he was just as nervous as she was. His face was dotted with fine beads of sweat, and the hand not clutching Viktor's dick was balled into a fist. "Will your delicate vampire sensibilities be offended if another man readies your woman?"

Viktor smiled. Diamond thought it was more a show of teeth than any real smile. "You can ready both of us, but don't make her come." He hissed again. "That belongs to me and no other."

Ranier met Diamond's eyes with his own. "Do you trust me?" His voice was feather soft. He didn't have to ask the question. Diamond knew what he was trying to do, and she truly loved him for it.

"With my life," she whispered back, her legs spread wide. "You don't have to do this, Ranier. I'm actually looking forward to it, though I do admit the thought of you two fucking turns me on quite a bit. I think I'm a touch perverted."

He barked a laugh. "I think I'm suffering the same affliction."

Ranier didn't waste any more time. He dipped his head to her cunt and swiped it from slit to clit.

Diamond sucked in a sharp breath. She'd been tongued there before, but always by women. A man's tongue felt different. Bigger. Even if she couldn't have seen who was eating her out, she would have known it was a man.

Moisture wept from her cunt as Ranier licked his way around her labia to suck on the little nub of her clit. He sucked each pussy lip into his mouth before letting them go with a soft "pop." Diamond moaned and closed her eyes, enjoying the wonderful sensations he was creating in her lower body.

She was about to lose herself in the pleasure of Ranier's mouth when Viktor grunted and Ranier deserted her parted thighs. She opened her eyes just in time to see Ranier envelop the massive head of Viktor's cock. Had she not been afraid of Viktor's reaction, she might have exploded right there. The sight of Viktor's dick disappearing inside Ranier's mouth was almost too much for her. As it was, she let out a whimper that got Viktor's attention.

"You like that." His voice was husky, gravelly, almost a growl. "You like watching Ranier suck me off." All she could do was nod. "Maybe letting him tag along was a good idea after all. I'm going to fuck you both until I'm sated."

Ranier's head shot up and he looked Viktor square in the face. Diamond had never seen Ranier look so deadly serious. "Not her, this time, Viktor. Just me."

"Oh, stars." Diamond couldn't help the breathy whisper. Was this really happening?

Viktor's eyes blazed, and neither of them gave an inch. "You *dare* deny me?"

"Only in regard to Diamond. If you wanted to destroy her, you'd have done so already. When this is over, you don't want a blood mate who's repulsed by your touch, do you?"

For a moment, Diamond thought Viktor might challenge Ranier. She almost spoke up to tell Ranier it was OK, but Viktor finally nodded. "This time."

Ranier ducked his head back to Viktor's cock. The big vampire let his head fall back slightly and closed his eyes, obviously giving himself over to Ranier's ministrations.

As large as Viktor's cock was, Ranier still managed to work more than half of it into his mouth. When Ranier pulled his head back so he had only the head in his mouth, Viktor's cock gleamed with saliva. Several times, Ranier did this until Viktor's hands tangled in his hair, and he moved Ranier at the speed and depth he desired. Diamond stared in amazement as Ranier took everything Viktor had to give and didn't gag once.

Before she realized what she was doing, Diamond dropped a hand to her pussy and began fingering her clit. The sensation sent ripples up her body. She pulled her fingers back and looked at them, staring in disbelief. She was wet. *Very* wet.

"Lick them," Viktor growled. "Lick your fingers and taste your essence."

She looked at him and, very slowly, brought her fingers to her mouth. She closed her eyes as she tasted the musky evidence of her arousal. When she opened her eyes again she held eye contact with the vampire. He bared his teeth and continued to direct Ranier's movements on his cock. Diamond brought her fingers again to her cunt and dipped them inside. When she brought them out this time, she sat up and brought her fingers to Viktor for his own taste.

He sucked the two digits into his mouth and

nipped one with one sharp canine tooth. Diamond sucked in a surprised breath, but didn't cry out. Viktor pulled at her fingers, no doubt sucking in blood to create a unique flavor. One more taste to add to his current craving.

"Enough!" Viktor yanked Ranier away from his crotch and practically threw him at Diamond. The force with which Ranier landed on her knocked Diamond to her back on the bed once more. The two of them made eye contact for a heartbeat before Viktor grabbed Ranier's hair and pulled him down Diamond's body until his face hovered above her pussy again.

Viktor pushed Ranier's face into Diamond's cunt, and Ranier stabbed his tongue inside her, eagerly lapping up her juice and making her moan. It only lasted a moment before Viktor pulled him away and descended on Ranier's mouth.

The kiss looked torrid. Both men struggled to get closer to each other, their mouths wide open. When they would part for brief moments, Diamond saw their tongues darting out and dipping into each other's mouths.

Viktor pulled Ranier away again, growling and snarling as he pushed Ranier's face toward Diamond's cunt once more. Again, he pulled Ranier back to kiss and suck at his mouth. This time when they broke contact, both men had blood staining their lips.

Ranier wiped his mouth with the back of his sleeve. "I owe you for that one." His voice was soft, but deadly serious.

"You'll have your chance to collect." Viktor didn't seem impressed, but when he met her gaze, Diamond saw something she'd not seen since this adventure began. The light went out in Viktor's eyes for only a moment, but she saw a sadness she hadn't seen before. The unexpected emotion was the hope she needed. It didn't mean no one would die before this was over if Viktor lost it like before, but she thought maybe Viktor was fighting as hard as he could to keep from harming her or anyone else. She hoped with every fiber of her being he won that battle, both for herself and Ranier.

This time, Viktor pushed Ranier up Diamond's body until he lay on top of her, his pelvis between her legs. "Fuck her." Diamond hoped Ranier would follow Viktor's command, wanted it with everything in her.

"Are you willing to do this, Diamond?" Despite the urgent nature of this entire scene, Ranier still took the time to give Diamond a choice as he gently stroked her hair and cheek.

"Are you kidding?" Diamond smiled at him. "If you don't fuck me now and give me a little relief, I'll draw your blood myself."

Ranier's laugh seemed more than a bit strained. "I have a protection implant. Viktor does, too."

"I know. It's OK, Ranier. You don't have to convince me. I'm a willing participant."

"For Viktor?" The vulnerability in Ranier's eyes surprised her. What did he want from her? What was she willing to give him? Ranier had always been kind to her, but he'd never given any indication he was interested in her. Viktor hadn't either, but that had been a choice she'd had to make without his consent. Whatever happened with Viktor later was something to worry about once this was all over.

Ranier, on the other hand, was in this of his own free will. Yes, he obviously had feelings for Viktor that might or might not go deeper than friendship, but he was also there for her. Ranier had put himself between her and Viktor. Looking into his eyes now, Diamond couldn't help but wonder if Ranier harbored any feelings for her he'd kept hidden, or simply hadn't explored before now.

"For both of you. Right now, I think you need me almost as much as Viktor does. I help Viktor because one of his kind once saved my life. I help you because not only did you save my life, you did so at great risk to your own." She grinned. "And because you're really cute."

He laughed once. "Well, I'm glad someone finally noticed." Then very gently, very carefully, Ranier eased into her.

* * *

Diamond's cunt held the most exquisite heat Ranier had ever felt. She fit around him snugly, holding him inside her like she wanted him there more than anything. He definitely wanted to be there more than anything. When she looked at him and smiled, he completely forgot the circumstances that had brought them to this point.

Until he felt Viktor probing his ass with that oversized monster he called a cock.

"Lube that thing up, you bastard." Ranier looked over his shoulder and gave Viktor what he hoped was a menacing glare. "I'm willing to let you do this to give Diamond a little break until she's fully healed, but I'll damned well kick your ass if you aren't more careful this time."

Viktor snarled, but complied. Ranier watched him climb off the bed and stalk across the room. He took the brief moment to focus on Diamond.

"When this is over, I want a chance to make all this up to you." It was lame, but it was the only thing he could think of to say.

She caressed his cheek and Ranier had to use all his force of will to keep his eyes open and not to groan. "There's no need for that." She smiled. "Just make this one time good. Besides, I told you. I'm really starting to enjoy myself. This most of all. Watching him fuck your ass is going to be the hottest thing I've ever seen."

He winced. "Oh, the things I do for the women in my life." He tried to make light of the situation, but he'd never done this before, and Viktor wasn't exactly the best man to ass-fuck you for the first time.

Diamond sounded like the woman who'd gone outside the *Black Star* and saved them all not that long ago -- strong and capable. Ranier knew she was probably fine to take Viktor again, maybe even a little eager, but truth be told, once Ranier had started on this path, he couldn't pull himself off it. He wanted Diamond. He wanted Viktor. If she was willing to let him indulge, he couldn't deny himself.

Gently, so very gently, he rested more of his weight on her and began to move inside her. He kissed her then. Softly. Tenderly. He'd admired her from afar since the day he'd helped rescue Diamond and the other women from Graves Station. Now he had this amazing woman in his arms.

Their lips parted, and they just stared at each other for several moments. Ranier knew his life would never be the same. He'd found a connection with Diamond. One he didn't want to let go.

Stars, how he wanted to savor this moment. This was *his* Diamond. *His!* Not Viktor's.

When Viktor returned with the lubrigel, the only warning Ranier got was when Viktor stuck the little capsule up his rectum and squeezed. The cool liquid rushed into his ass, followed by one then two of Viktor's fingers, and Ranier winced. At least he was making an effort to prepare this time.

"I know you love her, Ranier." Viktor's raspy voice sent shivers down Ranier's spine. The statement also embarrassed him, as he wasn't really ready for Diamond to know how he felt. Hell, he wasn't sure about it himself. "I know having my cock spearing your ass right now is the last thing you want. But if you'll help me get through this, I promise I'll never ask another thing of you again."

The sadness and desperation in Viktor's voice tugged at Ranier as surely as seeing Diamond lying in the doorway broken and bleeding had. The proud vampire was at the very edge of his sanity and admitting that loss of control to anyone hurt him deeply. Right now, Viktor knew Ranier wanted nothing more than to be with Diamond. He and Viktor had been inseparable since Ranier came aboard as the *Black Star*'s pilot. The vampire sometimes knew Ranier better than Ranier knew himself. In truth, Ranier knew he'd be lost without Viktor.

Not only that, but Ranier owed Viktor his life. He'd have been sucked out into space when the Hand of God had attacked them the first time if Viktor hadn't grabbed him and held on with every ounce of cybernetic enhancement he had. Viktor wasn't a bad person. He was just in an impossible situation at the moment.

"I'll admit, the timing of my feelings toward Diamond is a bit poor, but there are feelings inside me for you, too, my friend."

Viktor gripped his ass hard. "Not now, Ranier," he whispered. "I can't think about that now. Not while I'm hurting everyone around me."

Diamond spoke then, and the musical tone of her voice warmed Ranier's heart. "You're not, Viktor. I don't know you very well, but I've seen and heard enough to know you stand by your friends. You don't intentionally harm them. You're not yourself. Let us help you. Let us give you what you need." Then she grinned wickedly. "We'll pay you back later."

Viktor's groan echoed Ranier's. The vampire used his finger to open Ranier's ass and insert the tip of his cock. Ranier expected his rectum to explode in pain, but thanks to the bit of stretching and the lube, he felt full, but not painfully so. Several careful strokes later, Ranier felt Viktor's coarse pubic hair rest against his ass.

All three of them were still for a few moments. Diamond had her legs spread and framing Ranier's hips. Ranier lay over Diamond with his weight resting on his elbows, his legs spread wide. Viktor knelt on one knee, his foot flat on the bed, and he held Ranier's ass cheeks in a death grip.

"Sweet stars," Diamond whispered. "He's fucking us both."

Viktor started to move, and he did indeed fuck them both. Ranier was seated deeply inside Diamond, and as Viktor's thrusts grew more and more steady and rapid, the shockwave as he pounded into Ranier had a ripple effect. Every time Viktor thrust into Ranier, Ranier was thrust into Diamond.

It wasn't long until all three of them were panting and moaning in their pleasure. Ranier kissed Diamond, thrusting his tongue into her mouth as surely as his cock mimicked the action in her cunt. Diamond clung to him, tangling the fingers of one hand in his hair and sliding the other hand down his body until she rested it on Viktor's big hand clutching Ranier's ass cheek.

Ranier had never experienced anything quite like

this. For sure, he'd never been ass-fucked by anyone. But there was something special about it all. His feelings were a jumbled mess. He wasn't sure where his love for one ended and the other began. Everything seemed to blur together until he wasn't sure he was doing this for either of them as much as he was doing it for himself. Viktor had proven himself a good friend. Diamond had proven her character several times over. He might not believe himself "in love" with either of them, but he was damned close. He wasn't sure how he felt about that.

As Viktor slammed his cock home again and again, Ranier became more and more addicted to the sensations. Making love to two people at the same time awakened senses he never knew he had. His ass burned, but in the most exquisite, erotic way, and only enhanced the wondrous sensations his cock felt buried in Diamond's pussy. Combine that with her lips moving against his eagerly, her tongue stabbing into his mouth every so often, the insistent way she tugged his hair to keep his mouth on hers, and Viktor's occasional slaps to his ass cheek as he fucked them both, and Ranier knew he wouldn't last long.

No way in the universe.

"Sweet stars, I'm going to come," Diamond groaned out. "That's it, Viktor. Fuck us! Fuck us!"

"Damned straight, I'll fuck you," Viktor ground out. "I'll fuck you until you both come."

"I'm coming, whether you want me to or not," Ranier heard himself say. The blood throbbed in his ears, and his vision narrowed. He couldn't even concentrate on the woman clinging to him so tightly. All he could do was breathe and let Viktor move him however he wanted to.

"Now, Ranier!" Viktor swatted his ass twice

more, landing stinging blows that only sped his orgasm. "Fill her sweet little cunt with your seed! Do it!"

Three hard and deep thrusts later, Ranier did just that. Diamond let out a scream and gripped Ranier with her legs. Her pussy contracted around his cock, milking him of everything he had to give her. It wasn't long before Viktor followed them. Ranier felt the vampire's hot sperm explode into his ass and trickle down his balls. Viktor pumped into his ass several more times before he finally stilled and rubbed Ranier's stinging cheeks.

Viktor rolled them all over so they lay on the bed. Ranier's cock was firmly imbedded in Diamond, though Viktor's had slipped out of Ranier. Viktor held him, though. He held him as tightly as Ranier held Diamond. All three of them lay there, breathing hard. Ranier's pulse was racing, and sweat dotted his skin.

Diamond looked at him with sleepy eyes and smiled. "I'm sorry you got dragged into this on my account, but I can't say I'm sorry it happened. I know it sounds crazy --" She looked over Ranier's shoulder at Viktor, who was even now nibbling Ranier's shoulder. "-- but I'm not sure I'd wish *any* of it never happened. Even the bad parts. You're both extraordinary men, and I'm glad to have had this experience with you."

Viktor licked Ranier's shoulder again, and Ranier shivered, his cock coming alive once more inside Diamond. She gave it a little squeeze and winked at him. Her eyelids seemed to struggle to stay open, and Ranier knew she needed to sleep, but stars help him, he couldn't deny himself her flesh. Especially with Viktor nibbling on him that way.

"Fuck her," Viktor whispered in Ranier's ear. "Fuck her like you mean to make her stay with you forever."

With his words, Ranier's cock came to full attention. He moved slowly inside Diamond, pulling her leg up over his hip. Viktor continued to kiss, and nibble, and lick his neck and shoulder until Ranier was pounding into Diamond. Her moans and whimpers spurred him on. She gripped his ass and pulled him into her harder and faster with each stroke.

"Oh, yeah," she cried out. "I'm coming, Ranier! I'm coming!"

Viktor bit down at the juncture of Ranier's neck and shoulder, sinking his fangs deep. Ranier shouted and lost the tenuous hold on his control, emptying himself into Diamond a second time. The pull of Viktor's mouth was the second most erotic thing that had happened to him today. The only way it could have been any better would have been if Viktor had been fucking him while he did it.

As if reading his mind, Viktor fumbled with his now hard cock and crammed himself back into Ranier's ass. Thrusting his hips madly, Viktor fucked Ranier harder and faster, all the while drinking from him. Impossibly, Ranier's cock stiffened again, insistent on another release. Fortunately, Diamond recognized the problem and promptly scooted down the bed and took him in her mouth.

Ranier actually wished it could go on for a lot longer, but too quickly, Viktor stopped his sucking and gripped Ranier's hips, still thrusting like mad. It wasn't long after that, Ranier felt Viktor dump a second load into his ass. A roar that Ranier was sure could be heard across the entire ship burst from Viktor, and the vampire's hips jerked and spasmed in his pleasure. Ranier's own orgasm followed soon after, and he just about shot a fourth load when he realized Diamond had swallowed every drop. She licked the head of his dick one last time before looking up at him and grinning.

Eventually, they all settled into the bed and lay still, too sated and sleepy to move. Just before he drifted off to sleep, Ranier could have sworn he heard Viktor mumble, "I love you. Both of you."

Chapter Five

Diamond awoke pleasantly sore, but alone. She stretched and got out of bed. Neither man was anywhere in evidence. Just as well. Diamond needed some time alone to think. She also needed something to eat.

After a quick search for something to wear, she settled on one of Viktor's off-duty shirts. It enveloped her as if she were a child wearing a parent's clothing. Still, it covered her. She really didn't care if other members of the crew saw her -- she was too damned hungry to worry about it.

The door slid open at her approach, and she stuck her head out to look around. The corridor was dark except for soft strings of lights lining the floor. Sleep cycle.

Just her luck. The galley would be closed. She sighed. Maybe she could raid the kitchen. Surely Phoebe wouldn't get mad at her for pilfering for something to eat.

She trotted down the corridor until she came to her destination. Again, the door slid open at her approach. Her stomach rumbled and her mouth watered in anticipation of the goodies she'd find. Phoebe always had something ready for the next day.

She opened the large walk-in refrigeration unit to find a huge plate of food wrapped and sitting on a crate in the middle of the floor. There was a note addressed to her.

Diamond --
Viktor said you'd be famished. Given all the noise earlier, I figured you'd sleep a while. Heat this and enjoy. If you need to talk, you know where to find me.

    Love,
    Phoebe

Diamond giggled. They *had* been a bit vocal.

The plate was heaped high with more food than Diamond thought it possible for three people to eat. She unwrapped it and shut the door as she went to the processor. Setting a timer preset, she waited a couple of seconds for her supper to heat.

When she opened the door, the strong aroma of the combined dishes in the one plate assaulted her senses like a wave crashing over her. Before she could find an eating utensil, she started picking up bits of meat and bread. Rich flavor exploded inside her mouth, washing over her tongue, and she was sure her eyes rolled back in her head. She simply set the plate down and stuffed one tasty bite after another into her mouth with both hands.

As she literally gorged herself on the delicious concoctions in front of her, she vaguely thought something was wrong, but she couldn't get past the severe hunger and need to eat everything she could find in order to replenish her body.

When she finished the last morsel, she picked up the plate and licked every crumb, every last drop of gravy. She was just about to go back into the refrigeration unit to scrounge up more when Viktor walked in. He looked more in control than she'd seen him since she boarded the *Black Star*.

"Did you get enough?" At first, she thought he was teasing her, or worse, making fun of her, but one look in his eyes and she could see he was very serious.

"Yes," she lied. Her stomach still grumbled, though she wasn't sure how she could possibly eat another bite.

Viktor stared at her a moment before going to the refrigeration unit and bringing out another plate full of the same delicious meal. After heating it, he set it down in front of her.

Diamond didn't want to do this in front of him. She didn't understand what was going on, and eating like a starving woman in front of such a gorgeous specimen of a man would be highly embarrassing. If he was regaining his control enough that he was allowed out of his cabin, the time when he needed her was coming to an end. She didn't want his last memory of her to be of her stuffing her face like she hadn't eaten in days. Unfortunately, her stomach betrayed her. The rumble was enough to turn her face three shades of red.

"You need more." He gave the plate a little push in her direction. "Eat."

"Considering the short work I just made of the last plate, you'll understand if I pretend to be a proper lady and insist you don't watch."

He lifted his hand as if he might touch her, but hesitated, then dropped it to his side. "It's part of what you are, Diamond. I took too much of your blood, and you need to replace your body's nutrients. As a *kaliish*, you're protected against most of the effects of losing too much blood during a feeding, but you can't survive indefinitely. You have to eat."

"*Kaliish*." The word was familiar to Diamond, but she hadn't uttered it in a very long time.

"It is a term given to those who have been changed in order that our kind may survive when they can not kill," he explained. "In the current society, it's almost unheard of for a vampire to actually kill unless the circumstances are dire. We normally keep one or more *kaliish* in order to maintain civility."

"But you don't." Diamond paused in the act of lifting a bite to her mouth. She hadn't even realized she'd picked it up. Looking at her plate now, she noticed several things missing.

"No. I've never needed to. The extended stay away from Draggoon affected me more than I was prepared for."

"So, what now?" she mumbled between bites.

"Once I'm past any sudden recurrence of the Blood Burning, we'll talk."

She wanted to concentrate on what he was saying, but the food was simply too wonderful. Each bite she took was pure ecstasy. Phoebe had outdone herself this time.

By the time she dragged her finger through the last of the thick, meaty gravy, she felt much better. Hunger didn't gnaw at her belly any longer, and she felt stronger. She felt almost normal again.

Viktor leaned against the table, his arms crossed over his chest, concentrating on her intently. "What?" Diamond asked. "Haven't you ever seen a woman eat before?"

Again, Viktor didn't say anything, only rifled through a couple of cubbies until he found a bowl of some bright pink fruit. They were elongated and round, and Diamond couldn't help but wonder if they could be used for something other than eating. She almost groaned aloud.

Viktor chose two from the bowl and laid them on the table. He found a laser knife and sliced one from end to end, pulling back the skin and exposing the meat inside. With another flick of the knife, he sliced several pieces and scooped them up in one big hand.

"Try this." He held out a piece he'd cut. His voice was still hoarse and gravelly, but he sounded more in control of himself. It was hard to tell, though. He had been well into the Blood Burning when Diamond had come aboard the *Black Star*. "It's high in nutrients needed by all *kaliish* after a mating during Blood Burning."

Diamond eyed the fruit suspiciously. She didn't like eating things she wasn't familiar with. She eyed him, and he nodded at the fruit. She reached for it, but he shook his head and raised the sweet-smelling morsel to her lips. When she didn't immediately take it, he sighed and touched it to her lips gently. "Please, Diamond. Just one bite."

She thought about refusing, but her stomach rumbled once again, though not as vocally as it had before she'd eaten. The fruit's flavor was sweet, yet slightly tart, and nothing like she'd ever tasted. It wasn't a strong flavor, but pleasant nonetheless. More, it seemed to quell her lingering hunger almost immediately.

"A *kaliish* is a being designed to take the abuse a vampire doles out during a Blood Burning. They heal remarkably fast and can withstand large amounts of blood loss for longer periods of time than other humans. But, as with any human, blood loss must be replaced. A *kaliish* can aid her own blood replenishment by eating foods high in both calories and iron. Meats are best, but foods like this fruit -- a ruby banana -- are perfectly adequate."

She had taken another bite of the fruit. Vampire fodder. She was nothing more than food for a vampire. She shuddered. "How do I *not* be a *kaliish* anymore?"

"Once you've been transformed, there's no going back."

"Didn't I just know you'd say that?" Diamond finished the fruit Viktor set out for her while he cut up another. Both of them ate in silence for a time.

"Feel better?"

"Yes. Actually, I do." She smiled nervously. "Much. I'm going back to my cabin now." She turned to leave, a little nervous being alone with Viktor even though he wasn't as scary as he had been. She'd love to think he was completely out of his Blood Burning, but she very much doubted it was over this quickly.

"Wait." His hand on her shoulder sent shivers down her body. Fear mingled with sexual hunger. She might be frightened of him, but there was something purely physical that called her to him with an intensity that scared her even more than the man himself did. "I need to say something."

For the first time since she met him, the big vampire actually sounded unsure of himself. She turned to face him. "What's on your mind, Viktor?" She tried to sound nonchalant, but wasn't sure she quite pulled it off given the fact she was shaking so hard the hem of the shirt she wore quivered.

"I'm sorry I hurt you." He caressed her cheek and gently tilted her face until she had no choice but to look him in the eyes. "If I could take back that first time, I'd forfeit my life rather than rape you as I did."

"You didn't rape me, Viktor. I knew what I was getting into, and I didn't tell you to stop. My whole reason for being there in your cabin at that time was to help you in any way you needed."

He winced slightly and turned his head away from her for a brief moment. "My Blood Burning hasn't completely run its course, but the end is near. When I'm myself again, my life belongs to you and Ranier. The two of you brought me out of this much sooner than normally would have happened."

She waved her hand in a dismissive gesture. "I'm

just glad you're better, Viktor. Really. I meant what I said. I'm really glad to have had this experience with both of you. You're a good man, and I'm proud to know you."

As she spoke, Viktor's brows knit together with each word. "But you do not want my life."

Diamond blinked. There was something she was missing, but she had no idea what. "I don't believe in any person 'belonging' to anyone, Viktor. You definitely owe me one, but that's as far as I go."

"I see." He seemed strangely… disappointed. "Will you at least let me make up for our first encounter?"

A wonderful thrill shot through Diamond's body. She had been sorely afraid Viktor would shun her after he no longer needed her. Viktor wasn't the kind of man who would appreciate being reminded how much he needed anyone.

She smiled. "I'd like that very much."

Diamond didn't have time to say or do anything else because Viktor pulled her to him and covered her mouth with his. At first his kiss was filled with an overwhelming hunger that almost consumed Diamond. Had she fought him, it probably would have. Instead she embraced him, and his kiss soon became gentler and more filled with passion than with the fear of losing her.

He held her as if he never wanted to let her go, and his kiss was so sweet she wanted to cry. She couldn't imagine never feeling this again. Truth was, she loved his special brand of loving. Even if he was excessively rough. She hated the awkwardness that seemed to exist between them now.

She kissed him back as thoroughly as he kissed her, wanting this moment to last as long as possible.

Truth was, she wanted more. Much more from Viktor. The mere nature of this one kiss revealed a Viktor she'd never seen before. This man was not the strong, self-assured second in command who hated being second-guessed by anyone. This Viktor was almost vulnerable in his need. It was a humbling thought.

When he broke the kiss, his hand dropped to her breast and gently caressed it. Diamond knew her nipple stabbed his palm, and she didn't care. She wanted him to know how he affected her. If she could prove she still desired him, maybe he'd realize she meant what she said when she'd told him she had no regrets.

He might have said something, but the ship's alert siren suddenly blared out.

"Bloody hell," he growled and gripped her shoulders, looking at her so intently she couldn't look away. "Go to my cabin and wait for me there."

So much for the vulnerable man she'd admired a few moments ago. "Is that an order, Commander?" She couldn't help the irritated drawl to her voice. She hated being ordered around.

"Does it have to be?" The Viktor she'd met when she first came aboard was back. It was hard to reconcile one with the other.

"I don't respond well to orders, Viktor. If you've learned nothing else about me, I suggest you learn that."

"In that case --" He lowered his eyes. "-- I respectfully request for you to consider being in my quarters when my duty is done."

The formality of the request didn't escape her. Neither did she ignore the ease with which he changed directions on her. Viktor might be used to being the dominant presence everywhere he went, but for some reason he was willing to defer to her in some instances. What was so important now?

"Well, who could refuse such an eloquent request? I'll be there." She gave him a little nod and would have turned away, but he held her still.

Viktor opened his mouth as if to say something, but shook his head and closed his mouth again. Instead, he pressed his lips to hers once more, briefly. Then he moved past her and out the door. She watched him trot down the corridor toward Command.

Chapter Six

He should have bloody well known Diamond wouldn't want anything more to do with him after his Blood Burning was over. Hell, he couldn't blame her. He'd gone more than a little nuts. Any woman would think twice before accepting his life as her own.

Later. He'd worry about it later. Right now, he needed all his concentration on the *Black Star* and everything around her. The ship had left him alone during his crisis, but she was like a jealous lover. She couldn't stay gone for long, and she hated it when other women had his attention.

That's not entirely true, Viktor, the ship's slightly superior sounding female voice said inside his head with a sniff. *I could care less what you do in your free time. It's when you're cavorting with others during* my *time that I have problems.*

"I'd give almost anything if you'd speak only when spoken to." He was irritated at himself and projecting it to the sentient mind of the ship.

And how would you work through all this frustration and self-loathing if I did? You need that girl, Viktor. As surely as you need Ranier. And air to breathe.

"You don't think I know that?" Viktor got on the lift that would take him to Command in a matter of seconds. "Now, shut up and let me work. What's going on?"

The Hand ships as well as the allies they picked up among the Vok'nair are approaching us.

"What are our odds?"

Not good, in my estimation. We need Sword Breaker. *We cannot withstand them as one ship alone.*

The door *shooshed* open, and the conversation was terminated.

"Did *Black Star* brief you on the situation?" Captain Damon Singh glanced Viktor's way when he entered the command center.

"She said we can't get out of this without help." When he got to his station, Viktor glanced at the monitors, though he was already getting most of the information he needed from the now open link between him and the ship. He tentatively reached for the information he wanted -- the location and number of ships -- and got more than he bargained for. He gasped as his head was flooded with information. Had it not been for his cybernetic implants, he would have probably been overloaded.

Damon swiveled his chair around. "Viktor?"

"I'm fine, Captain." His head spun, and he had to shake it to clear it.

"If you aren't up to this, say so now. I don't want to have to toss you out an air lock." Viktor knew Damon was only half joking.

"No. I'm fine." He shook his head again before looking at his screens, trying to verify what the ship had dumped into his brain. "*Black Star* just loves information dumps, and I have trouble keeping up sometimes."

Ah! The first way to win both their hearts is not being afraid to admit you're less than perfect. Viktor hadn't even realized what he'd done until the bloody ship pointed it out. He hated looking inferior to anyone or anything.

Ranier snorted from his pilot's station. "There's a first time for everything," he muttered. In another life, Viktor would have had the man's head on a platter. Now, he merely gave him a stern look that was totally wasted. Ranier wasn't intimidated at all, though the rest of the bridge staff visibly cringed.

"How far away is the *Sword Breaker*?" Damon

punched at his personal computer.

"Not far," Viktor responded, deciding to ignore Ranier for the time being. "One sector away. He should intercept us in the next five minutes."

Damon scratched his chin a couple of times before giving the command Viktor had anticipated. "Raise deflectors. Laser status?"

"Fully charged, Captain. Pulse torpedoes awaiting your order for armament." Viktor punched a few buttons, still processing the data stream flowing through his head.

"I'm reading twenty-three war class ships and another twelve carrier class. All heavily armed and armored. Carrier complement unknown, but I estimate each can carry at least twenty one-manned fighters."

"Damn," Ranier muttered while his fingers tapped his console. Viktor felt the subtle movement as the ship readjusted. *Black Star* protested the new settings, but Viktor could see the position Ranier was putting them in and understood the reasoning. Surprisingly, the ship didn't put up a fuss, and let Ranier move her to a more dominant position. Well, as dominant as one ship could be against thirty-five enemy ships. "This isn't going to be pretty. Can we fight our way out even with the help of the *Sword Breaker*?"

"Unknown." Viktor used every processor available in his cybernetically enhanced brain to make sense of what the ship was telling him, and he still didn't believe what he was seeing. He could even feel the tension in the *Black Star*. The ship was trying to deny the data as well. "Captain, unless I'm greatly mistaken, I think they mean to destroy this ship, not capture her."

Damon didn't hesitate a moment. "Battle

stations. Notify *Sword Breaker* not to enter the area. Stand down. Mark it Priority Alpha. Get us out of here, Ranier." Viktor barely got off the message before the fight began.

Laser pulses surrounded them and slammed into the *Black Star*'s shields. The positively charged particles danced over the shield resonance and created a lovely aurora that belied the danger they faced.

"Primary shields holding," Viktor barked. "No damage reported. Awaiting your command to open fire."

"All stations, fire at will." Damon gave the command calmly enough, but the sweat trickling down his temple betrayed his agitation. Had Viktor not known the man so well, he'd have thought the captain unaffected by the threat.

Laser fire streaked across the distance into space. Some connected with targets, some didn't. The whole mess of a firefight in space was surreal. It was sometimes hard to tell what had been hit and what hadn't because there were no huge explosions due to the vacuum and lack of oxygen. Thankfully, *Black Star*'s sensors kept score. Viktor knew exactly which ships posed a threat and which ones had been damaged beyond being a danger.

"Concentrate some fire to the port flank." Viktor took up his role as second in command again as if he'd never been deep in a blood madness. His head was beginning to buzz again, and he knew he'd have to get away from the violence and adrenaline rush soon or he'd sink back into the mire. For now, however, Viktor had to concentrate all his energy on the battle. The odds were almost impossible, especially without backup. "Those two ships are the most immediate threat, and the strongest of any save the damaged one to starboard."

The ship rocked with the impact of heavy fire against the shields. The damaging lasers and torpedoes were unable to penetrate the defenses, but the concussion knocked them about horribly, creating its own danger.

"We're going to be shaken to pieces if we don't get out of here soon." Damon's grip on the armrest of his command chair was white knuckled, but otherwise he remained seemingly unaffected. "Ranier?"

The younger man frantically stabbed the computer console at his fingertips. The data stream Viktor got from *Black Star* told him Ranier was trying to plot a course, but the sheer number of enemy ships prevented anything but sublight propulsion.

Damon gave Viktor a sidelong glance. That was when Viktor realized he'd started to growl. Immediately, Viktor stopped the threatening sound and gritted his teeth tightly together. The adrenaline rush was starting to get to him.

Ranier wove between damaged ships, using them as a barrier between the *Black Star* and the rest of her enemies, but neither the Vok'nair nor the Hand seemed to care. They shot through any ship that got in their way. The Hand might have thought they'd bought an alliance with the mighty empire, but they were paying the price for their mistake.

Ranier swore under his breath. Viktor knew the young man was doing his best to get them clear so they could jump.

"Look!" One of the men at weapons -- Taren -- pointed at the viewscreen in excitement. The unmistakable flash of a ship coming out of hyperspace dominated the upper right corner. "It's the *Sword Breaker*!"

"Damn it!" Damon swore. "Did you send our message for them not to approach?"

"Yes, sir."

Damon stabbed the ship-to-ship comm. "Mikiel! What the fuck are you doing?"

"We can't leave all of you to fight so many. If we're to go down, we'll damned well do it together," Commander Mikiel Anjoom answered seriously from the comm unit.

The *Sword Breaker* engaged three Hand ships an instant later. He had thought the real challenge would come from the Vok'nair ships. However, each Hand ship proved to be almost as great a battle. With so many enemies against them, Viktor knew they had to get rid of the ships easiest to defeat in order to even up the odds, and they had to do it quickly. Also, they had a finite number of torpedoes, and lasers weren't as effective. Running out of ammo wasn't an option.

"Three carrier ships destroyed," Viktor reported. "Three war ships are gone, too."

Damon's smile was positively vicious. "Now, let's get the rest of them."

The two ships engaged the fleet from opposite ends of the field, each using the special talents they were designed with. *Sword Breaker's* speed and agility proved to be a handful for their enemies as he spun a deadly dance through them, leaving a trail of destruction. *Black Star* did much the same, but her armament and firepower were much greater, and her larger size made for an easier target. Viktor noted she often ended up between the *Sword Breaker* and danger as if protecting him with her greater strength. If he concentrated, he felt the love and worry *Black Star* felt for her counterpart. It was too much emotion. He couldn't handle it in his current state.

"What's the count, Viktor?" Damon issued commands calmly, as he always did. Now, Viktor wondered how he managed it. Stripped of his control, his instincts were pushing him hard. He wanted to run around the room screaming to relieve some of the tension. A kill would sate him even better. He shook his head and tried to focus on counting ships instead. How many were destroyed, how many disabled, how many still fought them.

"Eighteen destroyed. Five unable to pursue. That leaves us twelve between the two of us." Viktor's heart beat wildly, and sweat broke out all over his body. Too soon. This was too soon. He needed to get away from everyone, but if he left now, it would destroy the concentration of the entire command center. Chaos in the command center was deadly in battle. He had to hang on until the battle was done.

Again, the *Black Star* rocked and bucked as her shields took hit after hit. *Sword Breaker* tried to fight through to her aid, but the Vok'nair ships held him off. Viktor got the distinct feeling *Black Star* was trying to get through to him, but he couldn't hear her. His ears roared, and his pulse beat loudly in his head.

Viktor reached out with his telepathic senses for the first time since leaving Draggoon. Other than communicating with the *Black Star*, he never used them unless he was on his home world because any time he had to use the skills he possessed as a vampire, the nature of what he was -- a predator -- made the temptation too great. The scent of blood drew him like a two-dimensional being to a cosmic string. His link with the ship -- and the constant use of the extrasensory skills given to his race -- was probably what had pushed him over the edge into the Blood Burning.

Diamond. He had to find Diamond. Her presence alone could help him hold onto what little sanity he had left. Ranier gave him a worried glance, but he was too busy to do much. Viktor nodded at the younger man, hoping to reassure him. Ranier needed his mind on the ship because Viktor was in no shape to help him.

"Look out!"

Viktor wasn't sure who yelled, but his attention snapped back to his control panel. "Collision course, Damon." He managed to get the words out, but his ears were ringing louder. *Diamond!*

She can't hear you, but I can, Viktor.

Black Star's voice was more tender than he could ever remember hearing it. How she broke through his haze of need for violence in the most non-obtrusive way he'd probably never know.

I'm losing control.

Just hold on a little while longer. I'll bring her to you.

Ranier --

Will be fine, the ship interrupted. *Don't worry about him. Focus on Diamond.*

If the ships collide at this pitch, everyone in the command center could be killed. I've got to get Ranier out of here. Everyone needs to abandon the command center. Viktor's heart pounded in his chest.

No. Something's not right. Black Star's whisper inside his head was distant, like she was focusing on something other than him. *Concentrate, Viktor. Look at their formations.*

"Where's *Sword Breaker*?" Viktor hadn't meant to speak aloud, but once the question was voiced, he got a sick feeling something was very wrong. He scanned his screens and tried to process what he was seeing.

Help me! I can't see what they're doing! Viktor

screamed in his mind. He couldn't focus enough to analyze their attack pattern. It *looked* like the Vok'nair and Hand ships were working together now, but his fog-filled brain couldn't wrap around the flight patterns. It all seemed too complex and random, but he *knew* it was a battle plan.

"Ranier," Viktor managed to squeak, "can you see the patterns they're using? Can you see what they're trying to accomplish? Are we the primary goal?"

"Stand by." Ranier broke away from his nav console and swiveled to an adjacent console that was a mirror of Viktor's own. Damon glanced at Viktor, but otherwise kept his focus on the battle. "No." Ranier moved his fingers from one console to the other and the *Black Star* had to compensate for his split attention. "Not us." He turned to face Damon. "*Sword Breaker*. They're coming at us, but the angle is slightly off. They'll miss us by meters, but they'll be going at the perfect speed to force *Sword Breaker* to dock with them. They're going to board him."

"Mikiel!" Damon stabbed the ship-to-ship comm. "Get your ship out of here! Now!" Damon jumped to his feet as he spoke. For a commander so in control to now show so much fear, he had to suspect something far worse than a collision. Something in his voice told Viktor Damon knew exactly what was going on.

"Don't worry, my friend." Mikiel sounded supremely confident in his people and his ship. "They can ram us all they want. They won't even pierce our primary shields, and the secondary shields would hold them if they did."

"They're not going to ram you. They're looking for a weak area in your shield for boarding." Damon was actually trembling. "They're after Nadira, I'd bet my life on it!"

There was no response from Mikiel, but Damon sprinted for the door. "Taren, with me! Rainer, keep my ship safe from them --" He stabbed his finger at the viewscreen. "-- and him." He pointed at Viktor.

Viktor bared his teeth and hissed.

Chapter Seven

Diamond ran down the corridors of the *Black Star* as fast as she could, shoving crew members out of the way as she went. She had to make it to the command center. Viktor needed her. If he was as close to the edge of control as the ship thought he was, she had no time to lose.

When she approached Command, Damon almost knocked her down. He barely acknowledged her, a frantic expression on his face, as he sprinted away from her as if demon spawn were after him. Something was definitely happening in a big way. Entering Command, she saw that red glow in Viktor's eyes again and knew he was in trouble.

"Get him out of here, Diamond." Ranier's fingers flew over his console. He didn't look up. "I'll join you when I can."

Viktor shook his head as if trying to clear it. "You need me here, Ranier. I can manage a while longer."

"Get the *fuck* out of here! You look like you're ready to eat someone, and I'd prefer it not be one of my command crew."

"And if I eat Diamond?" Viktor couldn't believe Ranier would risk Diamond this way after his earlier protectiveness. "I suppose that would be better?"

Ranier swung his chair around to face Viktor. "I heard what you said after we all made love, Viktor." Diamond thought she'd die right there. Did he *have* to announce it to the whole damned ship? "If you truly love both of us, you won't harm her, no matter how far into the Burning you are."

Viktor growled. "I meant exactly what I said, Ranier."

"Then take Diamond, go get your jollies off, but

most importantly, get the hell out of here before you scare the command crew into making a mistake that might cost us this battle, which would make your problems a minor inconvenience."

Diamond wanted to sink into the floor. She'd come here to help Viktor, but she might kill Ranier while she was here. She shot him a threatening look, but he'd already turned his attention back to more pressing matters.

Viktor grabbed her by the upper arm and guided her toward the door. "I'll deal with him later. Come with me."

He practically dragged her down the corridor before finally just scooping her up in his arms and carrying her back to his cabin. Diamond, while still annoyed with Ranier, got a perverse thrill from Viktor's barbaric handling of her. Being swept off her feet and taken to the troll's cave for his plundering of her body for his own pleasure was a heady aphrodisiac, and she'd be damned if she knew why.

When the door to Viktor's quarters slid shut with a hiss, Viktor laid her on the bed and immediately began removing her clothing. Diamond practically trembled with anticipation. As grateful as she had been to Ranier for trying to protect her when no one else in her life had ever done so, she really wanted Viktor's cock. She wanted both men, but she had a feeling that would happen soon enough. Right now, it was important to both of them to have this time alone.

"I'm afraid I won't be gentle this time either, Diamond." He sounded sad, lonely. Afraid. The red glow in his eyes was more pronounced now. "It seems to be a trend with you, but the more I think about you, the worse it gets."

Diamond grinned. "I'll take that as a

compliment."

"Well, don't," he growled. "I'm perfectly capable of killing you."

"But you won't." She lay back on the bed and spread her legs, inviting him to take what he wanted. "Not now. Maybe before, but not now."

He ripped his own clothes off, exposing his fangs in a snarl. "You don't know that. I'm as on the verge of out of control as ever. I could easily drain you dry and never realize what I've done."

"You're lying. You would have done it the first time if that were true." She was surprised to find she actually believed that statement. "Now, shut up and fuck me."

Viktor fell down on top of her, his cock pressing against her pussy. Instead of sinking into her as Diamond had expected, he plunged his tongue into her mouth and let his cock ride between them as his body made contact with hers.

She loved kissing him. Even the occasional nip from his fangs was a painful pleasure. He grunted with each breath, and his cock twitched between their bodies. Diamond clung to him, needing him closer. She wanted to feel the burn of his huge dick inside her again.

"You're mine, Diamond," he said against her mouth. "I won't let you leave me. I can't."

She grabbed two handfuls of his hair and pulled him back. He hissed, exposing his fangs. Had she been a lesser woman, a woman who hadn't gone through all she'd gone through with the Hand of God, she would have been frightened. As it was, a sexual thrill shot through her. This was a man on the verge of control. A man who could seriously hurt her if he wasn't careful.

But he wouldn't. Her life was in his hands in this

most intimate of acts, and she wouldn't have it any other way.

"Did you really tell Ranier you loved us?"

"I didn't tell him. I thought he was asleep."

She gave his hair a sharp tug. "Did you *say* it?"

He grunted. "I did."

"Did you mean it or was it simply the heat of the moment?"

"A vampire would never say something like that in the 'heat of the moment,' as you put it. More likely, he'd say the opposite. I *do* love both of you, Diamond, but I really need to have this conversation another time. If I don't get inside you soon, I might die of this incredible need."

She giggled, which prompted another growl from him. Again, he kissed her, plunging his tongue inside her with thrust after thrust. She clung to him until he pried her fingers loose from his hair. Diamond started to protest, but when he started kissing, licking, and nipping his way down her body, she didn't.

Viktor paused at her chest long enough to suck each nipple once before licking a path down the center of her belly and dipping his tongue into her navel. He hovered above her pussy for a brief moment before dipping his head and taking a long, slow swipe with his tongue.

He latched onto her cunt with his lips. The groans and slurping sounds mingled with her whimpers of need and created a beautiful melody Diamond would remember for a long time. She arched her back when he found a particularly sensitive spot and clutched his hair with her hands when he flicked her clit with his tongue. It seemed Viktor was making up for lack of foreplay earlier. Diamond thought it was definitely worth the wait. For a man who claimed to be dying to get inside her, he was prolonging his suffering a great deal. Diamond could feel him tremble beneath her touch and knew what the effort was costing him.

When he raised his head, his eyes glowed brightly. "Enough!" Her moisture made his lips and chin glisten. She watched in fascination as he wiped the lower half of his face with one hand and licked her intimate moisture off his fingers, never breaking eye contact.

"I love the way you taste, little jewel." His husky voice sent shivers through her. "It's a taste I'll never be able to get enough of."

"Just shut up and fuck me."

He barked a laugh as he reached beside the bed and picked up a capsule of lubrigel from the table. "You are truly a vampire mate. You might have been altered to make your blood perfect, but there's no way you could have the heart of a vampire mate unless you were born with it. I've never met a human who could hold such an esteemed position. You're truly a special woman, as Ranier is a special man. I almost feel guilty claiming you both."

He slid into her as he finished speaking. It took three strokes before he was all the way inside her, but the burn felt good. Diamond whimpered as she clutched his ass and pulled him into her.

"Sweet Stars!" Diamond gasped. "That's it, Viktor. Fuck me."

"Oh, yeah," Viktor answered her. "Definitely."

They moved together easily, but Viktor still thrust carefully within her. Diamond loved him for it, but she craved more. She pulled him to her and kissed him deeply.

When she pulled away she gave him her best wicked grin and said, "Are you going to play all day, or get down to some serious fucking?"

Viktor pulled back in surprise, then flashed her a smile that was positively sinful. His eyes glowed red and he started moving in earnest. The burn in her pussy was a wonderfully erotic sensation. The pain added to the pleasure Viktor created within her body.

He roared as he drove into her, his own pleasure obvious. Diamond dug her heels into his ass and held him tightly to her. Sometimes they kissed; sometimes they simply clung to each other. Whatever else, they held to each other.

Diamond felt like she moved in slow motion. Everything was perfect between them. As wrong as it was the first time, this time was right. She looked into Viktor's eyes, and they no longer glowed with anything other than his love of her. He knew more about the symbiotic relationship they shared, but she knew he loved her. She knew it was because of her brazenness in offering herself to him when he needed it most. What she didn't understand was how she could love him back so fiercely.

The force of his thrusts propelled them across the bed until her head hung off the side. Still he pounded into her and still she urged him on.

She let her head fall back and hang off the edge, exposing her neck to him. It was a conscious gesture on her part. She wanted him to know she was still here to give him what he needed.

"You are the most perfect gem in the universe, Diamond. My life will forever belong to you."

"And Ranier?" She had to ask. She had to know that Viktor wouldn't deny himself or Ranier the feelings they so obviously shared for one another.

"Ranier has been a part of my life since he came here from the *Sword Breaker*. He's my exact opposite."

"But you love him. He loves you."

He smiled before descending to her neck. "Don't worry, my little gem. Ranier and I will work out our own arrangement."

"But --" Before she could ask how it would affect her relationship with Viktor, he sank his teeth deep into her neck.

The pain was intense, but not as intense as the pleasure he created when he continued to move inside her. She squeezed him tighter with her thighs and tilted her pelvis, bringing the maximum amount of friction to her clit. He sucked at her neck, and the sensation seemed to mute the brief pain he'd caused when he broke her skin.

It didn't take long for Diamond to come. Pulsing, pleasurable sensations emanated from her clit where it brushed his body. Her pussy burned from the size of him, adding to her excitement. She loved that small amount of discomfort. It amplified her pleasure beyond anything she'd ever thought possible.

The room started to spin slightly before Viktor stopped pulling at her neck. He licked at the wound a few moments to stem the flow of blood, and Diamond used the opportunity to collect her senses.

How in the universe had everything changed so quickly? She'd gone from helping Viktor out of a sense of obligation, to willing participant, to needing him as much as he needed her in a disgustingly short period of time. She sighed. She wouldn't change any of it for anything in the universe.

Chapter Eight

The battle was over, but the war had only begun. Ranier stormed through the corridors of the *Black Star*, needing to find Viktor and Diamond. She had a choice to make -- Ranier needed very much to have some time with both of them before all hell broke loose.

He entered Viktor's cabin to find Viktor's massive cock gliding lazily into Diamond's cunt. She appeared sated, and Viktor didn't seem in any hurry to finish.

Ranier hurried out of his clothes and wondered how much Viktor had learned of what was happening from the *Black Star*. Apparently not much, or he'd probably be in a bit of a tizzy. It couldn't have come at a worse time for the vampire. He was only just regaining his footing. He still had problems, but the crisis had almost passed. This might be enough to push him a giant step backward. If he had formed an emotional attachment to Diamond, the possibility of losing her might push him over the edge. Either way, he needed this time with both of them. If this was the last time they had together as a unit of three, he needed the closeness and physical contact in order to stave off the grief.

"Ranier." Diamond smiled and reached toward him. Viktor looked his way and smiled -- actually *smiled*. Ranier crawled onto the bed as Viktor moved himself and Diamond away from the edge and closer to Ranier. Viktor rolled them to their sides. Ranier used some lubrigel on his manhood and positioned himself behind Diamond. Carefully probing with his cock, Ranier slid inside Diamond's pussy with Viktor and held himself still so Diamond could adjust to the new sensation.

"Oh, my!" Diamond gasped. "Oh, yeah!"

Viktor's groan echoed Diamond's. Ranier knew how they felt. The sensations were almost overwhelming. He could feel Viktor's steely erection mashed pleasantly against his own, and surrounding them both was Diamond's silky cunt.

"It is too much, Diamond?" Ranier breathed the words. It was all he was capable of. So many emotions coursed through him he simply couldn't process them all. His emotions needed an outlet, and sex was the easiest way to lose himself.

"No. I love the burn. It makes everything better. More intense."

Ranier made eye contact with Viktor. There was surprise on his friend's face. Surprise and concern.

"Not now, Viktor. I need *this* now."

"Then take what you need." Diamond turned her head to look at him.

Viktor reached out to Ranier and grasped his shoulder. "From both of us."

Ranier almost sobbed. The only thing that kept him from it was the need to let Diamond and Viktor enjoy this with no worries. He didn't know why the *Black Star* hadn't told Viktor what had happened, but it could wait a few more minutes.

Both men moved independently, and Ranier found the slide of Viktor's cock against him just as stimulating as the grip of Diamond's cunt around him. The residence cabin was filled with the music of their groans, grunts, and whimpers as they took their pleasure of one another. Ranier tried to drown himself in sensation, but the future was more uncertain now than ever.

The three of them continued to move, but Ranier could tell the other two were picking up on his mood.

Ranier became more urgent in taking his need. He was ever conscious of not causing Diamond any more pain than was erotic for her, but he needed to take all he could. It was selfish, he knew, but he wanted to remember every sensation of this experience.

Finally, the pleasure became so great he could totally submerge himself. His urgency increased, and he felt Viktor's cock swell slightly as the other man began his orgasm, as well.

Ranier shouted as if in pain, which he thought was accurate given the pain in his heart. He filled Diamond's pussy with his seed and knew from the pulses in Viktor's cock his friend had done the same. Diamond's body tensed, and she threw her head back as she screamed. Her cunt spasmed around both their cocks, squeezing out every drop from them.

When it was over, Ranier dropped his head to Diamond's shoulder and squeezed his eyes shut. His love for these two wonderful people was overpowering. The uncertainty yet to come was a dark cloud blotting out the sun and all warmth save where his body touched either Diamond or Viktor.

"Do you want to tell us what's wrong?" Diamond's rebuke was gentle, but he could tell she didn't like him keeping anything from her, even for a short time.

"I just want to let everything be good for a few more moments."

"That moment's long past, Ranier." Diamond's voice was still gentle, but he knew she wouldn't let him delay any longer.

"I'm surprised Viktor doesn't already know. Didn't the ship fill you in?"

"She's trying to give me the time I need to get the Blood Burning under control again. Now --" He squinted his brows together. "-- she's blocking me altogether." He frowned. "That's odd. Despite all my complaining when I couldn't make a connection with her, she's never truly shut me out." He kissed Diamond and -- surprisingly -- Ranier's fingers that rested on Diamond's arm before pulling himself from Diamond and rising from the bed. He'd never thought of Viktor as showing affection this easily. Yes, Ranier accepted the fact that he loved Viktor. The man grew on him after a while. He couldn't imagine Viktor not being in his life, but his feelings for him had never been tender. Mostly because Viktor had never seemed to need -- or want -- another person's love. This was a pleasant surprise.

Diamond turned in his arms and kissed his chin. Ranier slipped out of her with her movement, and every part of the spell was broken. It was time to face reality. Ranier sighed and closed his arms around Diamond tightly.

"Tell me what's happened, Ranier." Viktor stepped back into the main room from the bathing room, a cloth in hand as he approached the bed. Ranier watched as he spread Diamond's legs and cleansed her, then Ranier, before cleansing himself. Ranier had to shake his head. This was definitely a side of Viktor he'd never expected.

"Nadira has been captured from the *Sword Breaker*."

Diamond sucked in a breath and sat up. "The ship? His crew?" Diamond voiced her concern.

"Two injured, one seriously. It could have been worse."

"There's more." Viktor's expression was as severe and hard as ever. He was all business now. "I can see it in your eyes."

Ranier sat up and scrubbed a hand through his hair. "Apparently there was more to the incarceration of the two people who now serve as the ships' consciousnesses."

"Nani and Darian," Viktor clarified, his full attention on Ranier. "I figured there had to be, but that's been the last thing on my mind for the last few weeks."

"I don't know all of it -- no one does except maybe Nani and Darian themselves, and they're not telling -- but there's a revolt in the Asalian Empire, and I dare say Vok'nair isn't far behind."

"What's happened?" Viktor dressed in jerky motions, obviously readying himself to return to Command. "What does it have to do with Nadira?"

"I don't know. I think it has to do with her being heir to the Vok'nair Empire."

"But she's *not* the heir. She's not Samair's daughter." Viktor crossed his arms over his massive chest. "She's Nani's daughter. Samair might have raised her, but Darian is her father."

"No one knows that other than Samair, and I'm sure he's not talking, but I think it's more than that." Ranier began putting on his own clothes and tossed Diamond hers.

"So, who has Nadira?" Diamond wanted to know.

"The Hand of God."

"Great Universe," Diamond swore. "What stake do they have in this? It's not like them to ally themselves with anyone. Not unless they are the dominant force in the alliance."

"I have no idea, but they were with the Vok'nair fleet, helping them, and their ships were just as strong as the ships from an empire that should be far ahead of them in technology."

"They scavenge from every race they encounter, but it would be highly unlikely they'd be more advanced than either the Vok'nair Empire or the Asalian Coalition." Viktor was thinking in practical terms, but Ranier knew there had to be more. It was just too damned convenient.

"That can't be all your news." Diamond zipped up her suit and approached him, resting her hands on his chest. Ranier's arms came around her instinctively.

"It's not." Ranier swallowed. "We've got to get that transmitter out of your head. You *and* Phoebe. The Hand and the Vok'nair both are using their signatures as tracking devices, and they know exactly where we are. From the reports we're getting from both the Empire and the Coalition, Samair has put a bounty on the *Black Star* and the *Sword Breaker*. He's trying to clean up a mess he should have years ago."

"No one was sure if those chips in our heads could be removed without damaging us before. Is the prognosis any different now?" Diamond didn't pull away from him. She didn't look fearful or resentful in any way. She simply took what he was saying as if they were talking about removing her appendix. Ranier was very much afraid she didn't understand the gravity of her situation.

"Dr. Mahat Zabin, here on the *Black Star*, thinks he can do it. He doesn't deny the risks, but having studied the data *Black Star* gathered on both you and Phoebe, he thinks he can do it without hurting either of you."

Diamond looked into his eyes, so trusting Ranier's heart ached all over again. "Do you trust him?"

He glanced at Viktor. "He's who took care of you

when I found you before."

"What was your impression of the man, Ranier?" Viktor asked quietly.

"He was concerned with not only ensuring Diamond's life, but also her quality of life. If he didn't think he had a very good chance of success, I don't believe he'd attempt it. I also think that if he starts the procedure and realizes it can't be done without hurting Diamond, he'll stop. No matter who orders him to continue."

"So, in both your estimations, this chip inside my brain has become a liability." Diamond looked at both men, and Ranier cringed.

"Unfortunately, yes." Ranier pulled Diamond to him and looked over her head at Viktor, who was approaching them. "There's too much going on around us that we don't fully understand."

Viktor came to stand behind Diamond and embraced both her and Ranier. "It's up to you, Diamond. If you don't want to do this, no one will fault you for it. It's a great risk, and it's your life that's in the balance." Viktor's voice was tender once again.

"I'm not a coward, boys." Diamond snuggled into Ranier's chest. She reached behind her to touch Viktor's leg. "If this implant in my brain is a danger to everyone, then I'm willing to do what it takes to get it out short of sacrificing myself on something that has little hope of working. If you honestly think Dr. Zabin can do this, Ranier, I'll volunteer with no regrets."

"That doesn't surprise me." Viktor kissed the top of her head. "Considering the kindness you showed me when I did nothing but hurt you over and over again, I've come to realize helping others is in your make-up."

Diamond snorted. "Don't bet on it, Viktor.

You've had all the help from me you're going to get."

Viktor chuckled. "If that were true, you wouldn't be here with us now. When *Black Star* sent you to me, you'd have run in the other direction."

"Shut up." Diamond gave them both a final squeeze before pushing them away and stomping her feet into her boots. "Let's go see the doctor before I lose my nerve."

* * *

Viktor paced Medical for at least the hundredth time. What was taking so fucking long? Diamond had been in surgery for more than two hours with no word from anyone. The *Black Star* was quiet, but Viktor could feel her worry.

As time wore on, he reached out to the ship, hoping to glean any information he could about Diamond's well-being.

She's doing as well as can be expected. The soft female voice wasn't like Viktor had ever heard before. She sounded sad. Worried.

There's more going on here than just preventing anyone from following and possibly capturing us, isn't there? Viktor caught impressions from *Black Star* instead of actual thoughts or solid information. Whatever it was, she hated what was now happening to Diamond and soon to Phoebe as well.

Unfortunately, yes. I'm afraid Phoebe and your Diamond are simply more casualties in a war that started twenty years ago. I'm very afraid they won't be the last.

I don't understand.

Please remember it's been a very long time since all this began, but I don't think the Hand placed those transmitter chips.

Viktor pondered her words for a moment. *You think someone else placed them there? Who? The same people responsible for making you a war ship?*

Very likely. But I can't remember. Something is familiar, but I can't say what.

Viktor nodded to himself. *Not surprising given the amount of trauma your brain sustained.*

I told you and Damon I believed Diamond and Phoebe to be the key to the salvation of both the Vok'nair Empire and the Asalian Coalition. Do you remember? She sounded weary. Given all he'd learned about the *Black Star,* she had probably used every resource at her disposal to come up with her postulation.

Yes. It was during the beginning of my Burning so I couldn't concentrate on it much, but I do remember. Viktor had a sickening feeling he knew what she was going to say next.

I think now maybe I had it wrong. The women aren't the key, but I think the chips inside them are.

Viktor's train of thought took a sharp detour when Dr. Zabin entered the room looking weary but wearing a slight smile.

Viktor and Ranier both snapped their attention his way.

"Diamond." Viktor found he couldn't get the words out.

"Is she all right?" Thankfully, Ranier was just as anxious as Viktor. The younger man got the question out when Viktor couldn't.

"She's fine. We had to keep her conscious during the procedure, but she assures me she was only mildly uncomfortable. Still, I've given her a sedative to allow her to rest for a couple of hours so the tissue around where the implant was can begin to knit. With her healing abilities, she shouldn't need more time than that."

Viktor felt the release of some of *Black Star's*

tension. The ship's essence had been sincerely worried about Diamond. Underneath it all, Viktor felt a sliver of guilt. He could gather enough of *Black Star*'s thoughts and feelings to know she hadn't actually implanted the chip, but Nani still felt responsible for at least some of the misery dealt with by so many because of her actions so many years ago. It was as if *Black Star* felt responsible for the invasion of the young woman's mind.

"Thank the Stars." Ranier clapped Viktor on the shoulder. The younger man looked weary and careworn. Viktor knew they had to address their relationship soon. Preferably before Diamond rejoined them. Viktor would like to have answers for her as to where they all stood. He owed her that much and more.

He owed her his life. If she wouldn't accept it, he'd still offer it to Ranier. Still, with either one of the two missing from his life, he wasn't sure he could ever be whole.

"When can we see her?" Viktor asked quietly.

"I'll notify you the moment she's awake. In the meantime, I suggest you get some rest." Dr. Zabin scrubbed a hand over his face. "The chip that came from Diamond is being analyzed as we speak. If I understood the technobabble Taren was spouting correctly, there's going to be a huge amount of activity in the next few days. I'm sure Captain Singh will need the two of you ready for anything when it all starts."

Before Viktor could question him further, Dr. Zabin turned and entered the surgical suite again. Ranier let out a puff of air.

"Well. There's nothing quite like being totally in the dark." He turned to Viktor. "Do *you* know what the fuck is going on?"

Black Star didn't say anything, but she didn't block Viktor when he tried to access the ship's computers via the data stream *Black Star* always seemed to be able to process, or when he reached for her memories. There was nothing she could remember other than a faint feeling that the tiny chip had something to do with either her or the *Sword Breaker*. The data stream from the computers, however, held a wealth of information, the implications of which raised as many questions as they answered.

"It's hard to understand." Viktor squinted his eyes as he concentrated. "If I'm not totally misinterpreting it all, I'd say that chip inside Diamond was placed there when she was still an infant."

"I thought Phoebe told Damon the implants were put there by the Hand."

Viktor shook his head. "She was speculating. She doesn't know any more than we do about it. It's certainly possible the Hand planted them there, but I'd say definitely not for the reasons Phoebe originally thought."

"So, if they weren't tagged to prevent them from escaping, then why?"

Viktor shrugged. "I'm not sure, but I'm betting it has something to do with these ships and the people they were before the transplant."

Ranier sighed. "This is giving me a headache. I'm going to rest a while. If you're right, there may not be much time for it later."

"Ranier --" Viktor suddenly felt awkward around his friend. "Come with me."

Ranier raised an eyebrow. "To where?"

"Home."

"To Draggoon? Oh *hell* no! I don't think I could stand a whole planet full of moody vampires out to suck my blood." Ranier laughed. "I'll have to pass, my friend."

"No." Viktor wasn't in a laughing mood. "Draggoon might be my home world, but my *home* is *here*. On this ship. I want you to come with me back to my cabin. Not as a friend, Ranier -- though you'll always be my best friend. I want you there as one who holds my life."

Viktor was sure his face was bright red, but still he stood straight and tall. He would not be ashamed of the way he felt.

Ranier's laughter died as quickly as it had come, and the man looked at him with a mixture of astonishment and wonder. "Me? Look, you don't owe me anything, Viktor. It's not that I don't have feelings for you -- I do. It's just that I don't want you to do this out of some sense of obligation because of what I did during your Blood Burning."

"Come with me, Ranier. We need to talk."

"Indeed."

Chapter Nine

Ranier had half expected this. He remembered Viktor's confession after they'd all three made love, but he'd half thought he was dreaming. Ranier loved Viktor in ways he'd never thought possible for him to love another man, but he absolutely would not join his life to Viktor's unless he knew for sure the other man loved him. And he wouldn't do it without Diamond, either. The short time he'd had with her had created an addiction. It wasn't just the sex -- he enjoyed spending time with her, though they hadn't done much of that since they'd started having sex. He grinned.

When the three of them had made love, he'd felt whole. Connected to another person for the first time in his life. He hadn't just shared himself with one special person, but two. True, he'd been a little pissed at Viktor for the way he was treating Diamond, but he'd been horny as hell just thinking about Viktor's big cock piercing his ass. It had been everything he'd hoped for and more. It had been the most explosive sex Ranier had ever had, and it included both Viktor and Diamond equally. If either of them had been missing, the experience wouldn't have been as intense or fulfilling.

Viktor's door slid open at their approach, and as soon as they were inside and the door closed, Viktor whirled around and pulled Ranier to him and held him close.

"How can you possibly think I don't love you every bit as much as I love Diamond?" When Ranier pulled back in astonishment to make sure he'd heard the vampire right, Viktor lowered his head and captured Ranier's lips with his own.

Ranier opened his mouth and plunged his

tongue into Viktor's mouth the instant their lips met. He was hungry for the other man. Hungry for the pleasure they could both gain. Hungry for his love. He actually clung to Viktor, as if afraid he'd never get the opportunity again.

Their kiss was drawn out. They kissed for the sheer joy of the sensation. Ranier's cock grew painfully hard. He groaned and let his head fall back when Viktor reached between them and squeezed Ranier's cock through his uniform.

"I felt a connection with you the first moment we met, Ranier. It was that attraction that kept me by your side when our differences became apparent."

Ranier snorted a laugh, but sucked in a breath when Viktor nipped his neck. "We're like sunlight and darkness, Viktor, in everything but Diamond."

Viktor paused in his exploration of Ranier's neck for only a heartbeat before continuing. The rough stubble of Viktor's beard abraded Ranier's skin where Viktor explored. The erotic scrape sent shivers through Ranier, and he didn't protest when Viktor urged him out of his clothes.

He stood before Viktor, proud in his lust for the other man and proud in his own body. He knew the way he looked when the sweat glistened on the fine hair of his chest. His muscles gleamed and his abdomen rippled with each breath he took. Viktor's gaze took in every inch of Ranier's naked flesh, and his features grew more severe with each passing second.

Viktor removed his own clothing then. Many times Ranier had seen the vampire naked, but this time was somehow different. Ranier took his time to inspect Viktor's body as he disrobed. Now that he looked, he could see the tiny incision sites where Viktor's cybernetics were implanted.

The hardware was part of what gave Viktor his incredible size in both height and body mass. Viktor's musculature was scary in its perfection. He had the perfect amount of bulk to go with his frame. Each muscle was toned to perfection in ways no non-cybernetic human could attain.

Ranier itched to explore this perfect body, but there was a question on his mind he had to have answered before he could enjoy himself. "What about Diamond, Viktor? As much as I feel for you, I feel for Diamond. I can't choose between the two of you. I won't choose."

Viktor shrugged. "I'm all for that. If she's willing, that is. I won't put her through any more than I've already done."

Ranier blinked. "Really?"

Viktor crossed his arms over his massive chest. "Of course. Not out of gratitude, either. There is something special about Diamond I don't want to get away from. She's proven her character more times than any person should have to, and she's a loving woman. Given all she went through with the Hand, that's a hard trait to hang onto."

"So, you don't have a problem with a life sharing arrangement with the three of us together?" Ranier didn't expect it to be this easy, though he really should have. Vampires didn't have the preconceived notions about family and life sharing most humans did. They accepted multiple partners easily. He guessed his misgivings came from Viktor's standoffishness with most members of the crew. Ranier had never imagined Viktor as a mate before.

"Of course not."

"It's just that you've never shown interest in anyone before all this. At least, not since I've known you, and the men you've worked with since your commission on the *Black Star* say pretty much the same thing."

Viktor smiled and knelt before Ranier. Ranier held his breath. "That's because I've never met anyone who cared enough to see through my gruff exterior. You, on the other hand, ignored my temper. I never had a conversation with you that felt awkward. And I know I never will."

From that moment on, Ranier could have cared less why Viktor wanted this union. All he could think about was his own cock disappearing between Viktor's lips.

Viktor gripped Ranier's hips and glided his mouth back and forth onto Ranier's shaft. The satiny slickness and sucking pressure of Viktor's mouth were sheer heaven. All Ranier could do was grasp Viktor's silky black hair, close his eyes, and simply feel.

"Sweet stars!" Ranier groaned. "That's it! Stars, I love what you're doing!" Viktor hummed and slurped as he took the length of Ranier until his nose brushed against the fine hair of Ranier's lower belly.Time after time, Ranier watched his cock disappear into Viktor's mouth, and he knew he definitely wouldn't last long if Viktor kept it up. He tried to push Viktor away, but the other man seemed to speed up his motions, wanting Ranier to come.

He was on the verge of exploding inside Viktor's mouth when the door slid quietly open and Diamond glided inside. Viktor glanced her way, but didn't stop his ministrations.

"Well, looks like you started the party without me." She grinned, but Ranier could see the hesitation in her face. "Should I go busy myself with something else for a while?"

"If you do," Ranier ground out, "we'll just drag you back. Do you want to do this in private or against a wall somewhere where the whole ship can watch?"

"Son of a bitch!" Diamond came the rest of the way inside and shed her clothes. Her fair skin was alive with a beautiful blush. "How is it you manage to get my juices flowing with the crudest of situations? I'm a good girl." The twinkle in her eyes said she didn't care.

Viktor let Ranier's cock slip from his mouth with a soft *pop*. "Because you're a thrill seeker. I knew it when you led Phoebe outside the ship during the first encounter with the Hand. You've got a wild streak that loves what we do to you."

"I won't deny that." She walked to them, her hips swaying and the fine musculature of her frame sleek as a Tyberian werecat. "I'm becoming addicted to the two of you."

"Good." Viktor reached for her and pulled her to him. He wrapped his arms around her until she leaned back, resting against his arms and offering her chest to him. Viktor dipped his head and took one nipple into his mouth. "I don't intend to let you go, Diamond."

"Neither do I," Ranier added. He knelt and wriggled his frame between their legs. He lapped the trickle of cream from Diamond's thigh and followed its slick trail until his tongue met her pussy. She whimpered and spread her legs farther apart, allowing him access to her clit as well. He flicked the sensitive little nub and plunged two fingers inside her, working her while he tongued her clit.

Ranier didn't remove his fingers when he turned his head to take Viktor's sac into his mouth and suck gently. It was the big vampire's turn to moan then. "Oh yeah! Don't stop!"

Ranier loved to hear Viktor so affected. He got the feeling the other man had rarely had much pleasure in his life. He was always so inflexible and arrogant, most people probably avoided him. No one had ever gotten to know the real man underneath the gruff exterior. Their loss.

Ranier alternated between them for several minutes, all the while pumping his own erection with one hand. When Viktor had finally had enough, he let Diamond go and stepped over Ranier. With one massive hand, he hauled Ranier to his feet and kissed him deeply. "Fuck me," he hissed. "I want to feel your dick inside my ass."

Viktor fell backward onto the bed and scooted toward the center. Raising his legs, he spread his ass apart, offering himself. Ranier swallowed. His hands trembled as he spread the lubrigel onto his cock and then into Viktor's ass. Without a word, Ranier slid himself easily inside Viktor's rear. Both men groaned.

When they'd gotten a good rhythm going, Diamond straddled Viktor and sank onto his cock. It didn't take long for the three of them to be moving as one unit once again. Their sighs and grunts filled the room, and Ranier could smell the clean sweat clinging to Diamond's skin as he bent his head to kiss her shoulder.

They moved that way for a long time. The men kissed and fondled Diamond, tweaking her nipples and kissing her as they felt the need. Finally, she increased her pace. Her breathing became erratic, and she screamed. "I'm coming! Now! Sweet Universe, I'm coming!"

Viktor shouted and gripped her hips as his own climax overtook him and he shot his seed inside Diamond. The resulting spasms squeezed Ranier until he, too, followed Diamond into bliss.

Stars swam in his vision, and his ears rang. He shouted so loudly that he feared someone would break the security code and barge in to investigate as he and Viktor had their friend and captain, Damon.

No one did.

The three of them collapsed on the bed. Ranier rolled to his side, taking Diamond with him, and he and Viktor sandwiched her between them. The only sound in the small room was their deep, heavy breathing.

"I won't stay on this ship without having both of you," Diamond whispered. "I don't know how it happened, but I love you both with all my heart."

"I said pretty much the same thing." Ranier smiled and caressed her cheek. "I don't think there's a problem with it."

"The only problem would be if you tried to leave." Viktor pulled her closer. "I think we'd both take exception to that."

"I'm tired." She closed her eyes. "Don't leave me alone this time." Her next breath was a contented sigh as she drifted off to sleep.

Ranier couldn't blame her. She'd been through a lot. The stars only knew what lay ahead. He looked at Viktor. The vampire had closed his eyes, as well. He lay there and watched the two of them sleeping so soundly, and warmth spread across his heart and soul. This was where he belonged. He had been nervous when he'd requested to come aboard the *Black Star* in exchange for Nadira, the former pilot, but all his doubts had been erased now. This was home. Not necessarily the ship, but with these two people.

Viktor. Diamond.

Home.

Epilogue

Black Star waited nervously. This was her time. Hers and *Sword Breaker*'s. The chips had, indeed, held more significance than she'd first thought. There were so many things she hadn't known when everything that made her a sentient, living being had been thrust inside a techno prison. Now, she wasn't sure she wanted to know it all.

But it was there. She'd hacked into Samair's personal archives. It was all there, just as it had happened twenty years before. Every detail. Every betrayal.

None of it mattered now. She and her beloved would soon be free from their bonds. Free, and back in their bodies. Even now, the doctors were using cells from their brain stems to create two perfect clones of the selves they had been. They simply grew them without brains, then used the genetic and neurological mapping specific to each of them inside the chips from Phoebe and Diamond to transplant their brains into the living clones. If all went well, they'd have their bodies back.

She reached out to Darian. *Sword Breaker*. Her soul mate. His excitement mirrored hers. Soon, they'd be united.

Soon. They'd be…
United.

Black Star United
A Sci-Fi Futuristic Alien Adventure
Marteeka Karland

The *Black Star* is free, and Nani, the woman who made up the essence of the ship, is determined to unite her family. But retrieving her captive daughter will not only be dangerous -- it could turn deadly.

Darian, her lover and himself a prisoner, is her rock in a sea of chaos. But as more and more trusted friends are revealed as complicit in their long-ago betrayal, it begins to seem that they can trust no one but each other.

The events of twenty years past that condemned them both to a living hell have inextricably bound everyone they hold dear. Now, their goal is to unite both the Vok'nair Empire and the Asalian Coalition. Impossible?

Not when everyone involved is United.

Chapter One

Nani floated somewhere between consciousness and oblivion in a void almost overwhelming in its threatening finality. She'd prefer death to this existence. If the transplantation didn't go successfully, that was exactly what she'd get. She tried not to think about it as the seconds ticked by.

Minutes.

Hours.

It was maddening. She was bereft of any sensation except consciousness and time. Both of which she could do without. Panic was a very real emotion, one she wasn't used to. She tried her best to stave it off, but not knowing anything, after the more than twenty years she'd known practically everything, was the hardest thing she'd faced since her baby daughter had been taken from her immediately after she'd given birth. She could look death in the face and smile, but she didn't like him sneaking up on her.

And that wasn't it. Her daughter, Nadira, had been taken by a fanatically religious sect called the Hand of God. She hated them with every fiber of her being. They were responsible for far more than Nadira's kidnapping and the injustices to her two friends. Rage threatened to consume Nani. She felt alone. So alone.

I am with you, my love. I always will be.

Immediately, her mind eased. Darian was her best friend. Her lover. The one person in the entire universe who knew what she'd been through and what she felt. What she feared. Nadira was his daughter, too. He'd insisted they put Nani back into her body first, not because he was scared he'd die during the process and wanted to hold on to life a little longer, but because he, too, preferred death to the void they both had to endure. He loved her enough, knew her well enough, to know she couldn't take this nonexistence much longer. It had been a long, unbearable process for both of them.

How the process had been explained to them and the hope they both shared at the prospect of finally being able to express their love physically again tantalized them. Hell. A simple touch of his hand on her cheek would be pleasurable beyond words.

Communication was hard for her. He'd always seemed to be the stronger of the two of them telepathically. She was merely an empath, but he'd taught her how to reach for him, to hear him when he spoke. When they'd found each other so many years later, their consciousnesses trapped inside their respective ships, she'd learned to make him hear her thoughts, as well.

She reflected on their time since their reunion. They'd done nothing but talk, catch up on their lost time. And cry. Both in joy and sorrow. They'd missed out on so much, both with each other and, more importantly, their daughter. Nadira had grown into a beautiful, talented woman and had married a man who loved her more than anything. At least they'd been able to help bring them together. Now, if everything went well, she and Darian would secure their own future.

That thought had just crossed her mind when she felt like she'd been kicked in the chest. Or that was what it would have felt like if she'd actually had a chest. The pain vanished as quickly as it had come, and Nani thought she might have imagined it. But it happened again. This time, she thought someone had hit her in the chest with a repulser weapon of some kind. She just knew she'd have broken ribs.

Except she didn't have a chest. Or ribs. Or a body for that matter. Rather, she hadn't.

The blackness brightened slowly until the next kick to her chest and everything came suddenly, painfully, clear and bright. She tried to scream, but all she could do was take in a deep breath. The pain was so intense she couldn't make a sound.

The light stabbed into her eyes like shards of hot metal, and her head felt like it might split. Her chest felt like every rib was cracked into tiny pieces, and her skin tingled and burned like a million needles sticking her from head to toe. When she was finally able to scream, her ears rang with the sudden explosion of sound.

"Easy, my lady. We've got you." The voice was male. Authoritative. For a brief moment, she had the fleeting hope that maybe Darian had beat her to this other world, but no. The voice belonged to the doctor aboard the *Black Star*, Mahat Zabin. He was a kind, capable man and one Nani admired greatly, but not the man she wanted to see at the moment.

She tried to relax and let Dr. Zabin do his work, but she was anxious and scared. She had to see Darian. Needed to assure herself he would be all right.

"I'm fine," she croaked. "See to Darian."

"We haven't started the process on him, my lady," Zabin informed her. "I'll get to work on him personally after a few hours' sleep. It's a very long, tedious process, and one I can't afford to do as tired as I am." He stopped his work with the monitors and leads attached to her body and looked her straight in the eye. "Do you understand I'm not prolonging his hell needlessly?"

Nani was surprised the doctor understood so

completely. She could see the anguish in his face, the need for her to understand his reasoning.

"I do." She smiled and watched some of the tension drain from his face. "You're a good man, and a miraculous doctor. You do your job. I'd never presume to question your judgment."

"You will rest now, my lady. As much as it pains me to rob you of your consciousness, the neuro connections and blood vessels I created and repaired need time to heal. When you wake, Darian should be through the process and sleeping as well."

"One thing," she said. Her throat hurt, dry from the medication that had kept her body asleep during the transplant. "My daughter."

"No word that I'm aware of." Zabin was matter-of-fact in his answer. "The captain and Mikiel are working relentlessly to find her. I'm sure he'll update you after you've rested." Unless Nani was greatly mistaken, that was an order. She'd be resting whether she wanted to or not. After so long giving orders -- whether others liked it or not -- this was going to take some getting used to.

"As you wish." Nani needed to believe his words. She wasn't afraid of death, but it would be cruel of him to take her when she finally had a chance to face the one person in the universe, other than Darian, she truly cared about.

Dr. Zabin pressed a few buttons and tapped a few keys above her head, and her vision narrowed into blackness.

Sleep well, my love. We will be together and bring our family together soon.

* * *

Nani clawed her way to consciousness once more. This time, she sat straight up and was surprised when the room started to spin. She shook her head. Slowly, she got her equilibrium and slid from the medical table to stand on her feet. She would be strong of body as well as mind. No one would see her in a weak moment.

Just as she felt it was safe enough to walk, the door opened to admit Dr. Zabin, two other men and a woman.

Diamond.

She owed this woman and Phoebe more than she could ever repay. She had to blink back tears, but they threatened to overflow her eyes and spill down her cheeks anyway.

"You have my gratitude, Diamond. Without you, I'd still be in a living hell." Nani didn't feel like the confident, all-knowing person she had been only a few hours before. It had been so long since she'd had to thank anyone for anything, it just seemed odd. She shuffled her feet slightly and looked anywhere but at Diamond.

"Well, it was either help you or get as far away from this ship and those two crazily annoying men over there as I could. They wouldn't let me leave, so..." She grinned awkwardly as she broke off, shuffling her feet a little. She didn't look any more comfortable than Nani felt. Finally she groaned and reached for Nani, and the two embraced easily. Nani felt like she'd finally come home. She didn't know this woman other than what she'd observed as the *Black Star*, but she knew she was a good person. She'd risked her life, not only for her men, but for the entire ship as well.

When they parted, they stared at each other for a long moment. "Thank you, Diamond. For my life. For my daughter's life."

"No thanks is necessary, but you're very

welcome. You should know that Mikiel is working day and night to find her, and I think they may have pinpointed her location." Diamond gripped her hand fast. "He truly loves her, my lady."

She smiled. "Call me Nani. I thought that woman was long dead, but I suppose I need to find her again."

"You will. Anyone who could endure all you have can do this. Remember, you're not alone." Diamond dropped her hand, but Nani had one more question. Before she could do anything else, she had to check on Darian.

"Where's the doctor?"

"Reviewing the data from your transference." She pointed to a small room in the other part of the medical bay, and Nani noticed a dark-haired man in a red lab coat hunched over a computer screen.

"Please excuse me. I need to speak with him."

With one last glance and a smile at Diamond, Nani walked out of the room. It was time to find out what came next.

Chapter Two

"Dr. Zabin?" It was strange how she felt hesitant to disturb him now. She'd never had that problem when she resided in the *Black Star*. Then, she'd called on anyone, any time of the day or night. She was an entity unto herself. Untouchable. Now she was dependent on the kindness of others, she didn't think she had the right to demand anything of anyone.

"Yes, my lady." He scrubbed a hand across a weary-looking face. "I'm glad to see you up and about. How are you feeling?"

"I'm fine." She blinked. She wasn't used to anyone being concerned for her except Darian. "You don't have to call me that."

He looked at her intently. "I think I do."

"I'm not his wife anymore, Mahat. He lost that right when he conspired to rob my people."

"I know that, my lady. But it doesn't change who you are, and you deserve the title more than he does."

"Why?" Nani was suddenly furious. "Because I had an affair, got pregnant, then caught, and ended up the soul of a hunk of twisted metal and computer chips? Hardly worthy of royalty, don't you think?"

Mahat Zabin stood suddenly and rounded on her as vehemently as she had lashed out at him. "Because he forced you into a marriage to gain your title and the empire."

They stood nose-to-nose for several moments. Nani was shocked. No one knew that. Not even Damon. "What else do you know?" She wasn't sure she wanted to know the answer to that question, but there it was.

"All of it. I know about your heritage as well as Darian's. I also know that you were perfectly within your rights to take any suitor you wanted, so don't give me that *yasat* shit about not being worthy of royalty. You are royalty! Whether you admit it or not."

He turned away angrily and stared at the computer screen on his desk. It was obvious he didn't really see it. "You lived a life no one should ever have to experience. But would you rather have been killed? That was your only alternative." He didn't look at her -- he just punched buttons on his console and watched as a stream of data scrolled quickly across the screen.

"At the time, I'd have preferred it. Many times over the years." She refused to leave even though she knew he wanted her to. "It was only when we actually encountered the *Sword Breaker* I began to have some hope. At least we could touch each other's minds. This --" she wrapped her arms around herself, closing her eyes as emotion threatened to overwhelm her again, "-- is more than I'd ever hoped would happen. I know how difficult this was to achieve. I'm not sure more than a handful of doctors in the entire known universe could have accomplished this. I thank you."

He looked at her, the anguish and anger in his face so fierce, Nani stepped back a pace before she could stop herself. "Do you know why I was able to do this, to put you back in your body? Do you remember anything about that day?"

"I -- no. Well, some of it. Only in bits and pieces." She crossed the room to sit in a chair across from the doctor's desk. She had a feeling she needed to take this sitting down. "I was in shock, I think. I'd just given birth and was grieving, begging Samair not to do it." She shivered and squeezed her eyes tightly shut at the memory. She'd fought fiercely, hoping Samair would simply kill her. But he hadn't.

"It was me, Nani." Dr. Zabin scrubbed a hand

over his face. He looked weary, grief-stricken. "I did the procedure. I did that awful thing..." He trailed off and dropped his head into his hand.

Nani sat in stunned silence for a long moment. She thought she might faint. Had she not been sitting, she probably would have. She'd focused her anger solely on her ex-husband. She'd never thought about the other men who'd had a part in it.

Instead of anger, fear overwhelmed her. This man was in charge of bringing Darian back to her. Would he sabotage Darian's chance at life?

She stood and backed away. She needed to get out of here. She needed to find Damon and be with someone she'd known in her previous life. She needed advice.

She needed Darian. Desperately. For a woman so used to being in control of everything, knowing everything, being so cut off from the technologies she'd grown to rely on was maddening.

Nani turned and fled out of the med bay and down the corridor to the mess hall. She was almost sure to find Phoebe there, and Phoebe would know where Damon was.

She ran.

Her arms pumped and her legs churned, hurling her down the corridor as fast as she could go. When she reached the mess, she ducked inside, only to be met by a dozen or so smiling faces. The crew, enjoying Phoebe's wonderful food and some relaxation, were oblivious to her plight. Some gave her a friendly smile and a wave, while others seemed to wonder who she was, but no one seemed overly concerned.

Nani was about to turn and run back to her quarters -- or perhaps back to the med bay to guard Darian -- until she could figure out what to do.

Thankfully, Phoebe came up behind her, pulled her back into the kitchen without a word, and wrapped her arms around Nani.

Nani was the cast iron bitch. She always had the answers -- at least more answers than everyone else -- and she had a sarcastic wit that made everyone cringe. Now, she felt helpless and completely out of touch with her true personality. She was strong. She never leaned on others. Others always relied on her to be strong, and now she felt weaker than she ever had.

She totally lost her hard-won control. Tears of anger, grief, and betrayal poured out of her. She only knew Mahat Zabin from his time aboard the ship, but it was like the ultimate betrayal. She had accepted him as part of her extended family -- the crew of the *Black Star*. Now this.

"What's happened? Dr. Zabin said you were distressed."

"With good reason," Nani sniffed. "I need to see Damon."

As if on cue, the klaxon sounded and everyone scrambled from the mess. The clatter was almost as loud as the alarm reverberating throughout the ship. Nani's head snapped up. Automatically, she reached for the ship's sensors, only to find nothing.

Dammit! As glad as she was to be in her own body, not knowing was simply terrifying. For more than twenty years, she'd been in control of almost every aspect of this ship. Now, she was blind and deaf.

When she whipped around to run out the door, Phoebe grabbed her arm. "You should stay here, or at the very least stay with me."

"This is my ship, Phoebe," Nani snapped harder than she intended. She took a breath and tried again. "If there's something wrong, I need to know."

Phoebe said something else, but Nani didn't pay attention. She knew the woman was just trying to help, but she couldn't stay here while the whole world went to hell.

It took her less than a minute to reach command, but she might as well have stayed with Phoebe. The captain and crew were using the internal comm system technology Mikiel had given them, and she didn't know any more than when she left the mess.

Not wanting to break anyone's concentration, she tried to peek at the display screens to get a sense of what was happening. Three Hand vessels to port. The *Black Star* was very likely not within their sensor range, so they had the element of surprise.

Nani had never been able to form a strong bond with her daughter, but she knew as sure as she was standing there Nadira was on one of those ships. She wished she could narrow it down.

"Damon," she whispered. The captain tilted his head in her direction but did not take his eyes off his console. "Nadira…" She trailed off as she felt her daughter find her telepathic link and grasp on tightly. Nani sucked in a breath.

Damon whipped his head around to her sound of distress. "What?" His eyes blazed, and he looked fiercer than she'd ever witnessed during her time as part of the *Black Star*.

"She's on one of those ships, and she's in trouble." Nani fumbled with her telepathic link and swore to herself when she lost it altogether. She knew the environment the crew was used to and knew not to disrupt it with needless noise.

She closed her eyes and took a breath, trying to calm herself and concentrate. It had always been difficult to touch Nadira in this way, more so now because of both their anxiety.

I have her, Nani. Darian's calm, sure voice whispered in her head. *She is on the smallest vessel of the three and frightened, but unharmed.*

Nani let all her feelings of gratitude and relief flow from her to Darian, though she had no doubt he already knew. He had always been adept at reading her, even when he was unable to communicate with her because of distance. He knew her feelings.

"Darian says the smallest vessel carries her. She's unharmed but terribly frightened." Again, she kept her voice quiet and for Damon only.

He acknowledged her with a slight nod of his head and punched several buttons on his console. Immediately, the *Black Star* banked to starboard and took up a new position off to the extreme left of the smallest Hand ship. They had still been a good way out of sensor range, but the drastic movement must have alerted the trio to their presence.

As expected, the other two ships took up defensive positions, protecting the ship that held Nadira. Nani saw Damon's lips twitch slightly and knew he'd been expecting such a move on their part.

As Nani watched on one of the vacant display screens, brilliant green and blue light burst into view at the two defending ships. The angles were all wrong for it to be the *Black Star* firing. Those were laser and plasma fire from the *Sword Breaker*.

She clenched her fists and leaned over the console. This was all so surreal. The essence of her one true love was in that ship, and she couldn't shake the instinct she had to protect the *Sword Breaker*. It was almost as strong as the fierce need to do anything necessary to get her daughter back safely. For the first time since she'd been forcibly placed inside the essence of the *Black Star*, all she could do was stand there and watch.

Not bloody likely.

The keys to the console seemed to take more dexterity to operate than her fingers possessed, but she gritted her teeth against the frustration and called up the information she so desperately needed. In a few seconds, she had a real-time readout of all psycomm chatter on the ship.

It took some adjusting, but she was used to intense multitasking. Pretty soon, she was following the conversation almost as well as she could have before she was put back into her body.

Forward warship sustained light to moderate damage port bow, sir. Shielding is compensating.

The Sword Breaker *is closing in to their starboard side. Lasers at full capacity.*

Increase to flank. Darian's command cut through all other communication in bright, bold letters. *Isolate the middle ship and cut her away from the other two.*

Nani clenched her jaw tightly. Knowing what was happening and not being able to help was worse than not knowing. She could tell by the lack of energy fall-off of the Hand ships' laser banks that they were holding back. It only made sense they were holding their main burst to get a good, clean killing shot. Looking at the typed text, Darian didn't know that.

She looked to the tactical station where Viktor should have sat. He was gone. The seat was vacant. Briefly, she thought about taking the station, but without a psycomm, she was worse than useless. She'd break their concentration by needing external communication.

Quickly, she hacked into Darian's personal comm. He was flying into a trap. True, anything the

Hand could throw at them probably wouldn't fatally damage them, but it might slow them down enough for the Hand to get out of the area with Nadira.

It's a trap, Darian. They're going to focus everything they have on you.

There was a pause, and for a moment, Nani was afraid he hadn't gotten her text. Then he typed, *That would buy them enough time for escape.*

I believe so.

There was a pause as she watched Damon punch a few buttons on his console.

Topside thrusters. Take us down. Ready the tractor.

Sir, using the tractor beam on anything with that kind of mass will take our power down to twenty percent capacity and disable our hyperdrive. Reading the transcript seemed to lessen the impact of the warning, but Nani knew the safest course of action would be to simply back off. Fortunately, Damon was never one to retreat if there was a reasonable chance of victory.

Understood. DO IT.

The outburst was uncharacteristic, but reflective of her own feelings at the moment. He was a brilliant tactician, so she had no doubt he knew what he was doing. The ship sank with a slight lurch, and Nani watched as power was taken from all systems, save life support, for the tractor.

Target the starboard ship with lasers and engage tractor on that smaller ship when I command.

Nani scanned the area and found the *Sword Breaker* again coming at them from the other side of the battle sector and above them. The Hand ships floundered in space, not knowing which way to go. Damon's target sank straight down, but he kept the *Black Star* out of the other ship's line of sight. Had the commander been experienced in battle, he'd have relied on his sensors more, but Damon's gamble seemed to be paying off. He'd definitely done his homework. The Hand, while they loved technology they could glean from other cultures, had little understanding of how most of it really worked. They obviously weren't used to the highly sensitive sensors the class of ship they flew used. Apparently, if they couldn't see their target out the window, they floundered. Damon obviously had a hint that might happen.

Target acquired. Tractor ready. Awaiting your command, sir.

Several blind shots surged through space, missing both ships easily. The Hand moved about, trying to protect the smaller ship, but all they did was give the *Black Star* and the *Sword Breaker* easier access to the ship from above and below.

Nani gripped the edge of the console hard. Damon's plan seemed to be working, but she didn't want to hope too much. She wasn't sure she could take that kind of disappointment right now. When Nadira had been taken, she'd felt like a knife had been plunged into her heart. Even now, her chest ached with grief even as hope tried to bloom inside her. She was finally able to hold her daughter in her arms and she might still lose the chance to do so.

She looked at Damon. His face was impassive, but his jaw clenched, and instead of simply pressing buttons on his console, he stabbed them with unnecessary force. He was as determined as she was. As she watched him, she was again thankful -- as she had been many times throughout the years -- that Damon had taken Nadira so closely under his wing. It was very likely she wouldn't have survived without him. If there was any doubt that Damon loved Nadira like a daughter, it was erased as Nani watched him fighting to get her back now.

Steady. On my mark. Nani tensed and locked her knees to keep from falling. If this didn't work, they might lose Nadira again. The thought that they might execute her flitted through Nani's mind, and she quickly squashed the evil vision. If she thought like that, she might drive herself insane.

Fire! Damon barked the command into the psycomm, and Nani jumped. Brilliant green light streaked through space and hit the Hand target squarely. It was difficult to assess the damage by looking at it, but a small puff of green plasma fire exited the ship near where the aft engine should be. The flare was brief but Damon didn't wait to see what happened. Apparently, he wasn't taking any chances.

Again! Disable her completely. Do not destroy.

Similar bursts came from the *Black Star* against the other ship, and it wasn't long before neither of the warships gave any signs of life. Nani checked the sensors. The only thing functioning aboard either warship was life support, and one of them only minimally.

Damon sprang from his chair, a testament to how high his emotions were running. "Engage tractor!" He used the psycomm, but spoke anyway. His fists were clenched as he bent over the shoulder of the crewman sitting next to him. He had full readouts from his own station, but he was apparently expending nervous energy. Nani couldn't blame him. She felt like she had a fifty-kilogram weight sitting on her chest. "Viktor! Are you ready?"

"What's going on?" Nani's quiet question was met with a slashing movement of Damon's hand. An order to keep quiet.

Ready, Captain. I have her coordinates as Darian believes them to be. If he's wrong, we'll have to get a boarding party together. Viktor's voice was calm and assured. Firm. He had supreme confidence in himself. Nani immediately reached out to Darian, trying to see the plan. He blocked her, but she fought her way through, needing to know what thing Darian would try to hide from her. When she found it, she staggered backward into the bulkhead.

"You're going to do *what*?" She looked to Damon, demanding an answer to her question. "You don't even know if she'll survive such a thing! It's not been tested!"

Damon rounded on her. "I hate to sound cliché, but every second she stays on that ship is one second too long. They'll kill her once they know there's no chance of keeping her. So, if you've got a better idea…"

Nani clenched her teeth together. She knew he was right. A rescue party would arrive in time to collect Nadira's remains. As Diamond and Phoebe had stated on several occasions, no one escaped the Hand of God. At least, not without a horrible fight, and this would be a horrible fight.

Viktor and Darian had apparently come up with a way to use that ship's food generator to turn Nadira into trillions of biological particles, funnel her signature through the filtration system to the waste outlet and into *Black Star*'s tractor beam. They then planned to put her back together in solid form once her particles were safely aboard. If it worked. If not…

She didn't want to think about that possibility.

"Whenever you're ready, Viktor. Do what you have to do." Damon reached for Nani's hand. "Come on, my lady. Hopefully by the time we get there, Viktor will already have her."

Chapter Three

Darian caressed her mind the whole way to Viktor. Damon took her to the cargo bay where Mikiel was already waiting. Viktor stood at a control panel at the very front of the bay. The tractor unit glowed an iridescent, shimmering blue as it pulled its target into the cargo bay.

"If the food processors on that ship are even remotely similar to ours -- which from everything I've found about that class and design of ship, they are -- we should have little difficulty with her," Viktor was saying to Mikiel. "I have her signature, and she's dissolved. Reconstruction in thirty seconds."

Nani walked in and up to Mikiel. "You tested this idea on yourself." It was a statement, not a question.

"It was too risky to try it untested. If anyone was going to die because of this desperate idea, it wasn't going to be Nadira."

She looked at Viktor. "It was your idea."

He didn't answer. Didn't even look at her.

Nani counted the seconds in her head. She felt Darian's touch trying to comfort her, but she refused to concentrate on anything other than the countdown going on in her head. If this didn't work, Nadira would come back to them as so much space dust.

Fifteen seconds.

Ten.

She held her breath. She said a prayer to every deity she'd ever heard of in every language she could remember. Ten seconds seemed like an eternity.

Finally, the tractor reined in as far as it could, Nani saw sparkling particles roughly resembling human form begin to take shape on the landing platform.

"Initializing optimization. Creating a pattern." Viktor's verbal checklist was for her benefit, she knew. As glad as she was to have her own body back, it was damned frustrating not to be able to tap into the ship's sensors. Even more so not to be in control. It was amazing what one could get used to given enough time.

She blinked back tears. Time. She'd missed so much of it. All of Nadira's childhood. Her wedding. Time with Darian. True, she had a chance to catch the rest of it, at least, but she was still very bitter about the rest.

Breathe, my love. Breathe.

Can you sense her? Is she OK?

She's pure energy right now and has no thoughts or feelings. It's a limbo state.

So if she doesn't make it…

She won't feel anything, Nani.

Darian's gentle assessment didn't ease her mind.

"Materialization in three, two, one."

Before her eyes, Nadira formed from particles of light. It took about ten seconds for the process to complete, but when it did, Nadira stood with her eyes tightly closed and her fists clenched. Her face was bruised -- presumably from a beating those people had given her aboard the other ship -- but seemed otherwise unharmed. Dr. Zabin…

Oh, God. Nani had put so much trust in him. How far could she trust him now? Certainly not with her daughter's life.

"Take her to Medical," Mikiel started.

"No," Nani said, quietly but firmly. "Mikiel, take her back to the *Sword Breaker*. Your doctor there can assess her injuries."

"Dr. Zabin --"

"Is not to touch her." For the first time since her rebirth, she found herself. She wasn't a weak woman, and not one to lie down and meekly let others decide her fate or the fate of the ones she loved. "Take her back to your ship and see to her there. I want her away from here."

Mikiel looked hard at her for a long moment. "As you wish."

Nadira looked at her, and Nani almost lost the control she'd only just reclaimed. She wanted to run to the young woman and throw her arms around her, but she wasn't sure Nadira would welcome her. They exchanged looks, but didn't approach each other. Nani inclined her chin slightly in acknowledgement, but otherwise didn't say anything. She'd figure out what to do when they were in private.

She turned her attention to Viktor now. Five slow, measured steps later, she stood almost toe-to-toe with him. He was so massive, she had to crane her neck to look him in the face, but she didn't care. His face was impassive, but she could see some of the vulnerability she knew lay underneath. It didn't make her next action one bit harder.

With one swift movement, she drove her hand hard into his chin. His head snapped back, but otherwise, he didn't move.

So she did it again.

"Nani!" Out of the corner of her eye, she saw Damon take a step toward them, but Mikiel stopped him with a hand on his shoulder. Nadira breathed in sharply, and Mikiel reached for her immediately, bringing her into the shelter of his body.

"You will never put my daughter in that kind of danger again." Her words were quiet when she wanted to scream at the vampire. More than once, she'd wanted to knock some sense into Viktor, so she took the opportunity she'd been given.

"Feel better?"

"Not even close."

"You could hit Mikiel, you know. He was part of this, as well as Darian." Viktor sounded petulant, like he always did when he knew he couldn't argue with her. To be the scariest person she'd ever seen, to have the worst possible reputation, Viktor really wasn't a bad guy, and he didn't deserve to be hit like she'd done. She couldn't, however, bring herself to apologize. He might not have done anything this time, but he'd infuriated her enough in the last few months to have deserved it at some point.

"Mikiel, at least, had the good grace to put himself through it before exposing Nadira to it," she snapped. "And I'll deal with Darian, have no worries."

"And if I'd done it to myself, who the hell was supposed to run the bloody thing?" Viktor gritted out his response. He was tense now, but unless Nani was greatly mistaken, it was his usual exasperation with her and not the dangerous, out-of-control anger she associated with his "time of the month," as she'd come to think of Viktor's Blood Burning. A vampire's need for sex and blood when they'd been denied them for too long was an emotional, violent thing, scary in its intensity. This was just Viktor wanting the last word, but unsure how to get it.

"Even without me, the computer is perfectly able to make the necessary calculations."

Viktor threw up his hands and turned away from her. "I don't fucking believe this!"

"Let it go, Viktor." Mikiel chuckled. "You never could win an argument with her."

"We bloody well saved Nadira's life!" He rubbed his jaw. "That was uncalled for." He was pouting now, Nani knew.

"Maybe this time," she conceded, "but I can't tell you how many times you've needed it over the past few months. Consider us even now."

She looked one last time at Nadira, who was suppressing a smile, and strode out of the cargo bay and down the corridor. Back to her room. She needed time to think.

She needed Darian.

Chapter Four

By the time she reached her cabin, Nani was actually sorry for what she'd done to Viktor, but there was no help for it now. He had been a pain in her side on more than one occasion, but this wasn't one of them. She'd taken out her fear and feelings of helplessness on him. She definitely owed him an apology.

He knows. And he's not really mad. It's a reflex on his part. The two of you have made your way like that together for several months. He didn't expect it would be any different.

Darian's voice caressed her mind. His love for her filled her, but he had to pay for his little part in the amazing but crazy feat that had ultimately saved her daughter, too.

"You could have warned me, you know. I'd have liked to have been part of planning that little stunt."

And what would you have done, hmm?

"Fretted, fussed, and worried myself to death. Not to mention never let you try it, but that's not the point." She was pouting now, but she knew it was OK. Sometimes she had to, and Darian always grinned at her and nodded appropriately. They were like an old married couple. Even before the horror of the last twenty years, they loved each other that completely. Over time, they thought they'd lost each other, but when they were reunited, all those feelings and comfort with each other returned as if they'd never been separated.

Then, my dear, what is the point?

"How should I know?" She shrugged out of her clothes and flopped down on the bed, naked, exhausted and exasperated. "I'm just looking for a little sympathy and understanding here. That was our daughter you and Viktor just shredded to subatomic particles."

You know I would never have agreed to it if there had been an unreasonable risk of her dying. Had we not tried, she would have died, anyway.

"And since when do you communicate with Viktor, anyway? He's had a connection with me, but never you. Why now?"

Believe it or not, he's a little afraid of you.

Nani was still for a moment, afraid she'd heard Darian wrong. Then she burst out laughing, clutching her sides after a while as she writhed on the bed. "Afraid of me? Viktor? I'd say you were out of your mind, but that would be cruel."

You are a strong woman, Nani. You always have been. You're thrown into an impossible situation yet again, and you're off balance. You'll find your place in this new world.

Her mirth died and her smile faded. "A place where I belong." Her voice was quiet. "The only place I've ever truly belonged was by your side. I feel lost. Disjointed. Nothing makes sense."

It's a new situation. That's all, Nani. You'll be OK.

"You sound like you don't expect to join me." Nani tried not to let despair fill her. Darian would know if she were too distressed. They'd shared their minds almost continually since they'd been reunited, and he was much more talented than she. He knew her mind almost as well as he knew his own.

His sigh whispered softly across her mind. *I admit, I don't know what to think about the very man who put me in this position to begin with trying to save me. I don't have much of a choice, though.*

"No. Death would be preferable to where you

are." She tried to breathe through the sadness and grief filling her. She'd just gotten him back. To have him taken from her again was unthinkable. "I just…"

I know. She could almost feel him embrace her. His presence in her mind was warm and comforting, and she felt horrible about it. This might be the last few hours of Darian's life, and he was comforting her because she was feeling sorry for herself.

"You're the most amazing man I've ever known, Darian."

And we'll be together again, Nani. Somehow, this will work. I know it will.

She lay there basking in the warmth of his presence. Her mind felt fractured by everything going on. It was as if there was no such thing as a "normal life," and she was stuck in a living hell from which she could never escape. Even being back in her own body, while much better in some respects, wasn't the relief she thought it would be. She was so used to being in control, the lack of knowing what was going on was maddening.

Do you remember the first time we made love?

His voice was a mere whisper in her mind. Darian always had a way of seducing her with the smallest things. She'd always loved that about him.

"We were underneath the garmon tree at Barron Lake," she replied with a smile. "The grass was so soft it felt like a *maharie* fur rug underneath me. Only the cool breeze coming off the lake tempered the sun's warmth. I was nineteen, and you were twenty-four." She smiled and shifted on the bed to put an arm under her head, her other hand resting lightly on her stomach. "We were both so anxious, it didn't take either one of us long the first time."

His sexy chuckle tickled her mind and spread a

happy warmth through her torso. The mere memory of his skin sliding against her own sweat-slickened skin thrilled her beyond belief. She wanted to feel it again. Darian. Her first and only love.

I still remember how good your mouth tasted, Nani. I loved hearing your sighs as I kissed and touched you. You were so responsive -- that time and every time after.

"I always loved touching your chest. You always had such a beautiful body, Darian. You were perfect in every way I could ever imagine, but I loved the feel of your chest hair against my skin. Any part of my body. And your hands were always so strong and rough. A man's hands. I loved for you to touch my body."

The memories, and voicing them out loud to the man inside her head instead of speaking them directly to his mind, brought back sensations she'd thought long dead. Desire coursed through her, moistening her core and making her fingers and hands tingle in anticipation. Her heart rate increased slightly, and her breathing came a little quicker.

Still beautifully responsive, just like you always were. He sounded happy. If she could have seen his face, she was sure he'd have been smiling at her. *Show me I'm right.*

Nani blushed, but she brought her free hand to one breast and cupped it gently, feeling its weight. The fleshy globe was plump, but firm. Its nipple was already pebbled and standing out against the rest of her flesh. She circled her nipple once before bringing her finger to her mouth to wet the digit, and circling the same nipple again. The cool air against her damp flesh made her shiver, and her skin erupted in chills.

That's it, my love. Feels good, doesn't it?

"Almost as good as I remember."

It will be better. You know it will. Touch yourself.

She spread her legs and brought her other hand from behind her head to the downy curls covering her sex. With tentative fingers, she delved into them to find her clit, which sent a jolt through her lower body, and she whimpered.

Sweet music, he crooned. *Do it again.*

She dipped her fingers deeper. When they came back wet, she rubbed her clit again, lingering this time. She circled the nub several times before wetting them again in her intimate moisture. Her belly contracted when she returned to her clit the third time and she squeezed her inner muscles, reaching for what she knew would come later.

"I'm wet." She wasn't sure why she was so surprised. Perhaps it was twenty years of not only abstinence, but the absence of any physical stimuli at all.

I know. Darian's voice in her mind was becoming more insistent. He was always so soft-spoken, but in bed he totally dominated her. She wouldn't have it any other way. *Do it again.*

Nani spread her legs wider, and this time she pushed two fingers inside herself, brushing her clit with her thumb. She pinched her nipple gently and gasped at the sensation. The inside of her cunt was slippery and warm. She moved her fingers in and out, mimicking the act she was beginning to need desperately.

Feels good, doesn't it? Darian whispered. *That's it. Use three fingers. Feel it burn when you stretch your pussy for me.*

"Sweet stars," Nani whispered. "It does feel good."

Pulling her knees close to her body, allowing her easier access to her cunt, she plunged a fourth finger inside herself. Darian had always loved watching her stretch herself. He knew she loved the burning sensation. Most of the time, their love play had been tame and simple. But sometimes, they'd used toys, or had rough sex. While it wasn't something she would have enjoyed all the time, Darian had used his talents to know when she'd needed it.

Now, more than ever, she needed it. She needed to feel alive. Loved. Even the mild pain was an aphrodisiac.

She concentrated solely on the sensations she created within her own body and the sound of Darian's voice in her mind. She loved everything about him, but his voice could do things to her without him ever touching her physically.

That's it. Fuck yourself, Nani. Rub your clit. I want you to come.

Frantically now, she pumped her fingers into her pussy. She could never deny him. Her breath came in little gasps, and she clenched her inner muscles, reaching for the orgasm she knew was just out of reach.

Finally, it started, beginning at her clit and pulsing through her abdomen. She pushed with all her might. The tingling and contractions grew and grew until Nani thrashed about on the bed, screaming her pleasure.

She panted, and her vision swam with tiny pinpricks of light. Even her face tingled with the force of that orgasm. Even after she'd stopped manipulating her pussy and clit, the sensations still swam through her for several moments before gradually falling off.

When it was over, tears formed and spilled from the outer corners of her eyes down the sides of her face.

Now, my love. Be the woman you were born to be. This was but a twenty-year delay. You and I both know what must be done. If I can't join you, you must take Nadira and do it alone. Her DNA will serve in my absence. You will unite our two peoples.

There were so many things that had to be done. So many things she had to do. She would have Darian back, and she would face Samair again. What would happen then, only the stars knew, but she had her focus now, and no one would stop her.

Chapter Five

Nani had rested for a while, alternately dozing and thinking. Her first order of business was to see Dr. Zabin. He was the only one who could help Darian, but she'd damned well keep an eye on him during the procedure.

She found him exactly where she'd found him the first time; hunched over a computer screen. If possible, he looked even more tired than he had before. She'd bet he hadn't slept at all.

"Dr. Zabin." She called his name from the door to his office when he didn't acknowledge her presence. He whipped his head around, fear on his face, before he schooled his features and straightened.

"My lady. I didn't know you were here. Please come in. Sit."

She watched him carefully. He was definitely uncomfortable. "What's happened?" She didn't need her meager telepathic skills to know something wasn't going as planned.

He fell into his chair and scrubbed a hand over his weary-looking face. "I'm having problems with the clone I grew for Darian. The cell structure was very unstable. I took only a very small amount of cellular material because I didn't want to damage either of you, but I miscalculated with Darian. I didn't get enough complete cells to grow a viable clone."

Nani narrowed her eyes. "So there's no place to put him. What are we going to do now?"

"Well," he began, punching a few buttons on his computer, bringing up a DNA strand, "I think I've found what I need in one of the chips I removed from Diamond and Phoebe. Apparently, one contained your DNA, the other held Darian's. There is enough physical material to make approximately ten clones of each of you. I could use this to grow another body for him, but I've got to be careful when extracting the material or I could destroy it."

"So why haven't you slept?"

His expression crumpled. Nani had never seen anyone look more dejected. "I've only got one shot to make it work, and I'm not sure I can. If I fail, I can't grow a clone of Darian, and he'll have to be put in another body."

Nani thought for a moment, looking intently at Mahat Zabin. He knew something he wasn't telling her.

"And?"

"Look, Darian always believed Nadira's genetic make up would be enough to prove he had an heir, but I'm not convinced. I'm not sure he'd be accepted unless he actually presents himself."

Nani narrowed her eyes. "How much do you know?"

"Everything. What Samair didn't tell me, I made it my life's work to discover. It's taken the better part of twenty years, but I know why Samair had the two of you exiled in such a manner."

"And, knowing this, you're convinced the only way to unite our two peoples is with Darian actually being there?"

"I'm certain of it. It can't be his daughter, or his mind inside a surrogate clone other than his own, and he can't be in a cyborg body. It has to be him. The climate after he went missing changed dramatically against everyone in the Vok'nair Empire hierarchy. Especially you. I think most people truly believe you killed him."

None of this mattered much to Nani, since she

was determined to have Darian back in his own body, anyway. She'd love him no matter what form he took, but it was the principle of the matter.

"What do you need to make this easier for you?"

"You don't understand." He stood and paced to the other side of the room. "This is technology I've never encountered before. I need whoever designed this to explain to me how to extract the cellular material. Since I don't have any idea who that is, I'm going to have to study it until I figure it out. I need time. And unless I miss my guess, time isn't something we have a lot of."

As if on cue, an explosion rocked the ship. Sirens blared once before the deadly silence she associated with battle aboard the *Black Star* engulfed them. The entire place glowed eerily red, but no one made much noise at all. Sometimes, battle could get loud, but most everyone used their internal comm. Which reminded her. She needed that from the good doctor.

"I need an internal comm. You owe me at least that much." She looked at him sternly.

He didn't even bat an eyelash, just took a medigun from the shelf, loaded it with something and held it to her temple. "Hold still." It was the only warning she got. He pulled the trigger, and her head exploded in agony for several seconds before the pain fell off. She saw stars for the second time that day, only this time it was from pain, not pleasure.

"Son of a bitch," she breathed before sitting down hard in a nearby chair.

"Relax a moment. Once the transponder clears your skull, it will attach to your synaptic system and gradually feed you data. You should be fully receiving in five minutes, able to transmit in eight."

She shook her head to clear it before standing up

slowly and taking a few tentative steps away from the chair. When she was convinced she wouldn't fall, she pulled herself together as much as she could, nodded once to Darian, and headed out the door.

She was still several minutes away from knowing everything going on, but she was being fed information from Darian as fast as he could glean it from Viktor. Her link with Viktor had been tenuous at best, but with so many things for her to deal with since her rebirth, she had only connected with him occasionally, and only then when he was reaching for her.

Reaching command, she quietly went to the same station she'd occupied before, again hacking into the comm channels to try to figure out what was going on until her internal unit kicked in. Viktor made brief eye contact with her before returning to his job, and she saw a note of approval on his face.

Vok'nair vessels starboard flank, Captain. Weapons hot and targeting. Viktor's usually calm voice filtered through her comm, but since no one else's did, she assumed he directed his statement toward her intentionally.

Is the Sword Breaker *in position?*

Captain Anjoom is standing by, sir.

And the Vok'nair fleet?

On the outer border of the sector. There are at least thirty war ships, sir. All state-of-the-art. Most look as if they've barely made it out of dry dock.

Communication was spotty now, but coming through her comm unit easily enough.

Damon Singh chuckled. *Thirty war ships to capture one Asalian Slaver and the* Black Star?

She was *the flagship, sir.* Viktor's dry tone came through loud and clear. He was neither surprised by the show of strength, nor impressed by it, judging by his tone. *They're obviously afraid she packs more of a punch than a mere man in command of a ship.*

No. They expect the Black Star *herself, no doubt.* He glanced toward Nani with a smile. *Maybe we'll have to give her to them. Just not the way they expect.* Damon was clearly in control, but he stepped down from the command center and gestured for Nani to take his seat.

At first, she wasn't sure she should. Her internal comm hadn't started working properly yet, and the last thing she wanted to do was usurp Damon's position, but she doubted he would have handed control of his ship over to her without good reason.

Do you know who leads this fleet? she asked.

Tyrelle Amos. And he's demanding our surrender.

Nani's heart sped up. Tyrelle had been her father's best friend and advisor. It wasn't surprising he headed the fleet. Samair would have been able to keep him away from the Vok'nair home world and out of the way without killing the admiral outright. With strategic moves like that to keep key sympathizers in the administration without them actually being able to do anything, he'd have been able to effectively take control without much change. If the people didn't notice what was going on in their everyday lives, they'd be less likely to care who was in power as long as they weren't inconvenienced. It was a brilliant move on his part, but one that would ultimately be his downfall.

Also, he had been there when they'd taken her from the hospital to meet her fate. He'd protested vehemently until his own family had been threatened. Even then, he'd argued with Samair, just in a more subdued manner. He was a good man in a bad situation.

Let me hear their message. My internal comm is not yet at one hundred percent.

Viktor flipped a switch, and Tyrelle Amos's voice projected commandingly over the external intercom. "*Black Star*, surrender and prepare to be boarded. This is Admiral Tyrelle Amos, supreme commander of the Vok'nair Empire. Please respond."

Nani took a deep breath. Her words in the next few minutes could change the future of her people forever.

"Be sure to respond with visual, Viktor. He has to see who I am." Nani straightened in her chair. She crossed her legs casually, waiting for Viktor to nod at her and for Tyrelle Amos to appear on her monitor. "Commander Amos," she said in a friendly manner. "It's good to see you again."

Surprise flickered on the admiral's face, but like the professional he was, he schooled his features almost immediately. "That ship belongs to the Vok'nair Empire."

"This ship belongs to me." Nani willed herself to relax. She couldn't show weakness or uncertainty. Not with a man like Admiral Amos. "I earned her many times over."

It was a while before the admiral said anything, but when he did he stood firm, looking at her hard. "It's still my obligation to bring this ship -- and you -- back to the Empire."

"You can try, Tyrelle, and you will probably succeed, but is that what you really want to do?"

"You know it's not. But I have my own family to think about now. Children and grandchildren who are innocent of any wrongdoing. You made your choice when you rejected Samair. Besides, once we bring back Samair's daughter, any claim you have will be disputed anyway. Nadira's his heir. As the male parent, he will be placed in control of her estate and the kingdom."

Nani had been ready for this. "And if Nadira is not his child?"

Tyrelle turned his head slightly, but sharply. This wasn't a question he'd expected. "Not possible."

"You know it is. You've probably even asked yourself that over the years. Why is it so impossible to contemplate it now?"

"Nani --" he began and looked around him at his command crew. His shoulders fell slightly, and he suddenly looked much older than he had a few moments ago. "It's not that simple. The general population believes you died in childbirth. Samair has a stranglehold on anyone involved with your disappearance. Dr. Zabin was the only one of us brave enough to defy him, and his entire family was slaughtered. I understand now why he never had children."

Nani felt an overwhelming relief wash over her. Knowing she could trust Mahat Zabin was the best news she'd had in forever. She was still uneasy, but she suspected she would be until Darian was at her side again.

I'm always with you, my love.

His love was like a warm column of air wrapping around her soul. Any uncertainty or doubt she had fled in his presence.

"Dr. Zabin has been a great help to us."

"So I imagine, seeing you back in your body. You had a funeral and everything, you know. It was very public and Samair was visibly distraught as he held his baby daughter. It won't be easy getting the people to accept you. Especially after being under Asalian influence. They're not going to believe you've simply been raised from the dead."

Something struck her then. Something that had been nagging her since she found out about the implanted chips within Phoebe and Diamond.

"There were two microchips that contained the DNA structure of both Darian and myself. Both have been recovered with no harm to those who held them." She watched Tyrelle carefully, but if he knew about these chips, he gave away nothing. "Who designed them?"

There was a brief silence before the admiral spoke. "A man named Grimm. Pardell Grimm. He was a friend of both your father and the leader of the Asalian Coalition."

"Is he still alive?" Nani's heart pounded. This was it. This was the key.

Admiral Amos raised an eyebrow. "Yes. As a matter of fact, he is."

Chapter Six

Nani tried to contain her excitement as she headed to Medical. She was hyperventilating, and she felt like her chest would explode with the pounding of her heart. She had to continually remind herself not to run. She had to be calm when she approached Dr. Zabin. Knowing it was hopeless, she detoured to her cabin. She had to get a hold on her emotions.

She felt Darian's presence inside her mind, but he was calm as ever. The man infuriated her sometimes. Nothing frazzled him. Nothing impressed him. He was the rock in their relationship. She was always on emotional hyperdrive. She wished she could be more like him.

Then we wouldn't be perfect for each other. We balance each other, Nani. Your strengths are my weaknesses and vice versa. We're perfect for each other.

You always know how to calm me.

And you know how to enflame me.

He deliberately sent an image to her of how she looked during one of their more memorable sexual experiences.

He had tied her to his bed, her arms and legs lashed to the posts at each corner. They'd been playing a game. He was the space pirate, she the captured princess. At first she'd giggled and even laughed at the absurdity of it, but she'd soon gotten into the game. Mostly after he'd pulled her over his knees and pulled her dress up, her underwear down, and spanked her bottom until it had glowed red.

She'd been up for anything after that. Nani remembered how that spanking had completely changed her attitude about sex. Never again had she been content with vanilla sex in the strictest sense. Yes, she needed tender loving from time to time, but not now. Now she needed -- no, wanted -- hard and rough.

After he'd tied her to the bed, he had shaved her pussy. Carefully and methodically, he'd scraped the razor over her delicate skin and massaged lotion into her newly bared flesh. He'd aroused her more than ever with that gentle action, but she knew that wasn't the end. Her clit had throbbed and ached for him to touch her. She wanted him to take it into his mouth and suck and lick it.

Then, to her dismay, he'd taken one of the many candles he'd lit around the room and tormented her with the wax and flame. Her skin had never been harmed, but the psychological impact had completely stripped her defenses.

She'd begged him not to harm her. Not to burn her. She'd do anything if he'd just not hurt her. He'd laughed his scary pirate laugh and dribbled hot wax over her chest. It had burned, but not horribly. It had been the thought of it that had terrified her. Soon her breasts were covered in warm, cooling wax. He'd taunted her as he gently peeled it from her skin. Did she think this was all he had to offer by way of torture? Oh, no. The night was young, and there were so many more delicious things he wanted to do to her.

He'd reached up to a drawer high on a shelf above his bed and pulled out a small, wedge-shaped butt plug and a larger, penis-shaped dildo. She'd used toys the size of the dildo before, but her ass had never been touched before in this manner. Not even by herself.

A tube of lubrigel had followed. He'd smiled evilly as he squirted a generous portion of the clear, slick gel onto the butt plug.

"This will hurt, my dear. But you'll get used to

it."

It was a side of Darian she'd never seen before, and it thrilled her to her toes even as fear consumed her. Her desire fed off the fear and created its own perverse excitement. She loved every second even as she dreaded what would come next. She couldn't tell him to stop.

Before she could even form the thought that she might not like what he was about to do, he dipped the plug between her legs and found her ass. He didn't cram it in, but used exquisite slowness and was careful to let her adjust to each new centimeter. Once it was in, he stepped back and looked at her, smiling that evil smile he'd adopted.

"Nice," he nodded as he looked her over. "But I want more."

He'd dived between her legs then and latched onto her clit. Occasionally, he dipped down to her pussy, and when he did, he seemed to go mad. He growled and groaned as he ate her. He nipped her flesh from time to time, causing her to cry out sharply, but again, she relished the small pain. She screamed every time he pulled at her clit, or stuck his tongue inside her pussy. It wasn't long before she pulled at her bonds, trying to touch him, wanting to make him stop all this nonsense and simply fuck her. In fact, she told him so. Quite vehemently.

"Stop playing around, you bastard, and fuck the shit out of me!"

He'd bit her then, pulling at her pussy and clit until she cried out with the sharp pain. When he let her go, the lower half of his face was shiny with her moisture. His eyes glittered in the candlelight, and she knew it had been the wrong thing to say.

"Bitch." His soft voice belied the intense emotion

on his face. "I'll do what I want with you, when I choose to do it and not before." Such extreme change in her lover gave her pause, but something in her mind told her all was well. Later, she would realize it was Darian himself. He knew she enjoyed the danger, enjoyed playing the role of scoundrel himself, but still had the need to protect her. Even from herself.

"I don't think you're man enough," she'd hissed, raising her head and shoulders off the bed as far as she could manage.

That had set him off. Just as she'd hoped it would. He'd grabbed the dildo angrily and shoved it inside her cunt without even using lubrigel. Not that it mattered. She was so wet, the toy glided easily inside her. The dildo had been made rather like the butt plug at the base in that it swelled out slightly only to form a neck between the hilt and the dildo itself. It would stay inside her until someone pulled it out. He pressed a couple of buttons on the end of it, and the thing started to buzz inside her. When her eyes widened in surprise, he'd pressed another button -- this time on the thing in her ass -- and it too started to buzz.

"The one in your ass gradually grows, you know." He'd stepped back calmly then, his agitation seeming to have evaporated as quickly as it had come. "It will stretch you until I can slide my dick easily inside that puckered little hole. Was your ass a virgin before I violated it with my little toy?" She didn't answer, but she knew he'd gleaned it from her mind. "Good. I'll be the first to come inside it. Before the day is over, I'll come in every hole you have. You'll be so full of it, you'll never get it out of you."

And he had. He'd come in her mouth, straddling her chest and shooting off as she sucked him. Nani had swallowed greedily, even licking the overflow from the corners of her mouth. She'd sucked him until she'd gotten every drop she could.

He then went back to work on her pussy and clit with his mouth. He'd licked around the dildo still buzzing away inside her, even licked the underside of it on the skin separating her pussy and ass. Nani could remember screaming until her throat hurt before he latched onto her clit and sucked for all he was worth. She had been on the verge of coming when he'd pulled away from her with a growl.

"You fucking bastard!"

"You will not come until I say so. Do you understand me?"

She wanted to say more, but he pressed a button on the end of the butt plug and the pressure that had been building in her ass suddenly released and he pulled it out. The sensation was short-lived, however, as he rolled on a condom, squirted on lubrigel, stroked himself stiff -- which only took a couple of seconds -- and stuffed his cock inside her ass in one smooth motion.

She'd expected it to hurt, but the only pain turned out to be a slight burning sensation which soon passed. After a few moments, he'd started thrusting with increasingly faster strokes. It wasn't long before they'd both been grunting and panting. Nani had wanted desperately to raise her legs, to bend them at the knee to give him better access to her, but she was still tied to the bed.

Several minutes later, he came again. His hot semen erupted into her, and she screamed, needing the relief herself. The combination of his cock in her ass and the dildo in her pussy vibrating like mad was driving her crazy.

He dropped the condom in the trash. "Now,"

he'd said, "I'm going to come in that little pussy of yours."

She knew he was giving her a chance to protest. They'd never had sex without protection before. "Unless you untie me, I'm not going to agree to anything!" she screamed at him, tears sliding from her eyes unchecked.

He'd roared at her, but released her. Once she was free, she'd attacked him. She'd flipped him onto his back, yanked the stupid dildo from her cunt and impaled herself on Darian's cock.

She'd ridden him to her own orgasm then, continued slamming herself onto him over and over. He met her with thrusts of his own, gripping her hips with bruising force. She'd borne the marks for several days. It was, in fact, what had gotten her into trouble.

When he came, she'd cried out in another orgasm of her own. They'd continued their lovemaking the entire night. He'd come inside her many times, but Nani had always been convinced they'd conceived their daughter that first time. Even now, she knew it was true. Reliving the memory reinforced the idea she knew Darian shared.

"Stars above, I need to come, Darian." His presence in her mind was a constant thing. She knew he was with her. The memory had been his. She had seen the events from his vantage point.

Then stick your hand down your pants and fuck your clit!

She did. Leaning against the wall of her room, she fingered her clit. It only took a couple of seconds for the contractions to start. When they did, her knees buckled and she slid, screaming and panting, to the floor.

"I -- I need you, Darian." Tears welled in her eyes

and slid down her cheeks. "I can't do this alone."

You won't have to, my love. Darian will be successful this time.

"I hope so."

It wouldn't matter, anyway. You're strong enough to do this without me.

"Part of it, maybe. But in order to bring both empires together, I'll need you. Besides, I've lived without you long enough. The fates couldn't possibly expect me to be this close to having you back only to lose you again."

She felt his comforting touch almost as if he were sitting next to her. *It will be OK. Go now. Talk to Dr. Zabin. I know you don't like it -- I can't say that I do, either, though after the conversation with Tyrelle Amos I feel better -- but we don't have much choice.*

"You're right." She took a deep breath. "Time to go."

Chapter Seven

"What else do you think is on the chips?" Dr. Zabin looked alarmed. This wasn't good.

"I'm not sure," Nani said, watching him carefully. "I'm hoping something that will prove Samair's a foul swine in such a way that my return from the dead won't be held in suspicion."

"Nani." He took a step toward her. "In order to extract the DNA from that chip, I'm going to have to destroy it. That's why I only get one shot. It will be permanently damaged. I was getting ready to start the extraction process when you came in." He looked angry and frustrated. "Do you want me to do this or not?"

"You can't get what you need without harming the rest of the chip?"

"No! Dammit, woman! I'm under enough pressure as it is. Do you want me to do this or not? I can't be worried about what's happening to the chip. It's either your lover, or any data that may be with his DNA. Pick one!"

Nani was shocked. This was not like the doctor. "Are you OK?"

"No. I'm not OK. One wrong move and I could destroy any chance you have of getting Darian back."

"Is the chip that fragile?"

"It was made twenty years ago, Nani. The technology just isn't there. If there's anything else on this fucking chip, you need to figure it out now. And I mean right now. Darian has been in stasis far too long. I need to get him in a body before he starts to decay."

"Sweet Stars."

"Exactly. You've got another hour before I take the decision from you. I'm not going to fail on this,

Nani." His drive and sense of urgency was infectious. Nani wasn't sure how much more of this she could take. She had been through one crisis after another.

All she wanted to do was rest. She wanted Darian with her, and they'd just disappear. They'd take a shuttle from *Black Star*'s hangar and find a little planet where no one knew who they were. They'd get a job and raise a family, and be left alone.

Darian's soft chuckle tickled her mind. He didn't need to say anything for her to know he knew she'd never be happy with that. They both had responsibilities. Whatever happened once the work was done, once the nasty evil bad guy was deposed, then they could be happy slinking off to nowhere. Until then, neither of them had much of a choice other than to move forward. It was part of who they were.

"Will intensive analysis harm the DNA sample?" Nani needed as much information as she could get at this point. She didn't have much time, and she refused to wait any longer if Dr. Zabin said doing so would put Darian in danger.

"It shouldn't. But I'd stay away from chemicals and anything other than computer scans. No ultraviolet or chemical scans. I don't know how these samples were protected."

"Understood." Nani activated her internal comm. *Damon. Does Admiral Amos have Grimm?*

He's on the way here now.

Good. Dr. Zabin has given us less than an hour to see what we can extract. After that, he has to extract the DNA, and the chip will be gone.

Not a problem. He should dock in ten minutes.

Make sure he gets here immediately.

I'll bring him there myself.

Nani hesitated. *Have you heard from Nadira? Is she*

OK?

> *Mikiel says she's fine. She's healing nicely. She wants to see you.*

She sucked in a breath. Her one encounter with her daughter had been rushed and unsure. Neither of them had known what to do. Nani desperately wanted to see Nadira, but she wanted to do it with Darian at her side. That was important to her, but if her daughter wanted her, she would not wait. Nadira had been put off long enough.

> *I want to see her too, Damon. Is she able to come here, or does she need a day or so to rest?*

> *It would probably be best to give her a few days. Mikiel thinks she needs some time to get her strength back. He said he wants her to enjoy her time and make the most of it. He also knows you've got big things going that you need to finish.*

Nani let her head fall forward. These people were simply amazing. All of them were so selfless and understanding.

> *I always knew you were a good man, Damon. I'm glad to see my daughter found a man just as wonderful.*

> *He's good to her, Nani. I wouldn't tell you that if it weren't true.*

> *I know.* She smiled. She really did know. Mikiel was a good man. Both she and Darian were thankful Nadira had found him. It was ironic too, given Mikiel was from the Asalian Coalition and Nadira was, for all intents and purposes, the daughter of the leader of the Vok'nair Empire. Just like her and Darian.

> *Thanks. Thanks for looking after her.*

> *It was my pleasure. I owed you that much.*

> *You owe me nothing. Any debt I might have once tried to claim you've more than returned by raising my daughter.*

Nani took several deep breaths. This was all so overwhelming, and there seemed to be no end in sight. Even now, she waited. One crisis after another.

It wasn't long before Damon helped an elderly man into Dr. Zabin's office. His white hair hung in long, dirty strands, and he had a wild look about him.

"Pardell Grimm?" Nani looked from the old man to Damon.

"I am, indeed." His words were slurred, and he seemed not to focus on anyone or anything. "Pardell Grimm. Das me."

Nani looked at Damon, who shrugged. Dr. Zabin nodded his head and advanced on her. "That's just great, Nani. What exactly is this old drunk supposed to do?"

"He designed the chip, doctor. He's the only hope I've got of saving Darian and uniting the Asalian Coalition and the Vok'nair Empire."

"My dear." Grimm staggered toward her. "You look somewhat familiar." He still slurred his words, but his eyes were focused and bright. Intelligence glistened there, but he continued to bumble around, going so far as to stumble into Nani so that she had to catch him. She scratched her arm on a huge ring on his finger and inhaled sharply, but did her best to steady him. "So sorry. How clumsy of me." He immediately looked at the ring she'd left a fair amount of her skin on.

Nani was dumbfounded. She wanted to burst into tears. She wanted to laugh. Of all the things she expected, this was the last. The man was definitely chemically enhanced.

She was about to tell Dr. Zabin to continue with his work when Pardell Grimm suddenly changed completely.

"I'm sorry." He grinned. "Blood sample. I had to make sure you were actually you. Well, as much you as you could possibly be considering I helped bury you twenty years ago."

"This has got to be the strangest day I've ever had in my life." Nani collapsed into a nearby chair. "All I want is to get my man out of stasis, take him to my room, and fuck like rabbits. Can no one understand that?" Damon turned away, but not before Nani watched him cover his smile with a hand. "Oh, stop it. It's not like you don't do that from time to time with your woman. I happen to know for a fact you make so much noise you alarm the whole ship."

"Um, right. Yes, yes. Well." Grimm cleared his throat. "Anyway. Your DNA is the same as that of the woman I helped imprison within this ship. I can only assume the good doctor here is responsible for undoing all that damage we did." He sounded apathetic, but the look in his eyes told a different story. This man was haunted by what he'd done, but had grown accustomed to hiding it. "I understand, however, you're having trouble with the chip?" This last question was directed to Dr. Zabin.

"It's too old for me to be able to extract the DNA without destroying whatever else is on it. Can you help?"

"Sure." Grimm grinned, walked over to the doctor's workstation, and picked up the second chip. "Use yours to extract his DNA. I'll use this one to extract the data."

Dr. Zabin blinked. "You're kidding, right?"

"Why, no." The old man grinned. "Only the DNA needed to be kept separate. It was actually essential the data be the same on both in case one was destroyed. I'd have put both sets of DNA on each chip, but I didn't have enough time to develop a method."

"But --" Nani's brow furrowed in concentration, "-- why do it at all? And why harm two innocent children?"

"I didn't," Grimm replied, waving his hand. Nani was really beginning not to like the man. He seemed to be the type of person who enjoyed the challenges he'd undergone in that grim project. "Those two girls were clones. I built them around the chips."

Dr. Zabin had apparently had enough. "You son of a bitch!" he roared, advancing on the other man until they stood nose to nose. "Did you intend to sacrifice them all along? Do you have any idea how dangerous it was to remove the chips? They both could have been killed!"

Pardell Grimm just looked at him, as if he could really care less about Darian's outrage. "Then they'd have died by your hand. Not mine. I did what was necessary."

The doctor's face was a mask of contempt and rage. It was quite possible he'd have hit the other man had Damon not stepped smoothly between the two. "OK. Let's everyone step back and try this again." Damon spoke to both men, but looked squarely at Dr. Zabin. "Phoebe and Diamond are fine. You saved them. Focus on the problem."

"There is no 'problem'," Grimm spat, his whole attitude changing yet again. "I saved this woman and her lover. That was the greater good! I may have harmed two in the process, but I saved two more." He grinned evilly, looking like a wild beast. Even his sparse hair was mussed, looking as untamed as the man himself. "And Samair still has no clue he's about to be exposed for the evil son of a bitch he really is."

Damon just shook his head. Nani was sure her

jaw was only a couple of inches from the floor. Was he serious?

"You're kidding, right?" It was the only sentence she could form.

"Are you too stupid to understand what I just said?" He whipped his head in her direction, but deflated visibly when his eyes landed on her.

"They understood you just fine, Pardell." Tyrelle Amos swaggered into the room, the picture of a man in control. "I told you to behave or I'd have to take you back to the ship early. You promised to retrieve the data for these people. Remember?"

This was it. Nani had had just about all she could take. "This man's insane."

"Yes. But you needed his information. Do you need him further?"

Nani turned to Dr. Zabin. "Do we?"

"How should I know?" Zabin threw his hands up in exasperation and stalked across the room. "I'm not a computer engineer. I can get the biological material out, but any data will have to be looked at by someone else."

"No matter what, Doctor, you need to get Darian's clone growing. You said there was limited time."

"Are you going to take a chance the data isn't on both chips?"

"I don't even know what this 'data' is. Besides, Darian is more important than anything on that chip." She leveled Dr. Zabin with what she hoped was a fierce, determined look. "Don't delay any longer. Get this done. If there's one thing that can be salvaged, it's him."

"Even at the expense of both our governments?" Damon asked quietly. "I agree we can't sacrifice

Darian, but he'd agree that the greater good has to come first."

"You're not listening, little man," Grimm said in a singsong voice. "The data on both chips is identical. Let him get the DNA he needs and I'll show you my little surprise on the other chip." He grinned maniacally. Nani wanted to cringe and back away from the man but she held her ground.

Dr. Zabin nodded once -- apparently his decision made. "Here. See what you can come up with. Darian's clone should be ready in three hours. That will make him approximately the same age as he was before. Just like you. After that, it will take me approximately ten hours to perform the procedure."

"So we have plenty of time to pick through this." Nani wasn't sure she wanted anyone else to see anything she found. Not yet. "I'll be in my cabin if anyone needs me." She turned to Damon. "I'll need as much computer power as you can provide me. The technology is twenty years old, but more than half the battle is finding something simple enough."

He nodded at her. "Done. If you need anything else -- or anyone else -- all you have to do is say so."

"Just see I'm not disturbed." She took the chip from Mahat Zabin, gripped it tightly, and headed to her quarters. "Admiral, bring your man here and come with me."

She had a lot of work to do in the next thirteen hours.

Chapter Eight

"Bloody hell!" Nani had never been more frustrated in her life. They'd been at it for hours and didn't seem to be any closer to extracting whatever data Grimm had put on the chip than when they started. She was beginning to think he'd been lying all along. "There's nothing there, Tyrelle. We've wasted hours!"

The only sound the admiral made was a grunt, though he looked as haggard as Nani felt. Pardell Grimm merely laughed merrily as if it were all a big joke.

"I know something you don't know. Neener neener neeeeenerrrrr." He'd been singing that phrase for hours now. The longer they worked, the louder he got.

Nani thumped her head on the desk where she worked. The computer screen flickered once as if in protest. "I'm not sure how much more I can take."

Again, the admiral grunted but didn't say anything.

"Wait a minute." Grimm went suddenly sober. Or, at least, as sober as he was likely to be. "What time is it?"

"Oh nine hundred," Admiral Amos murmured, but said nothing else. He'd bent back over the computer screen he'd been working at for the past twelve hours. Nani had hoped she'd be done with the chip by the time Dr. Zabin finished with Darian. She hadn't had any communication with Darian for a couple of hours, but he'd said he didn't want to distract her when the doctor started the procedure. With him deliberately blocking her, she had to simply wait for him to contact her. That was almost as maddening as this absurd project with a mad scientist.

"Good, good!" Grimm clapped his hands together like a child about to get a cookie. "Move over, girl. Let me show you how it's done."

He practically shoved Nani from her chair and sat down. Quick as lightning, he keyed a set of commands and passwords faster than the computer could keep up. Nani had never seen anyone move so fast. There was no way she could follow what he was doing, but she had no doubt she could backtrack him later and figure out exactly what he'd done if she needed to. He continued this for several minutes before a video popped up. There, on the screen, was Nani herself, begging for the life of her child.

She felt like the bottom had just dropped out of her world. Her knees gave way and she fell hard to the floor. Admiral Amos was at her side almost immediately but she was sure his look of horror matched her own.

"Stop playback," Pardell Grimm said, all hint of madness gone from his voice. Nani wanted to look at him to see if he looked as sane as he sounded, but she couldn't take her eyes off the screen. In that one instant, she relived all the pain and horror of her past.

Her newborn baby literally ripped from her body and the pain -- both mental and physical -- was tremendous. Not only childbirth itself, but all the hideous things that followed. She could almost feel the blinding pain as they cut into her skull. Unable to move or even scream because of the paralytic she'd been given, she remembered, of all things, one tear leaking from the corner of one eye to run down the side of her face. That moment had shaped her psyche for the years ahead.

One tear was all the satisfaction she'd given

Samair. From then on, she'd swallowed her emotions. Until she'd been reunited with her body, it had become easy to prevent herself from becoming too emotional. Now, however, she ached from anger, sorrow, and despair as well as joy, happiness, and anticipation. Emotions threatened to overwhelm her in a way she hadn't experienced since the day she was staring at now on the computer screen.

She reached out for Tyrelle Amos blindly. The older man pulled her to him and held her carefully, patting her head sympathetically. She got the feeling he was very uncomfortable, but he didn't push her away.

"That was harsh, Pardell. You could have simply saved the file instead of playing it," the admiral admonished quietly, still patting her comfortingly.

"Yes. I could have." Pardell Grimm looked more sane than he had since this ride had begun. "But when would she have watched it and who would she have been with? This isn't something she should watch by herself, nor something she could have been prepared for by anyone so she could have been with her beloved. Neither of them should have to see this alone, and in each other's company doesn't count."

Nani got to her feet with a little difficulty, tears now freely streaming from her eyes. "This was all an act. You did this when you were sure Darian wouldn't see it without the support of friends and people who love him."

"Absolutely." He laid his hands on Nani's shoulders and hunkered down a little to look into her eyes. "It's all documented. Every second. Everyone involved. Samair even said enough to get him forcibly removed by your family."

"You didn't keep any other copies of this video?"

Nani knew she had to pull herself together. She had to have all the facts and think the situation through before acting on it.

Grimm straightened and let go of her, shaking his head. "Absolutely not. I couldn't risk Samair finding out. I faked a brain injury shortly after that day so I could work on making those computer chips and growing clones to place them in. Believe me, smuggling out the video was simple compared to getting viable DNA samples without anyone important finding out."

"I'm the only other person who knew," Amos said from behind Nani. She turned to look at him. "I helped Pardell every step of the way and kept him under my protection all these years."

"So, how did the Hand of God end up with Diamond and Phoebe? Why make them suffer so much? It's unthinkable." Nani had been horrified about this most of all. This man created two lives designed solely to carry the means of giving her and Darian back their lives and to hold information to overthrow a tyrant. No matter how noble the intention, no matter how grateful she was to be whole again, nothing could justify what had been done to those two women.

"It was a risky decision, to say the least, but we knew if they survived, we'd always know where to find them. That's why I imbedded the beacon within the chips. To keep up with them."

"But, Diamond and Phoebe finding their way aboard either the *Black Star* or the *Sword Breaker* was nothing more than blind luck. Why would you leave something like that to chance?" Nani was growing more and more angry the longer this went on. "You made them suffer so much. Why take a chance it might be in vain?"

"There was an unacceptable amount of chance involved, but we didn't have much choice." The admiral sat down heavily in the chair he'd occupied most of the evening and into the morning. "Those chips were the only chance of righting so many wrongs. At the time, the Hand of God was merely a religious colony with a few radical beliefs. They didn't treat their women so abominably, and both girls were placed with families we thought would take care of them."

"We didn't count on one family dying and the other alienating the adopted girl out of fear." Pardell Grimm placed a hand on the admiral's shoulder and gripped it in a show of support. "It was luck Phoebe actually made it aboard the *Black Star* when she did, but we'd had people down there for months subtly planting the idea it was time to go. We knew Damon and Mikiel were trying to decide what they were going to do since they'd basically stolen the flagship of the Vok'nair Empire. So we made sure the outer boundary patrols drove them toward Graves Station. Again, subtly. We didn't want either of them to feel like they were being set up."

"Them coming back for the rest of the women was a given, though." Amos looked at Grimm and put his own hand on the other's, which was still resting on his shoulder. The intimate gesture was telling. "We both knew neither of them could look the other way. So, yes. We were lucky. But we tried to make some of our own luck as well."

"You know, Diamond may very well kick both your asses when she finds out."

"No, she won't." Grimm raised his chin. "She'll know her life served a great purpose. All her suffering was for a greater good, and she'll understand that. Look at what she did for Viktor. Look at what she did for this ship and her crew. She's risked her life many times over for people she didn't know. She's not going to be upset about what she did for you, however unintentionally. Phoebe either. Not once they've had a chance to think about it."

"There's more to this than you're telling me, isn't there?"

"There always is." Admiral Amos looked even wearier than she felt, the worry and sorrow showing clearly on his face. He looked like he was about to say more, but his composure finally collapsed, and he dropped his head in his hands and shook slightly in despair.

Grimm's jaw clenched. She could see the muscles working as he looked at his friend. "Those girls were more than mere clones. They were genetically engineered from our own DNA. I altered one X chromosome to make them both females, but they're essentially our daughters. They're just grown like clones instead of allowed to develop naturally."

"Sweet stars," Nani whispered. "You did this to your own children?"

"It was the only way." Grimm looked as if he'd argued this point with himself and Amos on more than one occasion and found it lacking. "We had very little time. We also had devised a way to give ourselves children even though we were a same-sex couple and unable to have our own children outside of adoption or use of a surrogate. Had we been found out, we'd have been executed for ethics violations in genetics, and the girls would have been destroyed. I would have gladly sacrificed myself for my children, but there is no way Samair would have let them live. At least this way, they not only served a higher purpose, but they had a chance to be happy. And they both are."

"This just keeps getting better and better," Nani murmured to herself. She was saved discussing it further by an internal comm chime from Dr. Zabin.

He's awake, my lady. He needs rest to heal, but he's alive and asking for you.

She looked at the two men, clearly miserable and hurting. What in the world was she supposed to say? She opted to keep her mouth shut and simply turned and left the room. They'd either find their way back to their ship or to Phoebe's mess hall. If they found the latter, she hoped they'd tell the young woman everything.

But that didn't matter. None of it was her concern at the moment. Darian was awake.

And asking for her.

Chapter Nine

He looked just like she'd remembered. Shiny black hair fell over one eye in unruly curls. She didn't even try to resist the urge to gently brush it aside. It was as silky as she'd remembered, and her fingers trembled. Masculine black brows slashed across his forehead over his cobalt blue eyes. Dark lashes fluttered at her as he seemed to try to focus blurry eyes on her. Chiseled cheekbones and full lips gave him that exotic look she'd always loved about him.

He was her beloved. Just as she'd last seen him.

Darian lay on the exam table covered with a thin blanket. Monitors overhead gauged his vital signs and brain function. It looked as if he were completely fine.

She laid a hand on the side of his cheek and smiled at him. "Welcome back."

"You're a sight for sore eyes." His voice was rough, husky, much as hers had sounded when she'd first awakened.

"How do you feel?" She continued to stroke his face, unable to help herself. He was so beautiful; the line of his jaw, the contour of his neck, the slope of his shoulders. His chest was wonderfully sculpted muscle. She had to pull herself away from him before she explored his body further. Now was not the time or the place.

"I'm tired, but I feel fine." He smiled weakly, his eyelids drooping. "We need to talk, Nani. I know about the video, though Dr. Zabin refused to let me view it. He said I needed to be prepared before I saw it."

She hissed in a breath of air, feeling his conflicting emotions. He, like her, didn't know whom to trust. It seemed like the lives of everyone around them were somehow connected to that fateful day.

Samair had touched more lives than simply theirs with his actions.

"I saw only part of it, but I have no wish to see any more. I was told it was a record of everything that happened that day with everyone involved and on what level."

"It will also prove Samair doesn't have legal claim over the Vok'nair Empire. That belongs with you and your family."

"We could have united this entire quadrant if we'd married back then."

"We still can." His smile was weak, but he held eye contact with her.

They stared at each other a moment, possibilities glistening all around them. All they had to do was go home and face the monsters who had put them in this situation to begin with.

"You should let him rest now, my lady." Mahat Zabin's voice was quiet and unobtrusive, but he still brought so many demons with him Nani felt as if she'd been ripped from a fairy tale into a harsh reality.

"I want you and that madman off my ship. Take the admiral with you." Nani hissed her order quietly, but judging by the doctor's expression, her meaning was clear.

"Nani." Damon walked slowly toward her. "No one will dispute your orders, but I urge you to think about what you're doing. Think about the people these men have become."

Darian gripped her hand as he carefully pulled himself to a sitting position. Nani tried to hold him back, but he brushed her away until he stood. He framed her face with his hands and forced her to look at him. "Mahat was but a young, idealistic person back then. He obviously regrets his actions, and he saved us,

Nani. Not just us, but look at what he's done for everyone here."

She placed her hands on Darian's wrists and held to him like he was her lifeline. "What he did was unforgivable, Darian. Not just to us, but to Nadira. How much better would her life have been if she hadn't been given to Samair?"

"And she might never have met Mikiel, either. She's happy now. Isn't that what's most important?" She'd never thought Darian would take this position. The fact that he spoke aloud and not by telepathy told her he was absolutely sure about his feelings. He wanted the others to know why he felt this way, and why he disagreed with her on this.

"I've been inside his mind, Nani. While he put me back in my body, he let me have access to everything he was doing. He didn't give me permission to go poking around inside his head, so I didn't, but his emotions were so high, I couldn't help but get a lot of bleed over."

Then it was clear to Nani what Darian had seen. "You felt his emotions. Not only current ones, but what he felt that day, didn't you?"

"Yes. I don't know the whole story, but what he did was not what he thought he'd be doing. He was forced into it the same way we were."

"I don't know if I'd put it that kindly, my lord," Zabin said. Nani looked at him for the first time since he'd shown her to Darian. Tears fell freely from his eyes, and he made no attempt to dry them. "I had a choice, at first. It just wasn't what I thought it would be."

"I knew Mahat back then." Damon spoke again. He looked all of his fifty-two years and then some. He looked tired. Weary beyond imagination, and for the first time, Nani saw Phoebe behind him. She was definitely young enough to be his daughter, but her eyes showed an age and wisdom of someone twice her age. Now, she put her hand into Damon's and squeezed, offering him her silent support. "He was a few years younger than me, but was a brilliant surgeon."

"That doesn't matter, Damon." Dr. Zabin waved him off. "I was given an offer I couldn't refuse, even though it violated every ethics oath I'd sworn to uphold as a physician. I shouldn't have been surprised when it turned out as evil as it did. It was evil to begin with, and I was evil to shrug off everything I stood for simply for the opportunity to combine biology with technology. Samair knew what he was doing when he chose me."

"He knew of your interest in biotechnology, and he knew you were good enough to make good on your research. He twisted your quest for immortality into the ultimate death sentence." Damon pleaded with the doctor while Nani listened intently. Something inside her wanted to believe Dr. Zabin wasn't as willing a participant as she believed him to be at first.

"Tell me exactly what happened, Dr. Zabin," she said. Darian had sat back on the table but held her hand firmly now. He gave her access to his mind, and she knew he felt stronger. He wanted this story, too. Though he knew the doctor's emotional state at the time of the original procedure -- one of horror and a disbelief he was actually doing something like that to another human being -- there were still many unanswered questions.

"I was told I'd be testing my theory that a human brain could actually be transplanted into a cyborg machine. I was told I'd be performing the test on criminals sentenced to death for crimes so unspeakable they weren't made known to the general public. I questioned whether people like that deserved a second chance at life, and I was told even if they survived, once the study was over they'd be terminated anyway. It was better not to use good people for the study phase of the experiment.

"Of course, I recognized Darian right away. I immigrated from the Asalian Coalition after medical school and Darian, being the son of the president, was always in the public eye. Naturally, I refused to do the procedure…" His voice trailed away and, if possible, he looked even more anguished than before.

Darian grunted. Nani felt his distress even as the images flooded her mind, and she cried out. The pain in her chest and stomach was so great, she doubled over. She was going to vomit. She couldn't hear another second of this. Even as the images of Mahat Zabin's family being slaughtered one by one played through her mind like a vid image on continuous playback, she ran from the room. That same room she'd seen on the computer screen in her cabin earlier was truly a hall of horrors. She knew Darian followed but she couldn't wait for him. She ran to her quarters and into the bathroom where she vomited violently.

She severed her link with Darian, but it was too late. She saw a tearful and begging Zabin doing as he was told until both she and Darian were encased in their new "bodies," only instead of android bodies, they had computer casings. What had happened next she was spared, only to know Zabin had left Vok'nair space as soon as he'd been able. It wasn't until Nadira had gone aboard the *Black Star* that he'd returned. He'd gotten himself on board as one of three doctors and quietly waited for an opportunity to right everything he'd done wrong.

A warm body pressed against her back and a cool, damp cloth was held to her forehead while she got her stomach back under control.

"I'm sorry, my love. I wasn't prepared for it, either. I'd have blocked you if I'd known." Darian held her hair back from her face with one large hand. She took the cloth from him and blotted her sweating face and neck, spitting out the last remaining nastiness in her mouth. He stood and ordered a glass of water, then handed the cool, synthesized liquid to her. She gulped it down greedily.

"It's probably on the video, too. How can I show that to the people when I can't stand to watch it myself?"

Darian thought for a moment. "Perhaps you only need to show it to one person."

"Samair."

Darian nodded. "That, combined with Admiral Amos's support, may be enough for him to voluntarily step aside."

"We're talking about a monster, Darian."

"We're talking about a man who did horribly nasty things in the name of gaining power when he was fifty years old."

Nani blinked. "I'd forgotten how much older than me he was. My father hadn't seemed to think much of it at the time."

"From what I've found out, your father may not have had much of a choice."

"True. Samair had contacts high in the inner government. Even though my father was king, he still had to answer to the parliament. Once Samair had his sights set on being king, his only choice was to marry me, since, as my father's only child, I stood to inherit the kingdom."

"I hate to say this, but he probably knew you and I were seeing each other even after your marriage. You carrying my child would be the perfect excuse to be rid of you."

Nani wiped her mouth one last time and stood. She looked into his eyes as the last piece of the puzzle clicked into place. "It's not just that, Darian." She laid the cloth on the counter and brushed past him into the living area of her quarters. The computer screen still showed her terrified and agonized face where Grimm and Amos had left it. "I'm betting Samair couldn't father a child by me, or any other woman."

"What makes you say that?"

"I'm not sure. I only know that he and I never consummated our marriage."

"Wait. He never had sex with you, and you didn't think something was wrong?"

"I was twenty at the time, Darian." She laughed a little, needing the tension break. "The only thing I was concerned about was avoiding him. I knew he only wanted my title. I figured he just didn't care about sex with me. Even when he had the baby tested to prove parentage, I didn't say anything. We both knew that child wasn't his, but I thought if I said so, that would just make things worse."

"Which it would have," Darian quickly supplied, pacing the room, obviously thinking. Then he stopped. "So, it was his plan all along to get rid of you. What does that tell us we don't already know?"

Nani shrugged. "I'm sure he didn't want the whole kingdom finding out he was sterile, or worse, impotent."

"And by getting rid of you, he destroyed the one person who could have hinted at either of those things, and he got an heir to the throne with his name. He was assured immortality through his descendants."

"Could all of this have been about a quest for the throne? It just seems so…" Nani struggled for the right word.

"Trivial?"

"Well, at the very least it was supreme overkill."

"Who knows what he was thinking?" Darian shrugged. "What matters now is making sure that record of events gets in the right hands to pull Samair from the throne."

"And I think I just alienated the two people who might have been able to help us."

"The admiral and Grimm?" When she nodded, Darian waved her off. "They're still here. Everyone is in Medical, trying to decide how to go about overthrowing Samair and wondering exactly how much a part you want to play in this. It's your kingdom, after all."

She smiled. "Well, if they're working on it, let them. At least for now. At the moment, there's only one thing I want."

Darian raised an eyebrow. "And that is?"

"You, Darian. I want you."

Chapter Ten

She knew Darian probably needed rest, but she also knew that they both needed this. Before she could say anything else, he'd wrapped his arms around her, pulled her to him, and mashed his lips against hers. She opened her mouth willingly, eagerly, and his tongue slipped inside her mouth, licking and sucking at her tongue.

She sighed happily. She'd never thought this day would come. The sensation of his hair-roughened skin against her made her shiver in anticipation. With one swift movement, he pulled the zipper at her throat all the way past her navel and slipped the fabric of her jumpsuit from her shoulders and down her arms. He bent to one knee as he helped her step out of it and caressed her skin, from her arms, down the length of her back, to the backs of her thighs.

When she stepped out of her jumper, he rested his hands on either cheek of her ass and pulled her pelvis toward his face. His tongue found its way through her curls to her clit where he latched on insistently.

"Ah, yes!" she cried as she pulled his head closer to her core. It was as good as she remembered. Better, in fact. Her body was alive with sensations only he had ever created.

It didn't take long for him to coax an orgasm from her. Given all she'd been through, given how he always knew how best to distract her with sex, she was more than ready for the eruption when it came. She screamed his name and her legs gave way. The only thing that saved her from a nasty fall was his strong arms. Just like always. He was there to catch her when she fell.

Darian gently laid her on the floor and continued his exploration of her pussy. He bent her knees and pressed her thighs to her chest. Nani reached around her legs to either side of her ass and opened her pussy lips for him. He grunted his approval before plunging his tongue inside her so far his nose brushed her clit.

Again, Nani cried out. The sensations she'd been denied for so long were almost overwhelming, but she loved every second of it. His lips and tongue on her pussy felt so good, and his moans and growls were like the most beautiful music. She always loved the sounds he made during sex. It was the perfect blend of masculine satisfaction.

Finally, he stood, whipped off the pants they'd given him in Medical, and bent to scoop her off the floor. He carried her to the bed with seemingly little effort and placed her in the center. He knelt in front of her, stroking his cock, the lust shining brightly in his eyes.

Slowly, deliberately, he sat back on his heels, still stroking his cock. Nani didn't need any more of an invitation than that. She immediately moved to her knees and knelt before him on all fours. Licking a trail from his balls to the tip of his dick, Nani grinned when he groaned and his cock twitched under her tongue. She took the head into her mouth then, sucking and dipping until she took almost half of his thick shaft down her throat.

Knowing that was about as much as she could take, she opened her mouth wider and stretched her tongue so that she could lick just that few millimeters more of him. The maneuver also let him slide just a little farther down her throat. She was afraid she might gag a little, but she managed to control it, and when she released him, his cock came back slick with her saliva.

"Enough!" His growl was almost a shout, and he pulled her up by her hair and pushed her back on the bed, pulling her legs high as he descended on her. "The first time I come will not be in your mouth." He hooked her legs over his shoulders and sank easily into her pussy. "I'm going to come inside this hot, tight pussy."

"Yes," she panted. "Please."

He didn't start out slow or make any pretense about a tender loving for their first time in twenty years. He slammed into her, each stroke harder and more furious than the last. Sweat coated them and helped them slide easily against one another. Nani gripped his upper arms where they bore his weight on either side of her head. She was sure she'd leave bruises, but she didn't really care. If it marked him as hers all over again, who really gave a fuck?

"I've always been yours, Nani," he ground out, but she could see the tenderness in his eyes, if not his face. "And I always will be." He did smile then. "But feel free to mark me any way you like."

She gave a little strangled laugh then, too, but it was soon replaced with whimpers of pleasure as another orgasm began building inside her where their bodies joined. He growled then and ducked his head to her neck and sucked. The little pain in that sensitive part of her body pushed her over the edge, and she screamed his name. All the while she bucked against him, helpless to control the spasming of her hips and pelvis and pussy. She drove against him erratically, and she knew her cunt pulsed around him, wanting to milk him dry.

With one final, hard thrust, Darian threw his head back and shouted his release. Nani felt the familiar sensation of his hot seed inside her, bathing her with love and the promise of life. She hadn't realized how much she wanted the chance again, but she did. Not as a replacement for Nadira, but as an addition to her family.

She clung to Darian as he finished, knowing now was the time. They both needed to see Nadira and Mikiel and plan their return.

"Yes, my love," Darian panted as he rolled them to their sides. "Now. But give me an hour or so."

"Oh, goodness!" She gripped his head and made him look at her. "Are you OK? We shouldn't have --"

"We most certainly should have," he chuckled. "And we'll do it again before we talk to Nadira and everyone else. But I do need an hour or so. It will be a day or two before I have my full strength back."

"I'll hold you, then. Sleep. I'll watch over you." Nani smiled at him and, again, pushed an unruly curl from his eyes.

"I love you, Nani. I always have." He kissed her softly before letting his head fall back to the pillow. "And I always will."

"I love you, too." She snuggled into the warmth of his body and pulled the covers with her as she settled in. "Forever."

"Forever," Darian said and closed his eyes.

Nani had intended to simply lie there with him and enjoy the feel of holding him again, but his deep, even breathing and soft, steady heartbeat soon lulled her into a comfortable drowsiness. She knew she'd sleep. And she didn't care. She was with the only man she'd ever loved. Somehow, everything would work out.

* * *

Both Nani and Darian sat straight up in bed

when the alarm klaxon blared throughout the corridors of the *Black Star*. Psycomm chatter filtered through Nani's mind, and she was amazed at the ease with which she sifted through it.

"I'm not." Darian smiled at her even as he dressed hurriedly. "There was never anything you couldn't do given enough time."

She threw a shirt at him she'd found in the closet. It fit him perfectly. "Did I give you permission to prowl around in my head?"

"No." He chuckled. She loved that about him. They both knew there was danger, but he never missed an opportunity to laugh, and it always made her feel better. "Get used to it. I'm never leaving you again. You'll have absolutely no privacy, so don't go look at that handsome pilot. I'm the only pilot you can have."

She winked at him, pulling on her jumpsuit. "Wouldn't dream of it."

"If you thought it would torment me, yes, you would."

Both of them stomped into their uniform boots and ran down the corridor to Command where they entered quietly. Darian went to a console directly behind the command center where he had a good view of everyone and, more importantly, their computer screens. Nani took up the station she'd hacked into before and simply watched and listened. The comm channels were wild with activity on the part of the Vok'nair fleet. She now truly understood the benefits of psycomm linkage.

Who's in command, Damon? Her quiet, unobtrusive question could easily have been ignored by Damon if he needed his attention elsewhere, but he answered her immediately, as if he'd been waiting for her.

I don't know. But they don't appear to be united as a fleet, and Admiral Amos has joined them.

Nani blinked, and the hurt and anger flooded her all over again until Darian's calming touch kissed her mind. She took several calming breaths before addressing Damon again.

What do you make of that?

It's hard to make out, but I think he's trying to mount a mutiny and take command of the fleet from whoever their supreme commander might be. He's on the flagship, which is cowering in the center of the ships he brought with him. Something's definitely up. Don't count the admiral an enemy yet.

Several minutes went by, and the bulk of Admiral Amos's fleet moved between the *Black Star* and *Sword Breaker*, acting as a shield from the new fleet. Enough was enough. Nani would not hide behind anyone. The Vok'nair Empire was hers to take, and she intended to claim her birthright. Now.

Damon -- she began, but he cut her off.

Absolutely you can have command. I might have the better military experience, but no amount of that will help us if all of those ships decide to attack us. We're two against a hundred.

She moved swiftly into the command chair with Damon standing beside her should she need him. He placed a fatherly, reassuring hand on her shoulder and squeezed.

Comm chatter among a hundred vessels was damned near impossible to filter through, and Nani had no intention of doing such.

Jam all outgoing transmissions from everyone but the Black Star, Sword Breaker, *and Admiral Amos*, she commed. *If that doesn't get their attention, nothing will.*

Immediately, the chatter ceased.

"About damned time, *Black Star*." Admiral Amos's gruff voice cut through to them clearly now. "I assume you have something to address?"

He was giving her the perfect opening. He, as a ranking officer in the Vok'nair space fleet, had just ordered everyone to listen to what she had to say. It might not carry weight with their supreme commander, but with their outgoing communication blocked, she'd have sent her message, and her proof, before anyone could order them not to listen.

Nani stabbed the transmit button and asked, "Who is supreme commander here?"

When a crewman raised an eyebrow at her and commed, *The ship in the center of their formation is addressing us*, Nani nodded her head and a chillingly familiar voice flooded the external communications system.

"I am the Vok'nair king, you idiot! Samair Kone! You will surrender that ship to me and face the consequences of your actions immediately, or I'll see to it your entire family -- your entire world -- pays for your insolence!"

"I've already paid, Samair." Her voice was calm and sure, but inside her heart pounded. Darian's familiar touch soothed her, and she clung to him. She also found Damon's hand gripping her shoulder with her own hand. She needed the physical presence of those she trusted. "Now it's your turn."

There was silence. Nani was afraid he wouldn't respond, but she should have known better.

"I don't know who you are, but you'll pay for your insolence."

"You know very well who I am, and I have the DNA to prove it. You've claimed the throne long enough, Samair. It's over."

"Nothing's over!" Nani could almost see the hatred on his face as he screamed at her. "I am the king!"

"Because of your marriage to me. Considering what you did to me and Darian, I doubt the religious council would have a problem granting my petition for a divorce."

"You'll have difficulty proving anything." He sounded so confident, Nani knew she'd enjoy letting him see the video. It was perverse, really, and she was a little ashamed of herself. But she knew she'd get over it.

"Actually --" She crossed her arms and smiled. He couldn't see her, but the satisfied smirk came anyway. "-- I can. The whole grisly procedure was taped and, as it turns out, I have a copy. Not only that, but you left witnesses alive, of which I have three. Now. Do I need to broadcast this thing to the entire fleet, or are you going to surrender yourself to me and go before the council to accept judgment?"

Again, there was silence. She was afraid he'd cut transmission, and she focused her attention on the fleet. All outgoing communications were still blocked from their end, but if they'd figured out a way around it, she wanted to know before anything happened.

Ma'am, there's another transmission coming through. One of the lead ships, the young officer handling communications informed her.

"Let it through."

"*Black Star*, we request to see your proof."

"To whom am I speaking?" Nani wasn't about to send data blindly, no matter what she said. This was too personal for just anyone to see.

"I am Karn, speaker of the High Council and member of the religious council. If you have information that will depose a king, it is I who needs to hear it."

Not one to take things on blind faith, Nani contacted Admiral Amos privately for confirmation. "Is he who he says?"

"Absolutely. I contacted high command when I found out Samair was coming to find the *Black Star* himself. They need the information you have more than anyone else. It's bad on Homeworld. They can help."

"I'm sending a copy of the file now, sir. If you have any sway with the religious council at all, I respectfully request you grant my petition for a divorce from Samair and return the throne rights to me and my daughter."

"If you're referring to Nadira, is she not the current king's daughter as well?"

"No. It's all in the video. Everything."

Nani's heart raced. Everything had happened so fast. She hadn't had a chance to talk to Nadira. She hadn't been able to plan anything with the captains of either ship. Great goddess above. This was really it!

There will be time, my love. All will be well.

As much as she wanted to take comfort in Darian's words, what if all wasn't well? What if this went against them? There was no way they'd escape. Her only hope would be to make sure Nadira lived.

Damon, if this doesn't work, I want you to set up a screen for the Sword Breaker *to protect Nadira.*

I've already got a plan in the works, my lady.

Minutes ticked by. Thirty minutes. Forty-five. The strain was becoming unbearable. Darian was in constant contact with her, but though it helped, she needed more. She concentrated, focusing all her attention on Nadira.

Mother?

Nani's breath caught. *Nadira. I'm sorry I've wasted so much time. I just didn't know what to say.*

It's OK. I'm not sure I knew, either.

I love you. I just wanted you to know. I've always loved you. The greatest day of my life was when you came aboard the Black Star. *Even though we couldn't communicate directly, it was good to feel your presence. I think you pulled me back from the brink of insanity.*

I love you too, Mother.

Darian's voice was soft when he added it to the conversation. *I owe you an apology, Nadira. When I told you I was your father, I was harsh. I took out my anger and frustration on you, and I had no right. You have always been an innocent pawn in this deadly game of Samair's. I treated you no better than he did.*

Nani felt Nadira's love for Darian through her connection to him and knew everything was right between them. *Considering all the stress you were under, I'm surprised you were as congenial as you were.*

I love you, Nadira. No matter what happens, I love you, and I hope you'll give me a chance to get to know you. Darian sounded more vulnerable than Nani had ever heard him. Give a man a daughter, and he turns to putty every time.

Nadira's giggles filled her mind, and she knew Darian had heard her as well. He grumbled something she couldn't understand, but she felt his happiness. All would definitely be well with the three of them. Assuming they all lived, they would finally be a family.

"I understand your meaning, my lady." The response from Karn was sad and full of emotion. It caught Nani off guard. She was so caught up in the conversation with her soon-to-be-husband and her daughter, she had almost forgotten she awaited Karn's reaction to her file. "We've authenticated the video and conferred with Admiral Amos and Dr. Grimm. Samair Kone will be placed under arrest. This file has been sent to the rest of the High Council and the religious council, along with our interviews of Admiral Amos and Dr. Grimm. By the time we reach Homeworld, they should have reached a decision. I cannot guarantee the outcome, but I have included my belief that your divorce should be granted as well as my belief that your husband should be punished as they see fit for his role in your… ordeal. Will you go with us to offer testimony and DNA testing should it prove necessary?"

Again, she conferred with Darian, Damon, Mikiel, and the admiral. All agreed with her it was a reasonable request. With the backing of the speaker of the High Council, it was doubtful anything he recommended wouldn't pass. She was going home to claim the throne.

"Also," Karn added before she could terminate the connection, "I've contacted the Asalian Coalition. Darian's father is anxious to see him and will be meeting us at Homeworld. I think with the evidence you have here, along with returning his son, you've single-handedly united both governments. Congratulations."

"Nothing is ever done single-handedly. I had more help than you know, and I intend to give each and every one of them full credit for their roles. There is not one of us on these two ships whose lives have not been affected by what Samair did. Some more than others, but it's been a hardship for everyone. My only hope is we all find the peace we so rightfully deserve." She turned to look behind her. She'd known the moment Dr. Zabin entered the command center. Darian had seen him, and she refused to relinquish her connection to him. "Especially those I've wronged for their unwilling part, and I hope they'll forgive my narrow-mindedness." She looked directly at Mahat Zabin, who closed his eyes and bowed his head, nodding slightly in acknowledgement.

"That's it, then. We'd be honored if you took the lead back to Homeworld."

"The honor is ours. We'll be wanting the *Sword Breaker* with us and bestowed equal honor. Nadira and her husband command that ship. She's a princess of Vok'nair, he a warrior of the Asalian Coalition. It is my hope that the marriage of not only myself and Darian but the union of Nadira and Mikiel will help unite our two governments as well. It will only strengthen our societies."

"As you wish, my lady. On everything. You will have the full support of the council if I have anything to say about it."

When communications were cut, everyone in Command cheered. Smiles and claps on the back were passed all around. Nani was happier than she could ever remember being, and Darian beamed at her in pride.

He looked at the young officer standing next to him and pointed to Nani. "That's my woman."

"Yeah. We know," he laughed.

Darian moved around the panels and stations separating him from Nani until he stood beside her. Nani turned to him and smiled. There was no other man in the universe she would have chosen to share this moment with. Darian was everything she'd ever wanted. He understood her, and he knew what all these events meant to her. Every heartbreaking one of them had a significance, and they were all tied together. They bonded all these wonderful people together with a common thread that could not be broken.

But I'm the only one who knows how to do that little thing to your clit you like so well.

Nani laughed in pure joy. She launched herself at Darian and kissed him soundly. *That's true. It's been a while since you've done it, too.*

Do you think now would be a good time to refresh your memory as to exactly how good it feels?

I think now would definitely be a good time.

Hand in hand, they left Command. Their future was full of possibilities. United, they could accomplish anything.

Marteeka Karland

International bestselling author Marteeka Karland leads a double life as an action romance writer by evening and a semi-domesticated housewife by day. Known for her down-and-dirty MC, out of this world Post Apocalyptic Sci-Fi, and Dark Fantasy action romances, Marteeka takes pleasure in spinning tales of tenacious, protective heroes and spirited heroines. She staunchly advocates that every character deserves a blissful ending.

Marteeka finds joy in baking, and gardening with her husband. Make sure to visit her website to stay updated with her most recent projects. Don't forget to register for her newsletter which will pepper you with a potpourri of Teeka's beloved recipes, book suggestions, autograph events, and a plethora of interesting tidbits.

Marteeka at Changeling: changelingpress.com/marteeka-karland-a-39

Want more? Check out Wanda Violet O. -- Teeka's BDSM Erotica side at changelingpress.com/wanda-violet-o-a-226

Changeling Press LLC

Contemporary Action Adventure, Sci-Fi, Steampunk, Dark Fantasy, Urban Fantasy, Paranormal, and BDSM Romance available in e-book, audio, and print format at ChangelingPress.com – MC Romance, Werewolves, Vampires, Dragons, Shapeshifters and Horror -- Tales from the edge of your imagination.

Where can I get Changeling Press Books?

Changeling Press e-books are available at ChangelingPress.com, Amazon, Apple Books, Barnes & Noble, Kobo, Smashwords, and other online retailers, including Everand Subscription and Kobo Subscription Services. Print books are available at Amazon, Barnes and Noble, and by ISBN special order through your local bookstores.

ChangelingPress.com